THE PALACE OF SHADOWS

LOCKE & STEEL BOOK THREE

L. E. MEDLOCK

STONE SOUL PUBLISHING

For Dad and for Kevin.

CHAPTER ONE

V ienna is famous for two things; music and coffee.

I wonder who told me that—Turner perhaps? Whoever it was, they were right: violinists play on every street and a coffeehouse sits on every corner. The one we've chosen, Kaffeehaus Herzog, is upholstered in crimson fabric with chevrons embroidered in the cushions. Wooden beams alleviate plain white plaster and cheerful gas lamps compete with the early December sunlight. A glass counter in one corner holds a display of cakes, each one sliced to reveal layers of sponge and cream and chocolate.

The other guests in the coffeehouse eye us with barely concealed curiosity. "They're probably wondering whether we're Austrian," I say, to break the uncomfortable silence.

"I know exactly what they're wondering." Eve levels a hard glare at them and they duck her gaze.

The waiter takes a while to come over and when he does, he greets Cassius, evidently deciding that the Phantom's sneer and smug sprawl make him the most likely among us to be paying the bill. But Eve answers his query in clipped and near-flawless German, making him blink and bow and hurry to the counter.

German hadn't been one of Turner's languages, so my understanding is limited, but I can glean enough to know she's ordered the cheapest coffee they have. It effectively dismisses the interest of the other guests.

"If this is how agents travel, I'm surprised you made it this far," Cassius says in light, drawling tones.

Steel, already wound up from spending the last couple of days in close proximity to the Phantom demon, bristles. "Whose fault is it that we were chased out of London with a handful of coppers in our pocket?" he says, in a hard undertone. "You and your partner were the ones who locked us up in the first place, remember?"

"I remember you killing my partner."

"Quiet."

"That's enough." Eve and I speak at the same time. We glance at each other ruefully.

"Some reunion this is turning out to be," she mutters, leaning her elbows on the small table between us.

"If only Jacob and Max were here," I add. "We'd be a complete set."

"Monaghan sent them to Ireland." Eve stares out the window, her brows pinched. "It's just his new agents in London, now. And Khurana."

"She'll be all right."

Eve nods. A month ago, I didn't think I'd see her again. I can't help but feel grateful that she's here, even if it does mean I have to tolerate Cassius' presence. She won't stay for long, though. As soon as we've found Bellemeure, she'll return to London to protect her mentor. And she'll want me to go with her, to face Monaghan together.

I push that thought to the back of my head. Right now, Bellemeure is our enemy. I can't afford to underestimate her by losing my focus. "Where should we start?"

Cassius waves a hand. "It's obvious, isn't it? This woman is going after House Asmodeus. We find them, we find her."

Steel glares at the man. He's sat next to me, as much distance as possible between him and the Phantom. "Asmodeus are Revenant demons. They can't be trusted."

"Von Tier was House Asmodeus." The demon had been halfway to establishing his own demonic House in Paris before we helped stop him. I keep my voice low, adding, "His people aren't going to look kindly on us for assisting in his murder, even if we weren't the ones holding the blade."

"They'd probably be grateful," Cassius says, lounging in his seat. Eve scowls and something thuds under the table. The demon winces and straightens, glaring at her. "At least Rayne knew how to behave in polite society," he hisses.

"Luckily there's nothing polite about you," she returns, without a blink.

Steel, whose gaze has strayed to the cake display, says, "Here's our coffee," diverting Eve from stabbing the Phantom with whatever weapon she has hidden on her person.

I pull my thick coat tighter around my shoulders and the revolver in its pocket thumps against my thigh. Before we left Paris, Dumont had made me a gift of a second Lefaucheux, along with a box of fifty cartridges that he'd had blessed by a local priest. Its weight grounds me.

The waiter sets down our drinks with professional inscrutability, ignoring the simmering frustration hovering around two of our party, and then retreats. The coffee, at least, tastes good; smooth, hot and bitter. Steel immediately dumps three sugar cubes into his.

"He's not wrong." I steer us back to the topic at hand. I'm uneasy about the idea of seeking out powerful demons, but I can't think of a more efficient plan. "If Bellemeure is targeting the Houses, it makes sense for us to hunt the same quarry. We'll be in the right place when she moves."

"I agree." Eve leans back with her cup of coffee in hand. "A pack of them will be easier to find than a single woman."

Steel stares down into his cup, his jaw flexing. "Fine."

"What about the Viennese agency?" I ask. "Austria doesn't have strong connections to Britain—Monaghan never mentioned them, at least."

"Maybe they can help us." Eve's fingers dance over the rim of her cup. "Point us in the right direction."

Steel snorts. "The last thing we need is a second agency breathing down our necks. We can do our own hunting."

"We need allies," she says. "Monaghan won't wait for ever."

I pick up a napkin and fold it into a small triangle. "It's a risk. If they do have a relationship with London, they could notify him that we're here."

"We're *supposed* to be following you. They'll only be telling him what he already knows," Eve points out. She gives me a thin-lipped smile that tells me that she hasn't quite forgiven me for running. "Cassius and I can go to the agency. You two pursue the Revenants."

"What if they don't take kindly to foreign agents on their soil?"

"Then we're no worse off than we are now."

"I suppose. Be careful, then."

Her smile widens. "I always am."

"Then what are we supposed to do, while you two are breaking down the agency's door?" asks Steel.

"Houses are aristocratic families, right?" I find a loose thread at the corner of the napkin, tug at it absently. "We follow the money."

"The season has only just begun; invitations will be sparse," Cassius says, sipping his coffee with three fingers held out, fan-like. "I'd suggest you find the Emperor. The House will be as close to the royal family as it can get."

"What if they *are* the royal family?" I ask, with a flash of apprehension.

"No. Lucifer's lot would intervene if any of the Houses started getting ideas above their station." A passing waiter throws us a disconcerted look at the name, though I think the unease is due more to the silver cross around his neck than to familiarity with the House.

"We're in public," I remind the demon.

He flashes a pearly canine in my direction. "Would you prefer to be alone?"

I scowl at him, then Steel plucks the napkin out of my hands. I've pulled half the threads loose. He tucks it under his own cup and then stares at it, as though it crawled there of its own volition.

Eve is watching me, a question in the uneven line of her brows. I turn to my coffee, which shows no apparent desire to unnerve me, and inhale half the cup.

"Are we agreed then?" she asks. At my nod, she stands and downs her own drink in a single gulp, scattering offended whispers across the coffeehouse. "Let's reconvene tonight, at the hotel." Never one for farewells, she shrugs on her coat and strides for the door. Cassius leaps up to stay within the twenty foot distance imposed by their summoning bond and follows her out.

When they're gone, our table feels oddly small. Steel rests his forearms on the surface, his hands clasped, the knuckles pale under his skin.

"Are you all right?"

He lets out a long breath. "House Asmodeus are Revenants," he says, again, as though he isn't sure I heard him earlier. "They'll blame us for von Tier's death."

It was Revenants who killed Steel's father before he went to his mother's family for protection. Before they were killed, too. "Then we keep our distance," I reply. "Bellemeure's our target, anyway."

"And *save* them?" His lip curls as he says it. "It was House Asmodeus that my uncle was planning to attack, before he and my mother were murdered. And you saw what von Tier did in Paris. They're dangerous." He pushes back his chair and it squawks against the polished stone floor. Instinctively, I reach for his elbow, then check myself and pull my hand to my side. Steel's eyes track the movement.

I press my traitorous hand to my side. "Asmodeus is just a means to an end."

"I hope that's true."

So do I.

CHAPTER TWO

I emerge from the coffeehouse blinking. The sky is clear and blue, stained with orange where the sun is falling out of sight. Crisp cold air shears through my wool jacket and I button my coat, Dumont's other gift. The white buildings that loom over me have a weight that makes the architecture of Paris look fragile. The Austrian city would scorn France's national call of *Liberté, Egalité, Fraternité*; it is the heart of an Empire and it does not deign to be anything else.

"Which way?" I ask.

"The ring road," he says, gesturing towards the setting sun. "It's thick with traffic; I should be able to pick up a scent."

We'd crossed the road on our way from the cheap hotel that Eve had picked out. It carves a path around the inner city in a large, voyeuristic circle, marking a clear divide between the city's heart and its outlying districts. As we approach it now, I slip my hand into my pocket, wrapping my fingers around the pistol's handle. Though my experience of using it so far has only been one shot, a failed attempt at taking down the opera's ghost, the feel of the wood warming my palm makes me walk straighter.

I can't deny the awe that flickers through me as we step onto the ring road. The buildings lining it are an odd compilation of architectural styles, but all of them are huge, shrinking the city's population to the size of ants. The road itself is wide enough to hold a royal parade along with a throng of eager citizens—or angry ones—divided in the centre by a strip of trees and unlit lanterns.

An open carriage drawn by two white horses trots by. The couple inside grin fiercely into the wind, bundled in furs from foot to chin. Steel makes a dismissive sound. "Tourists."

It takes us a few moments to cross the wide road, and I examine the faces of each person we pass, looking for the unusual eyes or unnatural beauty that might indicate demonic blood. As we near the pavement on the other side, the faint strains of an orchestra reach us. The sound seems to be coming from a stretch of green ahead.

"Is that music?" I ask.

Steel has already paused, as if the noise has embedded lures into his heart and tugged. "It's a concerto, I think." He drifts towards the sound and a thought comes to me, unbidden; if someone wanted to trap Steel, this would be the perfect bait.

"A what?" My knowledge of music is as vast as my knowledge of fashion.

"Schubert," he says, as if that explains it. The name rings a bell, a dream-memory I had in a Paris cemetery; a memory not my own. "Vienna is home to some of the greatest composers in Europe," he adds. "If there's anywhere to start, it's a concert."

It's easier, now, to quiet my mind and listen to the seed of Steel's emotions at the back of it, brimming with trepidation and wonder. I'm conscious of my own anxiety and try to temper it.

But Steel doesn't seem to notice. He crosses the road—dodging a carriage and earning a shouted curse—and reaches a low wall on the other side, hopping straight over it. I nip through the open gate a few feet to the side. In summer, these gardens must bloom in verdant glory, a riot of colour. Now the grass is thin, the trees sagging. The winter cold seems to have driven away all but the most dedicated naturalists.

We follow the music towards the centre of the park. Two little boys in matching blue coats and thick scarves chase each other across a manicured lawn. An urchin in a torn coat and filthy cap watches from the shade of a pine tree and one brave painter sits on the lawn with an easel, attempting to capture the image of a large white pavilion; the source of the music.

As we drift across the lawn, the sound of trumpets comes to an end and the air is filled with polite applause. The sides of the pavilion are made of tall arched windows, and through them I can see a collection of tables filled with couples and young families. Their feathered hats and striped suits would mark them as aristocracy, even if the delicate china on the tables didn't.

"It looks like a cafe," I say, turning to examine the orchestra, which is only a small band arranged on a low stage.

"Invitation only," Steel adds, and I see the entrance, where the owners of the two boys are presenting a slip of paper.

"Would Asmodeus be here," I ask, "out in the open?"

"Why not? It's not as though anyone here can stop them."

The applause has died off and the orchestra takes up their instruments again. The first notes spill into the quiet and my lips part unconsciously. Cellos, slow and mournful at first, then they swell, rising on the crest of a wave like the sky before the dawn. And then violins, soaring, so perfect I could weep.

I *am* weeping; tears track a damp path down my cheek. I inhale shakily and wipe my face. Some of the pavilion's patrons are crying, too. I drag my gaze from them to Steel. He has his eyes closed, his lips pressed tight together, but his hands are held out, palm up.

"Steel," I say, so quiet the word is little more than a breath.

He twitches and glances at me, startled. His eyes are pale, the pupils thin and long and serpentine.

"Your eyes—"

He shuts them quickly, rubs one hand over them. When he opens them again they look normal, the pupils round and human. He makes a startled sound. "Are you—crying?"

Hastily I swipe at my damp cheeks. "It's the music." Then I recall what he'd said once, about magic being like music. "Unless... Was it you?"

"I can't feel it," he says, in a low, hard tone. "I can't feel anything."

"But it's been nearly a week." Bellemeure's poison should be out of his system by now, surely?

"I know that!" His hands clench, then he exhales, lets them fall open. "My magic should have returned by now."

Unless the result is permanent. I don't say it, but he takes one look at my face and makes a *tch* sound, turning his face away. "She'll have an antidote," I say. "She must, to protect the demons working for her. We'll have to persuade her to give it up."

"I'll make her give it up." It's said with the air of a man about to take on an invading army.

"Just don't—" A shout cuts off my attempt to soothe his temper. The boy in the dirty cap shoots out through the entrance to the cafe and bolts past us.

Steel stiffens. "That child's a demon."

"Stopp!" The waiter shouts, as a nobleman at his side curses and pats down his jacket. "Stopp ihn!"

That's easy enough to understand. As one, Steel and I run after the thief. As small as he is, he's quick on his feet, and he disappears into the park as though he knows it well.

"This way," Steel calls, darting down a deserted path.

I stay as close to his heels as I can, running with pounding feet through the park and emerging somewhere to the east. We race through a narrower street lined with the heavy cream buildings so prevalent in this city before we reach a divide. An open arch leads to a small alley. Without hesitation, Steel races through it.

His movements blur and then he's snatching at the boy's jacket, yanking him to a halt in the middle of the empty alley.

"That's enough," he says, not even out of breath.

I stumble to a stop, pressing at the sting in my side and panting. If we continue to work together, I'm going to need to develop stronger muscles.

"Why were you running?" I ask, when I've caught my breath.

The boy glares at me from under the brim of his cap. His cheeks are full and round and his hair is shorn close to his scalp, giving him the appearance of a trapped mouse. Except for the unnaturally bright gleam of his eyes.

Steel shakes him gently. "What did you steal, you little scamp?"

A mutinous glare is all the answer we get.

"He might not understand English."

Steel says something in a language I've only heard once, from the mouth of a Stalker demon we confronted in London. The words are guttural, stone scraping against stone.

The child wriggles in his hold. An exclamation bursts from him, one that I don't need to translate to understand as an expletive.

Steel looks amused. "He curses my heritage and your interfering nose."

I touch the object self-consciously, then say, "It isn't *my* nose that led us here."

"Well, he had to pick *something*."

"Tell him we don't care what he stole," I say, tugging my hand down and meeting the child's gaze. "We want to know about demons."

To my surprise, the child spits on the cobbled stone and curses again.

Steel shakes him, harder this time, and makes a demand in that odd language. The boy's reply comes with a jutted jaw and a scowl.

"He thinks we're after him and his people," Steel explains. His grip on the boy's jacket relaxes.

I wave my hand. "Nein, nein," I say, making use of the little German I know. "We're looking for Revenant demons. Asmodeus."

The child's eyes widen and he goes limp, staring at me with horror written clear across his face. Steel lets go of his collar. The child doesn't move.

I crouch to make myself smaller, less threatening. "We're not here for you, or any of your family," I say, slowly and clearly. My old warrant card sits in my other coat pocket, the only thing tying me to the Agency. I pull it out, show him the Queen's crest. "English," I add, tapping my breastbone. "English polizei."

He flinches at the last word. Steel asks him another question in that demonic language and he mumbles a response.

"He says they're at Schönbrunn," Steel translates, his brow crinkling. "Isn't that a palace?"

"He can't be talking about the Habsburgs, can he?"

Steel's attention goes to me as I speak and the lapse is enough for the child to dash away through the alley. Before I realise it, the flap of his jacket has vanished around the corner.

"Damn it." Steel tips his head back, scowling at the amber sky. "We should have asked him more questions."

"That's enough to go on, for now." If Asmodeus are living at Schönbrunn, they must have ties to the Emperor. Which will mean guards, legal protection, and perhaps even links to the Viennese agency. "Let's go back to the hotel and tell Eve. She might have learnt more."

Agent E. Wilson

It's easy enough to find Vienna's police station; the building is huge and white and perches on a stretch of the Ringstrasse like an overstuffed bird of prey. Staring at it from across the street, Eve's palms start to sweat. She pulls them out of her coat pockets and touches her fingers to the stiletto dagger tucked into her corset. Dumont had arranged to have it blessed back in Paris, along with Hazel's bullets, and she draws courage from its solidity.

"Well?" she asks Cassius. "You said there were demons here. Where?"

Cassius burrows his chin into his turned up collar, his vivid blue eyes shaded by the brim of a trendy bowler hat he'd nicked in Paris. "Not the main entrance," he says, examining the officers that stand there. "I'd guess around the back."

"I'd prefer to have more than a guess."

"Then perhaps you should find another demon," is his arch response.

It's been two weeks of dealing with him as her partner, and she still can't suppress the frustration and annoyance that surges through her whenever they argue. Not that she really tries. "Lead the way, then."

He trounces off as if he'd been waiting for the order, heading straight for the far side. The setting sun casts shadows over the gap between the station and the building beside it. The door to the latter is flanked by two guards.

"Ah, well," says Cassius. "Close enough."

Eve huffs. She doesn't falter, keeping her stride even and her face stern. Both soldiers are pale-skinned and dark-haired, and they stare at her warily as she approaches. Neither reaches for the rifle resting against their shoulders, though.

"Evening," she says. "I'm here to see your regional commander." Khurana had taught her Prussian-German, and the words are more clipped and abrupt than the Austrian-German she's heard in this city. The soldiers blink rapidly. It's probably not her accent that surprises them, but the fact she speaks their language at all.

"Your—your name, Fräulein?" one ventures. Cautious but polite, and her muscles relax a little. She'd feared that the further east she went the harder it would get, but this wary civility is a reception she's familiar with.

Part of her can't help but recognise it's a reception *Hazel* would never meet. She squashes that thought quickly. They each have their barriers to cross, and if Eve faces more of them it just makes her better at smashing them down. That's the plan, anyway.

She pulls out her identification card, flicking the leather wallet open. "Agent Wilson." Just saying the title is enough to fill her with a bubbling kind of confidence. "Assigned to the

British Investigation Agency. This is my colleague, Cassius." The Phantom demon grins at them and their eyes widen. "We're tracking a rogue agent through your city and would like to discuss the potential dangers with your commander."

The words *rogue* and *dangers* have them twitching, as she thought they would, and the men reward her with crisp bows. "Please proceed to the first door on your right," one says. "The secretary will direct you, Fräulein."

"Agent," she corrects and marches past them.

It takes her a moment to adjust to the darkness inside the building. The walls are panelled in some kind of dark wood and light comes only from electric bulbs in the shape of drooping tulips. Wooden shutters frame the windows, but though they're open, their awkward angles restrict the view. The entrance lobby is spacious, furnished with a few leather chairs and paved in marble.

"I could..." Cassius trails off, making a rolling gesture with his left hand. She's unreasonably annoyed that she understands what he means.

"No," she replies. "If you're invisible and they sniff you out, we'll have more to explain than we're prepared to."

The first door on her right stands open. She heads for it, pausing on the threshold and knocking twice. A woman with a high-necked blouse and greying hair looks up from her desk. Eve makes her request and the woman frowns.

"The Commander is not in Vienna at present," she says. "Perhaps you would be better off visiting the police next door."

"I will settle for his deputy. Or," Eve adds, with a flash of inspiration, "the foreign office liaison. You do have someone who deals with international agencies, I assume?" Her blend of assurance and condescension pulls colour to the other woman's face.

"Of course the Gendarmerie has a foreign liaison. This is Vienna. There are more than one hundred agents here."

"Is that so?" Eve does her best to keep her face blank. That's ten times more than Britain.

The secretary makes a derisive noise and Eve realises she might have been better off letting some of her awe slip through.

"That's impressive," she says, trying to recover. "Our resources back in Britain are not nearly as numerous." The irony of comparing one empire to another does not escape her. "We would only need a moment," she adds. "I believe that the rogue agent we are tracking arrived in the city yesterday."

The secretary arranges a few of the papers on her desk. "Herr Gruber will be in his office on the third floor," she says. "You may be able to catch him between his appointments."

"Thank you, Fräulein." The deliberate error in address makes the red in the woman's cheeks fluctuate and Eve leaves her trying to suppress a pleased expression.

A staircase leads from the far end of the lobby up to the next floor, and Eve marches through a series of large open parlours before she finds the next staircase. The second floor is full of grand offices, the leather polished and the wood varnished. When she reaches the third floor, she expects to find cracks in the skirting boards and chips in the paintings hung along the walls—regardless of their posturing, all agencies structure themselves the same way; the longer you have to walk, the less important you're deemed. But here, the floor is lushly carpeted and the paintings are framed in gold.

The offices here are smaller though, the doors marked with tiny gold plaques. Eve slows her pace and peers at them. *Intelligence Agent* one reads, and the next *Dog Handler*. The Agency had used bloodhounds in the past, but they weren't as good at picking up a demon's scent as the government had hoped, cutting short the plan to replace the Agency's female Hound agents. Vienna must have figured out a more productive approach.

An office at the end of the corridor reads *Foreign Liaison* and Eve raps her knuckles against the wood. She gives it a moment, then, when no answer comes, tries the handle. It opens under her touch.

Contrary to her hopes, the office isn't empty. A bearded man leaps up from behind the desk, staring at her, aghast.

"Who do you think you are, barging in here?" he demands. His shirtsleeves are rolled up to his elbows and his fingers are stained with ink. "Who are you?"

Eve calculates quickly. "Forgive my interruption, Agent. The secretary sent me," she adds, throwing blame on the woman without hesitation. "I'm here to speak to you about a rogue agent."

"Do you have an appointment?" he asks, pointedly.

"The danger was too near for me to arrange one." The man is the only one in the room; he has no demon. "You *are* the Foreign Liaison, are you not?"

He draws himself up and tugs at the bottom of his waistcoat. "Agent Gruber," he says. "And you are?"

"Agent Wilson." She shows him her identification, with less finesse than she'd used on the soldiers. "This is Cassius." She enters the room to stand opposite the desk, Cassius following her languidly.

At the intrusion of the demon, Gruber runs one hand over his balding head. The other he settles on the desk. "I see. You are partnered, then?"

She relaxes at the acknowledgement. They're in the right place. "You are not?"

"Only field agents undergo the joining."

Perhaps that's why the Gendarmerie can afford to employ a hundred agents. "I told your secretary that I was tracking a rogue agent, but it's closer to the truth to say I'm hunting a very dangerous demon. I'll require your assistance."

"What kind of demon? Our field agents are on location and our soldiers are busy guarding His Majesty—"

"It's not force I need," Eve interrupts. "My partner can manage that. I need to know if there are any areas of the city where demons congregate. A powerful group, for example, that might be harbouring our suspect."

The man eases back into his chair. "You should visit Favoriten," he grumbles. "The schrei demons are on the verge of inciting riots." The German word he uses could mean a Strike demon or a Scout, with their bat-like calls.

"Is that all?" she asks.

He eyes her. "What else are you expecting? You said you need no support."

Eve considers asking about Asmodeus, but plucking that name out of thin air will only be met with more suspicion. She and Hazel can try this Favoriten district first.

"Thank you," she says. "I will report on my progress, so you need have no fear that I will let this demon continue to run free."

"Yes, yes, if you wish." He waves a hand at her. "If that is all, then I must return to my work. Good day."

Bemused, Eve retreats, closing the door behind her. In the corridor, between a portrait of an ancient robed king and one of a dark-haired woman in a cascading white gown, she looks at Cassius. "He didn't seem worried."

"They have a hundred men," he says, with irony. "What do they have to fear from one rogue demon?"

"At least they won't be in our pocket, this way." She touches the corner of the painting as she passes. The frame is solid gold.

Agent J. Horner

Cerulean ribbons wind through Clara's bodice and tie in a bow at the front. They have the effect of highlighting her natural assets, so Jacob thinks it's safe for his gaze to linger there. The ribbon must be silk by the way it shines.

"Do you know why he wants to see us?" he asks. Golden motes of dust dance in the air. It used to be only Maia who was permitted to clean the professor's study. Now, the man's here so little that her absence doesn't seem to make a difference.

"He has a job for you." Clara's voice is crisp, authoritative. She stands with her hands clasped behind her back and, though she wears ribbons on her dress, her hair is pulled into the same tight bun that Hazel favours.

"It'll be nice to work together," he offers, and when she stares at him belatedly he realises she'd said *you*, not *us*. He tries to think of something to break the awkward silence and only succeeds in opening and closing his mouth a few times. He wishes, not for the first time, that Hazel or Eve were here. They'd know what to do.

Clara's new demon clings to her shadow. The woman is built on broad lines, hard in the places Clara is soft. Only Max's confirmation had convinced him she was a Hound; she carries herself like a Reaper. Something about her makes him reluctant to turn his back.

The door clicks open and Jacob straightens. "Professor," he says, as the man walks past him to the desk. Tiberius takes up his usual station by the window, watching. His amber eyes seem to swallow the afternoon light.

Taking a seat, the professor brushes a wayward strand of blond hair off his forehead. The man's jaw is clean-shaven, his eyes clear. A navy chequered suit makes the most of good shoulders and a physique that has stayed slim even into middle age.

The ever-present alarm at the back of his head starts to chime, telling him he's been looking for too long. Jacob tears his gaze away.

"Thank you for joining us, Agent Horner," the man says.

Jacob can't tell which *us* he means. "You have a task for us, sir?" His us is simple; he and Max are a team. They will be until he retires—or dies, which is probably more likely.

"Our newest agents need training." The professor starts shuffling through a stack of papers. He's been getting more correspondence since his appointment as Shadow Commissioner, and he's at the Houses of Parliament more than the agency. "You and Khurana will take them to Belfast. There have been a number of attacks against Catholics there. I suspect there is more behind them than your typical social unrest."

"Do we have any leads, sir?"

"Not yet." It's Clara that answers, and the professor lets her. "Khurana is compiling a list of areas to investigate. You'll sail from Portsmouth in the morning."

"The morning? But we'd have to leave London straight away."

"Yes. You have rooms booked at an inn by the docks."

"We haven't packed."

"The servants are taking care of it," she says, and that's new; servants.

"Do you require more time, Agent?" the professor asks.

He thinks of the half-finished landscape in his room. "N-no, sir. We'll be ready."

"Good. I know that Blythe and Cooper will appreciate your guidance. Ensure that Khurana stays by your side during the journey."

It's all said in the same level tone, with the same half-stern, half-thoughtful expression the professor always wears, so Jacob almost misses the strangeness of the order. "Yes, Professor," he says. First Hazel flees with her demon, then Eve summons Cassius and gets ordered to follow her. Now he's accompanying their best Hound agent out of the country? What on earth is going on?

"I am glad to hear it." A moment passes, and then the professor looks up from whatever new government order demands his attention. "That will be all, Agent."

Jacob startles, embarrassed, and pops down and up in a quick bow. "Thank you, Professor." He hesitates, then adds, "Agent Ward."

Clara blinks, as though she hadn't expected him to use her title. Jacob tries not to feel offended at that; perhaps another man wouldn't, but he can remember the rap of Turner's verbal reprimand as though she were still in the room. Still alive.

Max sticks so closely to his back as they leave that Jacob feels like he should be carrying a sack of diamonds on the way to a vault. "What is it?" he asks, when the door has clicked shut behind them. The professor's assistant had left a couple of days ago and his desk is still empty. Another thing that's new.

The Reaper demon stares into the distance, quiet, and Jacob waits. Before he was promoted, he'd spent time with Maximus at the side of his mentor, but the close quarters of their partnership is something different; it had taught him that Max kept his opinions to himself unless Jacob invited them into the air. It had also taught him that Max wouldn't say a single bad word about anyone—not even the Blood Drinker demons they'd faced a few months ago—and that if he saw a stray cat he'd stop to pet it even if it meant they'd miss their train.

"Tiberius," says the demon, and nothing else.

It's enough to make Jacob tug his jacket, make his neck ache with the urge to look behind him. "What about him?"

"He's been watching us."

"You mean back there, in the office?"

"Everywhere." They reach the staircase that leads down to the lobby and Max actually does look behind them then. The afternoon light casts shadows under the demon's curls, lends fire to the amber of his irises. "He's always looking at me."

A hole opens in his stomach. But no, it can't be what he thinks. Tiberius would never be so open about it if it was; no one would dare, even a demon. More likely, the other Reaper is considering their performance.

He casts about for something reassuring. "You two aren't the only Reapers at the Agency, anymore. Perhaps he's thinking about a promotion." The words come out hollow. Max might be powerful enough to earn a harder caseload, but Jacob wouldn't be able to keep up. He doesn't have Hazel's knowledge, or Eve's courage. He'd only hold Max back. "Or perhaps the professor's thinking about giving you to someone else."

Max stiffens, turning away from the empty corridor. "I wouldn't go," he says, loyal to a fault. Jacob tries not to read into it; Max is a good partner. Of course he'd say that.

"Let's go," he says. "We should find the new agents."

Jacob had attended the ritual to bind the new demons, just after Eve had left. One Phantom and one Reaper. The Phantom had been summoned and bound without difficulty, but the first Reaper who'd answered had been a woman. The Professor had broken up the gathering and dismissed them, and the next time Jacob saw the agent, he had a new demon—a male one. He never found out what happened to the woman. He hadn't asked.

They find the two men in the lobby, already in coats and gloves, their demons dressed to match. Two suitcases and a portmanteau wait by the front doors. Max rolls his shoulders as they draw close and the new Reaper works his jaw, his stare belligerent.

"Agent Blythe." It comes out with the tone of a rebuke, though Jacob doesn't mean it to.

The agent purses his lips, but he calls his demon to order with a brusque, "Valerian."

"Evening, Horner," says the other agent, the one with the Phantom. His demon is a waspish young man that reminds Jacob of Cassius.

"Cooper. Where's Khurana?"

"Braiding her hair, probably," Agent Blythe mutters. Jacob elects to ignore the comment. If they start fighting now, the whole case could be jeopardised.

A servant trots past them to set down another bag and Jacob recognises his own walnut leather trunk, the one he'd had engraved with his initials after they'd completed their first case. His skin crawls at the idea of someone going through his things, folding them, choosing which ones to take and which to leave. He rubs his palms together, asks, "Who has the tickets?"

"We do." It's Khurana, coming down the stairs with her usual gliding gait, her demon Isis at her heels. Her stern ash-grey gaze pins them in their place. "So, if you are finished gossiping like grandmothers, we will proceed."

It's almost comedic, the way the new agents bristle. Cooper's demon speaks first, smooth like Cassius, too. "As ready as we can be, miss. Ladies first," he adds, picking up a trunk with one hand and Khurana's portmanteau with the other.

"The train leaves in an hour," Khurana says, walking past the demon as if he doesn't exist. As Isis passes Jacob, she murmurs, "We will speak when we reach Portsmouth." The words are clearly only meant to be heard by him.

Jacob bends to pick up his trunk, hiding his face; Dominic always told him that his eyebrows gave him away. Perhaps Khurana already knows about the professor's order and wants to persuade him that she doesn't need supervision. He'd be happy to let her; this whole thing feels unnecessary, and he can't imagine why they're being sent so far away so soon after the ritual.

The trunk feels oddly light. Hoping the servants haven't forgotten anything important, he follows Khurana and leaves the
agency.

CHAPTER THREE

Having a bank account behind us makes a difference to our reception at the hotel. After naming the bank, the concierge's bow almost touches the floor as he hands us two keys. Two rooms, for the four of us. Eve takes them without a change of expression.

The bellhop waits for us to squeeze into the gold and blue elevator and then drags the doors closed. He pulls a lever and the compartment inches upwards. We stand in silence, Eve and I beside the bellhop and the demons behind us. Only the creaking of the chains as the elevator rises accompanies the sound of our breathing.

I grow more tense as the arrow above the doors ticks closer to our floor. I'm used to sharing a room with Steel. We work around each other with distant caution, doing our best to ignore the details that would otherwise make the arrangement uncomfortable. Now, with Eve and Cassius crammed into the small box with us, I'm reminded that our arrangement would be considered indecent to anyone else.

We reach our floor and the bellhop rattles the doors open, professionally inscrutable as we evacuate. Patterned paper covers the walls, glimmering in the light of a few gas lamps. Eve turns the two keys over in her fingers, counting the rooms out loud as we pass.

"Here." She opens a door and indicates the one next to it with the other key. "We have that one, too." She ventures inside, followed closely by Cassius. Swallowing, I brave the room.

It's larger than the one we'd procured in Paris. The walls are duck egg blue, the twin beds covered in white cotton so clean there's not a mark on it. Three chairs are clustered around a low coffee table near an adjoining door, which must be a little over ten feet from the nearest bed. I glance at Eve. She's studying the beds.

"Well, isn't this cosy." Cassius drops into one of the chairs, just within the edge of the ritual's boundary.

"How is this going to work?" Steel asks, bluntly. "Because if I have to share a room with him, one of us is going to end up dead and it's not going to be me." The two glower at each other.

"I'm sure you'll manage," Eve retorts, just as blunt. She drags the bed closer to the adjoining door. "Besides, I had to put up with him for two weeks hunting you down. This is the least you can do."

"So, the agency liaison suggested Favoriten?" I ask, picking up on the conversation we'd begun earlier, diverting their attention.

Eve turns from Steel with one last glare. "It's a poor district to the south. Mostly migrants and factory workers."

"We won't find Asmodeus there," Steel interjects, starting to pace. "They'll surround themselves with wealth. It's what they do."

"A palace, though?" Eve's voice is doubtful. "That seems excessive. And wouldn't the Habsburgs have a problem with that?"

Cassius kicks his legs out and crosses one ankle over the other. "Schönbrunn is the summer palace. The imperial family will winter in Hofburg."

"How do you know that?"

"What do you think I was doing while Rayne was pretending to work?" he responds. "Clipping my claws?"

"The liaison wouldn't have suggested Favoriten for the hell of it." Eve moves around the bed to unpack her case, nudging Cassius' feet out of the way as she goes. "There must be demons there."

"They wouldn't live in poverty," Steel replies. He scowls when Cassius moves his legs to cut off the small track he'd been wearing into the carpet.

"You said Bellemeure had a grudge against these demons. Surely she wouldn't stay near them?"

Bellemeure had been annoyed at von Tier's concept of 'entertainment', the way he'd pit Revenants against weaker demons for the pleasure of his guests. "In Paris, she moved among the aristocracy as if she was born to it," I reply, working through my reasoning aloud. "And it worked—it led her to von Tier."

"She doesn't know we're after her," Steel points out, and flicks Cassius' legs out of his path using the toe of his boot. "There's no reason to think she won't do the same again."

"Fine," Eve says, with a sigh. "We'll try this palace first, then Favoriten. Now leave us alone," she adds, to the demons. "Unless you object to us changing clothes?"

"Are you inviting us to watch?" Cassius asks, smirking.

Eve taps her sternum, returning his smile.

The Phantom levers himself out of his chair with an exaggerated sigh. "Fine. Come along, Dragon." He takes the second key and saunters through the adjoining door.

"Don't call me that." Steel pauses on the threshold, glancing back at me. "You'll...call if you need anything?"

"I will."

He nods and closes the door behind him with the air of a man going to the gallows. I feel an odd moment of disconnection—the last time we were apart, it was because Bellemeure had drugged him while her companion abducted me and dumped me in a cemetery.

Eve scatters her things on the bed. She's travelling light; a second blouse, a couple of nightgowns, a silk hair scarf for sleeping and a single penny dreadful, its cover depicting a masked highwayman.

"Some light reading?" My own luggage is just as sparse; the two outfits from Paris and the journal Steel gave me.

"I needed something to distract me from the company."

"It's going well, I take it?" I ask, as I brush and hang the dresses.

She snorts. "He's a nightmare. But you don't need me to tell you that."

I falter, remembering the dark alley in Whitechapel, the struggle with Rayne as Cassius fought Steel. The spill of blood on my hands. "No. I suppose I don't. What are you going to do with him, afterwards?"

"That depends on what afterwards looks like." I feel her gaze on the back of my neck and turn around. Her expression is assessing. "If I prove myself, he might let me choose another demon."

He. I go back to my luggage, picking up my journal. Its leather cover is soft under my fingertips.

"Of course, that assumes neither of us end up dead before we get back. The option may well be taken out of my hands."

"One can only hope," I quip and surprise a bark of laughter out of her. Then she gives me a narrow look, as if she's seen something on my face she hadn't noticed before.

The room has a modest writing desk tucked into a corner and I sit down, opening my journal. The Compendium of Demons ends on a portrait of Dragon demons, my and Steel's exchanges written in the margins. I turn to a fresh page and title it *Language*. The Agency holds no information on the language Steel spoke earlier, though it's used widely enough that it's understandable by an urchin in Vienna and a Stalker demon from Whitechapel. I make a note to ask him about it when we get a chance.

"This is nice." Eve touches the corner of the page, careful not to obstruct my work. "Good quality paper. How much was it?"

"It—it was a gift." My pen blots and I shake it out, ignoring the warmth travelling slowly up my neck.

"Really." At the non-question, I glance up. Eve's expression is pensive. "From who?" she asks, with a pointed arch of her brow.

I have a sudden childish urge to reply, *Nobody.* I focus very hard on dipping my pen into the hotel-provided ink pot. "It was Steel's idea, actually. For the case."

"For the case."

"How much do we have for the hotel?" I ask, seeking an escape from Eve's too-keen eyes. "If we're here for more than a few days, we may need to look at other options."

She sighs. "We'll have to put it on the Agency's account and settle at the end of the month. Assuming…"

"That we're not dead by then, yes."

"And that Monaghan doesn't come after us."

"He won't. He'll give you some time, at least." He won't want to be seen as concerned, not about a lone woman travelling around Europe, even one with a demon. Not unless we give him a reason to be.

Eve changes into her nightgown to oil her hair. "Have you been sleeping in that?" she asks me, as I strip down to my chemise.

"I didn't get much chance to go shopping, in Paris."

"I figured. I brought a spare." She gestures at the second nightgown, a simple white cotton dress with draped sleeves.

"Thank you." I change while Eve wraps her hair in the scarf, tucking the end under the front.

"You're just like Turner, you know," she says, as I'm sliding into the bed.

My breath catches on old grief. "Oh?"

She turns down the lamp, then climbs into the bed nearest the adjoining door, the faint street lamps casting her figure in blue-grey and gold. "She had the same expression when she was puzzling out her next steps. Khurana's the same. Everyone has their tells." Eve's voice carries an undercurrent of suppressed strain.

"You're worried about her."

"Of course I'm worried about her," she replies. "Who knows what Monaghan is going to do? When I left, he'd started hunting down every demon in London. If he finds out about her and Isis—" She cuts herself off. "I can't turn my back on our home so easily."

That hurts. "You think it was easy for me to leave?"

"That's not what I meant."

"It tears me up that I left." I speak to the ceiling, searching the cracks in the plaster like it might give me an expression. "That I wasn't able to stop him and Tiberius. He's a monster."

"But you're still here."

I bite the inside of my mouth. "Steel needed my help."

"Right."

The faint clopping of horse hooves comes from somewhere outside, until a gust of wind drowns the noise. I thought we could forget the argument we had before we left; that I had suspected Khurana of murder, how Eve had suspected Steel of swaying me. Evidently I was wrong.

"I can't stay," Eve says.

"In Vienna?"

"In Europe. If we don't find this Bellemeure within the next week, I'll take Cassius back to London."

A week, that's all she's giving me? "It might take longer than a week," I reply. A shadow passes over the ceiling as a cloud blocks out the moon.

Something rustles and I glance over to find Eve propping herself up on one elbow. Her expression is hidden in darkness. "Come with me," she says.

"What?"

"Come back with me. You can't stay here. What will you do, when he doesn't need you anymore?"

Stupidly, I think of the idea I'd had in Paris, of forming my own agency. "I don't know, yet," I evade.

"We can make a difference. With Jacob and Max—we can stop him. But we'll need your help."

I glance back at the ceiling, at a sliver of dark space where the paint has chipped. "I can't leave Steel now, not when we're this close. Not after he helped me in London."

There's a pause, then Eve says, "This is going to be a problem, isn't it?"

"What is?"

"You, falling in love with him."

A gust of air whistles through a gap in the windowpane. "I don't know what you mean."

"I know you better than that."

My gaze is drawn to the door that joins our two hotel rooms. Steel is asleep now—one of those things I just seem to know, thanks to the spell; where he is and whether he's awake or not. "I am in control," I say.

Eve makes a doubtful sound, but she flops back onto the bed. "If you say so. Regardless, you'll have to leave eventually. Perhaps you should think about what you're going to do then."

I turn on my side, facing the window, and despite my desire to forget the conversation and join Eve in sleep, thinking about it is all I do until the sun rises.

CHAPTER FOUR

The wind sneaks through the sturdy buildings on either side of the street and carries a fresh, humid scent to the open window of our carriage. Vienna must rise later than London, as we meet only a handful of people and very few carriages.

Our hansom cab takes us through a square dominated by a cathedral. Its pyramid spire seems tall enough to reach the heavens, and it towers over a steep roof decorated in geometric patterns. Even though people hurry through the square, their voices drop to a whisper around the structure, as if God himself is sleeping inside.

We turn from the cathedral and head south, winding through the huge hulking buildings. Vienna wakes around us, generating cabs and open air carriages, draft horses pulling huge barrels, the drivers calling to each other in brassy German. Along the sides of the road, pale awnings shade potted trees and figures crouch over steaming mugs. Pairs of women and young men promenade across the cobblestones. We pause to circumvent a horse-pulled tram and a whistling street performer regales us through the window.

None of us speak, and it seems an age before we break away from the city and the cab finally comes to a stop. I hop out while Eve pays the driver and Cassius complains about the seats. We stand by a thin river on a bridge three times its breadth, the bulky architecture replaced by leafless trees. Beside me, Steel stretches one arm over his head, yawning.

I consider telling him about Eve's time limit. But that won't endear her to him, and arguments aren't going to help us find Bellemeure. "How was your night?" I ask, instead. We'd all tumbled out of the hotel and straight into a cab without much chance to exchange more than a bleary greeting.

"Wonderful," he replies, dryly. "I've always wanted to spend more time with that asshole."

I wince. "I take it he was his usual charming self?"

"I'm sure he would have been thrilled to provoke me into a fight." A sideways glance. "I restrained myself."

"Thank you."

"I wouldn't want to cause the hotel staff any additional work. Blood is so difficult to get out of the carpet."

"I *do* appreciate it, you know," I add, quietly. "We can use all the help we can get."

"Next time, perhaps we can be a little more discerning about the help in question."

I snort. Eve and Cassius join us and we go silent, gazing across the river. Palace seems too simple a word to describe the structure on the other bank. Its pale orange walls and pure white windows glow under the rays of the rising sun. Tall plinths topped with some kind of bird flank the entrance and lower buildings stretch out on either side. The central edifice must be three stories tall, and the staircase leading up to its first floor curves around a pillared entrance. Statues bristle from the roof like spears.

"Not bad," says Cassius. "Although orange is not the colour I would have chosen."

"By all means, let the decorators know." Eve glances at Steel. "How do you plan on getting past those guards?"

Two soldiers in white cloaks stand guard in front of the plinths. We're far enough away that our gawking could be taken for the awe of tourists, but the way they cup their rifles in their hands indicates they won't be as easy to pass as the Gendarmerie's guards.

"He can distract them," answers Steel, poking at the Phantom demon. "Go on. Distract them."

Cassius gives him a disdainful look. "You must be joking."

"You're the only one here who can turn invisible."

It's not a bad idea. Not one of our better ones, but we won't get anywhere out here. "We'd only need a moment," I add.

"I don't think—"

"Come on." Eve thumps him on the back with her fist, making him tip forward before he catches himself. "Push them over, or something."

The Phantom demon tuts at her, straightening his coat. After a long, harried-sounding exhalation, he vanishes. We start along the bridge that crosses the river, Steel on one side of me and Eve on the other.

Along with their cloaks, the soldiers wear metal caps topped by feathers. They gaze straight ahead, much like the Queen's Guard outside Buckingham Palace, undisturbed by the occasional pedestrian that passes. As we get close, Eve raises her voice and adopts a soft northern accent.

"Look at that!" she exclaims, pointing at the palace. "Ain't that grand. And you said it weren't 'owt."

Steel looks at her, wide-eyed, and I pick up her cue, leaning into my natural clipped London accent. "I didn't say nothin'," I protest. "I said we oughta see the church, that's what I said."

We exchange a couple more sallies, carrying our pretence of being British tourists almost to the gate. I'm starting to despair of Cassius doing anything when the soldier on my left abruptly pitches forward onto his face.

The man scrambles up and scrabbles for his rifle, yelling in German.

"Was?" calls the other man, his grip on the rifle tightening, adding something else I can't parse.

Again the first soldier stumbles, and this time his gun flies out of his hands, spins through the air, and lands almost on the river bank. Both soldiers stare at it in silence. Then they erupt in a shouting match. The one on my right gestures wildly at the gun, getting more and more red in the face, and the other yells back. Finally, he marches off towards the rifle, stiff-legged in embarrassment, and as the second glances down the street to see if anyone noticed, Steel grabs me by the wrist and pulls me between the plinths into the courtyard.

The space is split down the middle with a line of potted trees, two fountains big enough to swim in on either side. It's framed by the two low buildings and faces the palace. Very few places to hide. We hurry along the edge of the building until we can whip around a corner, out of sight of the guards.

"There must be a servant's entrance around here some-where," I breathe.

"We'll draw less attention if we split up." Eve had followed us and peeks around the building's corner to watch the guards.

"Meet back here, or the hotel," I say and she nods. We split apart, Eve—and, I assume, Cassius—heading right and Steel and I going left. Though lower compared to the palace, the buildings on each side are still tall enough to obscure any glimpse of the world beyond.

"That could be a servant's entrance," Steel points out, indicating a humble white door. We walk closer, sticking to the wall, and the building on our left ends. A colonnade connects it to the central palace, letting us glimpse the start of what must be a vast park. We're far enough from the city centre that it's probably used as a hunting ground.

Steel stops, stiffening. "Guards," he mutters.

There's nowhere to hide but the colonnade. "The gardens?" I whisper.

"Do you trust me?" The words are uttered in an odd, stilted tone.

"Yes?" I hazard, wondering what on earth he's going to do.

"Just remember," he says, as he grabs my hand, "we're sup-posed to be married."

"What—"

He drags me into the colonnade and presses me against one of the creamy stone columns, then ducks down, covering me with his body and tucking his face close to mine, tilted so he can see the courtyard.

I stare at the expanse of greenery past his shoulder. "I have concerns about this plan." I say it partly because the situation is indeed ridiculous, and partly to divert his attention from the way my pulse has quickened.

"I'm hoping no one will notice us," he replies, under his breath, "and if they do, that we'll get a warning and not an arrest."

He's tense, carefully not touching me beyond what is necessary to make it look as though we're two lovers snatching an illicit embrace. Both his hands are flat against the column, one above my right shoulder, the other just by my ribs. It's only his torso that touches mine—which is enough to send my stomach into mad flutters—and his breath, hot on my neck.

The silence is too much. I search for something to say and, because my brain has apparently decided to beat a strategic retreat, come up with, "You're very hard."

Steel makes a choked sound.

Flushing, I raise my chin to stare at the colonnade's ceiling. "That's not what I meant."

His shoulders shake.

"Are you laughing at me?" I ask, suspiciously.

"Yes," he says, admitting to an utter lack of chivalry.

Shadows catch my eye, passing between the columns. I grip Steel's jacket at the waist and tilt my head back so I can watch the fraction of the courtyard that I can see. The stone chafes against my head, catching a few stray hairs.

After a moment, the shadows disappear. "They're moving on." Steel shifts a little, moving his hand. The rasp of his skin on the stone resonates through my body.

"So it worked." My voice is breathless. I pretend the pressure of Steel's torso against my chest is restricting my ability to breathe. Nothing to do with the heat of him winding through me.

"Indeed." He pulls away, brushes dust off his hands.

I cautiously probe my hair, but although my bun has been somewhat flattened by the experience, it's intact. Steel is still brushing his hands together, though I can't see any dust on them.

"Let's try that door before they come back," I suggest.

We stick close to the columns as we move towards the building. From the street comes the clip-clop of a horse passing. Everything else is quiet.

"I can definitely smell Revenants here," mutters Steel. "Not any other demons, though."

"At least that means they shouldn't be running any illegal fights."

Steel quickens his pace, heading straight for the door. If we can get inside, we can disguise ourselves as servants and infiltrate the palace. That way, we'll be able to head off any attacks from Bellemeure before she gets here.

Abruptly Steel draws up short. His expression tightens and he mutters, "Shit."

Footsteps ring against the flat cobbles behind us. I whip around and face two handsome men in white cloaks and feathered helmets. Guards. One says something to Steel.

Steel shakes his head, says, "Do you speak English?"

Both men's faces stretch with surprise. "Are you not—" one says, in firm accented English, "—the ambassador?"

"Ambassador?" Steel looks at me, but I have no suggestions to offer. If we could speak the language, we could pretend to be this ambassador for long enough to extract the information we need, but our blank expressions would have put an end to that idea even if Steel hadn't just admitted our ignorance.

The soldiers glance at each other, the feathers in their caps bobbing, then one puts his hand on the sabre hanging from his waist. "You will come with us," he says.

Steel braces himself. "Or?"

In answer, the man draws his blade. The soft ringing sound echoes in the courtyard. "You will come with us," he says again.

"As you wish," I interject. "We don't want any trouble." I'm not sure if they understand me or not; their expressions still register confusion and they keep their attention on Steel.

"We don't?" the demon asks, under his breath.

"Not until we find Asmodeus. And," I say, as we're shepherded to the door, "this might lead us to them."

Agent E. Wilson

Eve clings to the white and orange walls. This is a foolish idea. Even if Bellemeure *is* here, walking into the home of a group of incredibly powerful demons is a death sentence. She should have put up more of a fight when Hazel suggested it.

She should have done more to persuade Hazel to go back to London with her. At this rate, she'll be going alone.

Eve tries to ignore the squirmy feeling in her stomach. Agent or not, she doesn't want to face Monaghan by herself. She doesn't want to face the fear that she might not be good enough stop him.

The central palace has two doors on either end, as well as a carved out space in the centre that could lead to a garden. Hazel and Steel have reached the colonnade on the far side of the courtyard. Her side of the courtyard has no columns, only another garden.

"Careful," whispers Cassius from somewhere on her right. "Guards ahead."

A pair of the white-cloaked guards emerge from a door just ahead and strike out across the courtyard. Eve tucks herself against one of the protruding white façades. The stone is coarse against her skin, rougher than it looks.

"This is stupid," she breathes.

"That's the first sensible thing you've said." The Phantom demon keeps his voice low, and without being able to see him she can't place where it comes from.

She hadn't intended to say it aloud, but she doesn't retract her words. Part of her wants to defend her friend's choice, argue the benefit of this approach, but at this point she's struggling to see it. "Are there any other guards?" she asks, not ready to agree with him.

"The ones at the gate look like they're about to change."

The two they'd met earlier are going through some kind of ritual with their guns, looking a little like they're struggling to remember the moves of a dance.

"What about demons?"

"I can smell Revenants nearby. None of the guards are demons."

Odd, she'd have thought that demons would make better guards. Perhaps humans are easier to control.

"Ah," he says. "That might be a problem."

She presses closer to the wall. "What?" Then she sees what he's referring to—the two guards who had crossed earlier are approaching the colonnade. Hazel and Steel have vanished, hidden somewhere in the shadows.

The distance between her and the guards is too great for her dagger, and even if she got close enough, an attack would draw out the rest of the soldiers before any of them could get away. Then Steel appears, heading straight for the door, Hazel on his heels. Why haven't they noticed the guards? The demon should, even if Hazel doesn't. He won't be any good to them distracted.

Eve curses. Without a better option, she strikes out across the courtyard to intercept them.

A hand on her arm yanks her back. "What the hell are you doing?" demands Cassius. "If you go over there, we'll both be killed."

"I can distract them."

"And then what? What will you do when they arrest you and hang you for trying to attack a palace?"

"I'll figure something out," she snaps, trying to shake off his hand. His grip is unforgiving.

"That's not a chance I'm willing to take."

"Listen—" She cuts off. The guards have run into Steel. It's too late to catch them. She braces herself for a fight.

It doesn't come. They exchange a few words and then Hazel raises her hands.

"What is that woman doing?" mutters Cassius, his hold on her arm slackening.

The group starts to move, Hazel and Steel in front and the two guards behind. They are marched to the door and into the palace. Shit.

Suddenly, Cassius tightens his grip. "Move," he commands and she sees a second pair of guards marching down the length of the courtyard towards the entrance.

Eve spins. The two at the gate have turned to face the group and are clearly waiting to be relieved, leaving them nowhere to hide.

"This way." Cassius yanks her towards the building on their right, the one she'd hid against.

Without a better option, she heads for it, keeping her pace unhurried, as though she belongs among the tidy trees and the pale gravel. The door is made of metal, with two large handles.

"Cassius," she whispers and the door thuds under his invisible weight. After a moment it slides open. Eve slips inside and forces the door shut behind her.

The impression she gets is of polished wooden floors and painted murals. She shrinks in on herself, clasping her hands in front of her like a dutiful maid, and turns to the right. There'll be a servant's exit somewhere, she just has to find it.

It's quiet save for the occasional whinny of a horse. Eve follows the sound, tracking it through gilt-infused corridors and ornate parlours. She almost overlooks one passage half-hidden by a tapestry. Its walls are plain white stone and no polish adorns the floor. Gratefully Eve slips into it. Then she pauses, putting her hand to the dagger sitting inches from her pounding heart.

Cassius shimmers into view beside her. "Now what?" he asks. A lock of red hair has fallen loose and curls over his forehead.

"We need to get back outside." They won't be welcomed if they're found here. More likely they'll be arrested as thieves and hanged. She keeps her hand on the dagger and starts following the passage.

"Outside is where the soldiers are," mutters the demon, but he stays with her.

"You could have let the guards catch me," she says, realising his opportunity. "If they kill me, you're free."

"And I'd have to spend however long it takes for them to convict you huddling in a filthy cell," he responds. "As much as I value my freedom, I have no desire to starve while I wait for them to hang you."

"I'll bear that in mind next time."

"If you could refrain from there *being* a next time, I'd be grateful."

Voices come from up ahead. The passage ends in a simple white door, so Eve cracks it open a finger's width and peers through the gap.

The door opens into a parlour, tucked away behind a huge white piano; a hidden corridor for the servants to move in. A maid in apron and cap is halfheartedly sweeping a duster over the instrument.

"And now they want us to open the central wing!" she complains. Her German is soft and languid, making the frustration in her voice sound like weariness. "They were only supposed to be here for a month, yet they still haven't left! They'll be here all winter, at this rate."

"Don't let them hear you say that," cautions a second maid over by a window. "They're vicious. Lena tried to go into their wing to clean it once and they hit her!"

The first maid gives a dramatic shudder. "Monsters," she declares. "The Emperor better hurry up and send them back to Esterházy."

"Girls!" someone calls from elsewhere in the building. "Are you finished yet?"

"She's always badgering us," the first mutters, then shouts, "Coming!"

The maids bustle away and Eve counts to ten before she opens the door. It's a music room, decorated with couches and chairs to observe whoever's playing.

"Not bad," whispers Cassius, out of sight again. A piano key sinks and makes a low chime.

"Stop that." The tall summer windows look out over a lawn and a low block of stables. Eve heads to one and unhooks the latch.

"Better hurry," Cassius says, "or you'll be seen."

She glares over her shoulder at the empty air. "Instead of whining, you could help me."

"I'm helping you by not calling for the soldiers."

Scowling, Eve jumps over the low windowsill. The stables cover a wide expanse of ground, hiding her from the central building. The main street lies on its other side.

If she goes left, she might be able to find Hazel and help her escape, saving her from House Asmodeus. Assuming they don't find her and kill her first.

She turns right. The street is busier now, and with the noise of horses from the stables and carriages from the road, it's easy enough to slip away and join the traffic on the pavement.

"I'm getting a little tired of asking," says Cassius, appearing beside her, "but what are you doing now? I thought the plan was to *find* Asmodeus, not run away from them. Not that I'm complaining," he hastens to add.

"We won't be of any use to Hazel in there." Doubt is an irritating companion at the back of her mind. "We need support."

Cassius laughs scornfully. "From who? I don't see anyone lining up to help us."

"From the Gendarmerie." She meets his surprised look with a flat one. "They're an agency. They're sworn to protect humans. With their backing, we can get Hazel out." And Steel, she adds silently, though with less fervour.

Cassius regards her with a grim expression. "We'll see."

CHAPTER FIVE

Walking into Schönbrunn palace is like walking into a dream, a dream painted white and gold and cream, filled with statues and chandeliers. A thick red carpet covers the gleaming wooden floor and our steps make no sound as we pass murals and paintings and ancient, expensive vases.

The guards split, one taking the lead and the other following. Both keep shooting glances at Steel. They lead us into a passage lined with the stuffed and mounted heads of dead animals. Rows of them tower over us; stags with beautiful spread horns, boar with bared tusks, even bears, their lips pulled back from their teeth in an artificial snarl.

"Charming," Steel mutters. His voice echoes in the corridor.

The animals' flat eyes watch us pass. I scratch the back of my hand and pull my hands apart when I realise what I'm doing.

After what seems like an age, the passage comes to an end and we're faced with a closed door. One of our guards enters and a soft conversation is exchanged inside. Steel rolls his shoulders as if he's preparing for battle.

"Let's see what they want before we make any hasty decisions," I whisper.

He glances over his shoulder at the other guard, the one who'd mistaken him for an ambassador. The man baulks at the look and Steel gives him a savage grin.

"Treten Sie ein," a voice calls and the remaining guard gestures at us to enter, keeping a respectable distance.

Steel slips in first, his hand held out before me, braced for whatever comes. But we enter the room unchallenged. It's dark, decorated in mahogany with a desk on one side and a small table on the other. Seated behind the desk is a man that could be von Tier's brother, only with a thicker moustache and a heftier build.

It seems we've found Asmodeus, after all.

He looks up at us and jerks a little in his chair. Ink from the pen he holds splatters across a sheaf of paper.

"Count von Tier, I assume," I start, before Steel can jump in. "Guten morgen."

The man takes a moment to lay down the pen. It's an old feathered quill with a long nib. "Es *ist* ein guter Morgen," he says. "Though I cannot understand why it has brought me such interesting guests." The switch to English is so smooth it's obvious that he holds more than a passing familiarity with the language.

I bow, wondering how much the man knows. "Forgive us for trespassing, sir."

"Yes," Steel replies. "Forgive us for not debasing ourselves at the altar of your kindness."

The sarcasm seems to slide right off the man's broad shoulders. "You have not answered my question."

I bite my tongue to keep from saying, *You didn't ask one.* "Your question, my lord?"

The Count stands, stepping out from behind the desk. His jacket is similar to the blue military jacket von Tier wore in Paris, but in a red so dark it could be mistaken for black. His hair gleams with pomade, his nails are clean and trimmed. As tidy as Monaghan. Nausea bubbles in my stomach.

"Why did my guards find you outside my palace?" he asks.

"*Your* palace?" Steel replies, who seems to have lost any and all sense. "I thought this belonged to the Emperor. Where is he, by the way?"

Von Tier's mouth purses and the over-large black irises in his eyes dilate even further. An animal sense of fear scuttles over the back of my neck. "It is almost December," the demon replies. "Emperor Habsburg is at the winter palace. Were you looking for him, or has something else brought you to my door?"

If he doesn't know about the Marquis' death, then telling him won't do us any favours. Bellemeure, on the other hand... "House Asmodeus is in danger, my lord," I say, drawing his attention.

"You came to warn me?"

"Yes. We believe she will attack soon."

"How charitable." His gaze returns to Steel. "What is your name, Dragon?"

"My name?" The direct question seems to throw him. "It's Lyr."

"Is it?"

Steel makes an impatient, cutting gesture. "There's a woman trying to exterminate the demonic Houses. Her next target is Asmodeus."

"And you know that, how?"

"She destroyed mine," he replies, through gritted teeth.

"Ah," von Tier says, as if the words have clarified something. "You are Leviathan's son."

Steel works his jaw from side to side and doesn't respond. Von Tier walks to the door, opens it, and murmurs a few words in German. Then he returns to the desk, leaving the door open. Somewhere a clock strikes.

"It is not often that I have the chance to entertain the heir of a House," the Count continues. "Welcome, lord of Leviathan."

Steel bares his sharp canines. "So glad to be special."

"Special," the Count repeats, quietly. "Indeed."

"You don't believe us," I interject. "The woman's name is Bellemeure. We met her in—in the west," I say, stumbling. "She drugged the members of House Leviathan and killed them."

"Yes, we learned of their fate some months ago." The demon shrugs. "My daughters are concocting an antidote to this drug. Their education was quite thorough, I assure you. We do not fear this woman."

"You have an antidote?" Steel starts forward half a step, then checks himself. "Where is it?"

Von Tier regards him with arched brows. "Why, have you been drugged?"

Steel clenches his fists at his sides and glares at the man.

"We have experience with it," I explain. "Perhaps we could help your daughters."

The Revenant demon turns to me again, his gaze pinning me to the spot. "I did not catch your name, Fräulein."

"You did not ask it." The words run away from me before I can bite them back. "Lyr," I add, hoping he'll let the rudeness slide.

"Also Lyr?" he muses, then he crosses the space between us in a few strides and holds my chin, tilting my face to the side. "You are blooded, then?"

Steel bristles like a dog facing down a bear. "Take your hands off her."

Von Tier releases me without complaint. "I mean no disrespect. My own daughters are blooded. But this one is not, it seems."

"Blooded?" I repeat, still feeling the imprint of his fingers on my face. I keep my hands at my side, pretend he didn't just demonstrate how easily he could kill me.

"Part demon, part human." The thud of approaching footsteps makes him glance at the door, then back at Steel, examining him with a look that makes my skin prickle. "It was your mother, wasn't it, that had the Serpent's blood?"

"What does that have to do with anything?"

"It's rare to meet the heir of a House. It's even rarer to meet a child of two."

Bellemeure had said something similar, back in Paris, but with the chaos that had followed, it had slipped my mind.

Someone knocks on the door and the Count says, "Allow me to introduce you to the Ambassador to the First House. Luciel."

Another demon strides into the room. Steel draws in a hissing breath and I almost swallow my own tongue. This demon could be Steel's twin, except where my partner's irises are the silver of hammered metal, this demon has eyes of liquid gold.

The stranger halts in the middle of the room. Whatever flashes through his expression upon seeing Steel is quickly hidden.

"Luciel is the grandson of the Lord of House Lucifer," the Count says, while the two demons stare at each other, and I at them. "He arrived in Vienna a week ago. It seems that you are pursuing the same goal."

The demon seems to recollect himself. "You may call me Luka," he says, his mouth curling down instead of up, his brows arching a fraction too high. His voice cradles a faint accent I don't recognise.

He wears a black suit over a gold and black waistcoat, gold repeated in his cravat and gleaming from the lobe of one ear. A fob chain dangles from one pocket. Now that the first wave of shock has passed, the differences between the two of them become clearer. The demon's hair is shorter than Steel's, parted neatly and swept back rather than left to fall haphazardly into his eyes. The way he carries himself is different, too; straight-backed and proper, as if he'd learnt how to walk with a book on his head.

"How—" Steel starts, then stops.

The Count slides his hands into his pockets and says nothing.

"You are Leviathan," Luka says. "I can feel your affinity."

"You can sense that?" I ask, forgetting myself.

Luka glances at me and then back at Steel. "It is a gift of my blood. And yours, apparently," he muses.

Steel takes a step back. "I'm not part of your House."

"Look in the mirror. Your countenance would disagree with you."

Steel keeps shaking his head. His pupils have gone thin and serpentine. "It's not true," he rasps. "It can't be."

"How else would you explain it? Your good-for-nothing father turned his back on his family for some—"

Steel lunges and the demon stumbles backwards. Von Tier takes a long step away, removing himself from the line of attack. Steel keeps going, raking his claws at the other demon. He's slower than usual, though, and all he succeeds in doing is tearing rivulets in the man's jacket.

"Steel!" I call.

"It's not true," Steel grits out, and I'm not sure he even hears me.

"This is ridiculous." Luka raises one hand, as if he's telling Steel to stop. Then lines of blue-white crackle out of his palm. They slam into Steel's chest and hurl him across the room, throwing him hard against the wall. Luka folds his fingers over his palm, watching.

I fall to my knees beside Steel, check him over. He's conscious and he sits up quickly. Trails of smoke curl from his clothes. "What..." he gasps, "...was that?"

Luka's head tilts fractionally to one side. "You don't recognise it."

"Well," interrupts von Tier. "I am looking forward to an entertaining winter. Show them to their rooms will you, Luciel?" He clasps the demon on the shoulder and leaves the room. Luka's eyes narrow at his casual touch.

"Are you all right?" I ask Steel, torn between watching the threat and helping my partner.

He stands, yanks his coat into place. "I'm not part of your House," he spits at the other demon.

"I certainly wish that were true." Luka smooths his torn jacket, regarding Steel with an impassive expression. "Have you not used your magic before?"

"That was magic?" Steel lets loose a scornful laugh. "What, you're saying you can control lightning?"

One cool eyebrow curves up. "Because you thought a demon's talents ended at fire and water? Our ancestors were lords of Hell. This is nothing." He flexes his hand and sparkles of static electricity dance between his fingers. "Why do you not use it?"

Steel's jaw clenches. Instead of rebutting the demon's question, or coming back with a cutting retort of his own, he strides to the door and storms out, leaving me behind.

CHAPTER SIX

I need to go after Steel, but my body is rigid, an instinctive fear of the demon still in the room holding me paralysed. He's handsome in a way that puts me on edge; the kind of beauty monsters use to tear out hearts.

Luka examines his hand, flicking away static like it's a persistent fly. "Has he never used this magic?" he asks, unexpectedly.

I swallow, trying to wet a mouth gone bone dry. "He's never mentioned it, not for as long as I've known him."

"And how long would that be?"

"A few months."

Where Steel would have made a quip about that not being long at all, Luka only says, "Are his serpent abilities active?" His gold eyes are as bright as electric lights, making it impossible to look away. "Why did he not use them, just now?"

"Bellemeure drugged him. He hasn't been able to use his magic since."

Luka's thin mouth grows thinner. "That won't do. I will speak to the Count about rectifying his state."

"Thank you," I reply, curtsying. "I will let him know," I add, using it as an excuse to flee. The demon lets me leave.

A servant in black greets me in the corridor, bowing. "Allow me to show you to your rooms," he says, politely impassive.

"Where is Lord Lyr?" I ask. "Did he pass you?"

The man dips his head in acknowledgement. "Lord Lyr was taken to his apartments in the west wing. If you will allow me, I will show you to your room."

"In the west wing?"

"Count von Tier suggested that you would be more at home in the lower levels."

"He is mistaken." Irritation makes my response tart. "Take me to Lyr, please."

The man hesitates. He has a broad face framed by thick sandy hair and the fledgling crop of a beard. Rather young to be attending the Count's guests.

"I will not be able to rest until I've seen him," I add. "Once we've spoken, you can take me to wherever my room is supposed to be."

With a nod, the servant straightens from his slouch and begins walking. I follow him up a carpeted staircase to a gallery with massive portraits on one side and wide windows on the other. The distant melody of a harpsichord winds through the corridor.

"How many demons live in the palace?" I ask.

"House Asmodeus holds fifteen demons this winter," the man answers promptly, without batting an eye at the word *demons*. How many people know the truth? "And another fifty servants on top, all human."

"Human? Not copper class?"

The servant stiffens. "Asmodeus does not lower itself so far. Most," he adds, "are the Emperor's servants."

"And they know what von Tier is?"

"They do not."

Von Tier is wary enough to keep some secrets, then. "But you do. It must be rare to be so favoured."

"Favoured," the servant murmurs, then seems to catch himself and says, "Your room is this way, Fräulein."

We move through the gallery into another corridor and then on to a winding staircase. I map the journey in my head, trying to work out a quick exit should we need one. Given the size of the place, the quickest exit might be through a window.

There are plenty of windows on the first floor, large and square and overlooking gavel paths and clipped trees. A glimpse of water further away might be a small lake. Paintings of angels and clouds coat the ceiling. I wonder if the demons find them amusing or annoying.

The guard halts finally and opens a door to reveal a large suite. One side of the room is taken up by a bed, complete with its own curtains, and two chairs and a washstand sit on the other. The window looks out over a patch of dense wilderness.

At first I think the room is empty, then I see Steel's legs sticking out from the other side of the bed. "Thank you," I tell the servant and shut the door in his face. "Are you hurt?"

"No," comes his response. I skirt around the bed. Steel sits with his back against it, legs stretched out in front of him, arms folded over his chest.

After a moment's hesitation, I toss my coat on the bed and sit down next to him, tucking my skirt under my knees so I can pull my calves under me. The skies outside the window are grey, thick with the promise of rain. At this temperature, it might even be snow.

"My father would have told me. He wouldn't have kept this a secret." Steel draws one leg towards him and rests his forearm on his knee. "It's a House, a *family*. He wouldn't..."

My instinctive urge is to agree with him, but what Bellemeure said lingers at the back of my mind. "Have you had other reasons to think that you might be..." I wave my hand vaguely. "Both?"

"No." Another, longer pause. "When I was leaving Italy I was attacked by Blood Drinkers. They said something about my blood, but I just thought—I thought they meant that both my parents were powerful. Not that one of them was..."

I think of the demon's face. It's difficult to argue with a likeness so similar. "Perhaps this is a good thing," I suggest.

Steel's head is hanging, his hair falling forward over his face, but I can still see the black look he shoots me.

"Clearly he's familiar with magic," I persist. "He might be able to help restore yours. And then there's the antidote." In a palace full of dangerous Revenant demons, we don't have a lot of cards to play. Steel's connection to Luka could be one of them. "You could try speaking to him."

"No," he snaps. If fire was his element, the air around him would be sizzling. "That demon has nothing to say that I want to hear."

I watch him, and after a moment he throws me another sideways glance.

"Don't look at me like that."

"Like what?"

"Like you can see straight into my head."

"Can I?"

His eyes flicker away. "More easily than I would like."

"It's probably the binding ritual," I say and my heart twinges with the ache of an old bruise. "You may not want to listen to what he has to say," I continue, "but I think it would be worth hearing it."

He lets out a long breath. "I hate it when you're right, have I told you that?"

"I'd be surprised if you hadn't." He rewards me with a slight smile. "It doesn't have to change anything."

"It changes everything," he says, bleakly. "If my father was House Lucifer—" He cuts off, lets his raised leg drop and runs a hand through his hair. "They never said a word. If my father hadn't died, I wouldn't have even known about Leviathan. Was she ever going to tell me about *this*? Would *he* have told me?"

All Steel has told me of his father is that he was a rogue demon with no House, no ties at all. If that's not true, if Lyr had cut those ties, or they'd been cut *from* him...

"They wanted to protect you. You can't blame them for that." I sigh. "I wouldn't want a child anywhere near these power hungry demons."

"That doesn't make it right."

"No, it doesn't." House Lucifer. The most powerful of the demonic Houses. I glance at Steel, only to meet his gaze.

"See," he says, his mouth twisting, "you're already looking at me like I'm the devil."

"I'm not," I protest, instinctively, wishing I was better at handling conversations like this. As it is I feel like I'm walking along the edge of a precipice. "It might take a while for me to get used to the idea, but you'll always be a Hound to me."

It surprises a chuckle out of him. "Glad to know I sit so highly in your esteem." The words are uttered with his typical sarcasm, but tension thrums through the air around him.

"You do," I say, wanting to take it away.

"Do what?"

"Sit highly in my esteem." His expression softens and I hasten to add, "I only don't tell you because I know how badly it'll inflate your sense of self-importance."

"What sense would that be?"

It's my turn to scoff, then.

"I'm glad you're here," he says, so quietly I almost don't hear it. There's space for an entire person between us, but he sits easier, his shoulders more relaxed. Then, shifting, he says, "If we're going to be dealing with House Lucifer, they might want to use my real name."

"Oh?" I say, very aware of the quiet of the bedroom, the rolling clouds outside.

"It's Raziel."

My heart clenches. "You're giving me your true name?"

"Well, you can't *keep* it," he replies, one corner of his mouth turning up. "And you can still call me Steel. Not many know me by that name. It might be useful."

"You don't mind?"

He shrugs, still with that half-smile. "It's grown on me."

We sit for a while in silence and my legs start to go to sleep underneath me. "We should probably go back downstairs," I suggest.

Steel gets to his feet and strides to the door. I peek over the bed and watch him open it. The servant is waiting on the other side. "Could we have some tea, please?"

The man bows, displaying no sign of surprise. "Of course, mein herr."

Emboldened, Steel adds, "And cakes, too. And have Luciel join us."

A few blinks, but the servant says, "At once, mein herr," and vanishes down the corridor.

Standing, I massage my numb calves. "Would you like me to leave?" If I'd just found out I had some kind of familial connection to a powerful aristocratic family, I can't imagine I'd want an audience for our first meeting.

"Absolutely not. I'll be damned if I'm going to face this demon without you."

"Why?"

"Because you're going to keep me from killing him," he mutters, wrathfully.

Agent E. Wilson

Eve salutes the secretary, ignoring the harried "Wait!" the woman throws at her back. She takes the stairs two at a time and makes her way to Gruber's office.

The door is ajar, which spares her the effort of kicking it open. "There's been a change in plans," she says as she enters. "I need your help."

A younger man stands opposite the desk, pen and paper in hand. He joins his colleague in staring at her.

"F-fräulein," Gruber splutters. "You cannot just—"

"My colleague has been captured by demons." She'd turned over a few different plans in the carriage ride back to the city, trying to figure out the best way to get them to help her without divulging their real purpose here. She hopes this one will work. "We need to rescue them."

The foreign liaison shuts his mouth, stares at her for a moment longer, then mutters something to his colleague. The young man tucks his pen into a waistcoat pocket and slinks out of the door, skirting around Cassius.

"Fräulein." The agent leans back in his chair, adopting the same disdainful expression London police officers give her before she shows them her warrant card. "I do not know how England expects its agents to behave, but in Austria we follow a certain etiquette," he continues, condescension thickening his German. He gestures at her, and possibly Cassius, too. "This is not only inappropriate, it is disrespectful."

"It's Agent," she replies, sweetly, "Not Fräulein. And I'll be sure to report your concerns about my behaviour to Professor Monaghan. In the meantime, my colleague has been captured and we need to rescue her."

The man murmurs something that sounds suspiciously like Women, but he continues too quickly for her to mount a counter-attack. "Demons in Favoriten do not kidnap people. They do not have the sense to organise themselves for that kind of crime, nor are they willing to act against the Gendarmerie. I am sure that your friend is simply lost—"

"I'm not talking about Favoriten," she replies, clasping the back of the chair in front of his desk so she doesn't wrap her hands around his throat. "I'm talking about the palace."

"Palace? What palace?"

"Schönbrunn. Vienna's summer palace, yes? There are Revenant demons living there. They have kidnapped a British agent."

"Nonsense." Gruber moves a stamp from one side of his desk to the other, then starts to fold a blank piece of paper. "The summer palace is being used by the Emperor's guests. No one has kidnapped your friend, Fräulein."

"Agent," she repeats, with a cold smile. "I would prefer not to have to correct you again."

The creases at the corners of his eyes deepen. "As I say, no one has taken your friend. They would not—" He coughs and moves the stamp back to the other side of the desk.

She presses her fingers deeper into the silken teal upholstery. "Who are they?"

"Fräulein—"

"Agent," comes Cassius' voice. He has positioned himself in a casual slouch against the wall, his smirk baring one lengthy canine. Eve didn't know he spoke German. "She did say that she wouldn't correct you again."

"The guests of the summer palace are here at His Majesty's behest," the man replies. "To accuse them of...kidnapping...would be an offence punishable by arrest."

Eve breathes out through her teeth. "Who are these guests?" she asks, changing her approach.

"Well, that is—"

"House Asmodeus?"

He had been reaching for the damn stamp again, but at the name he pauses. "You are familiar with the Houses?"

"I have a source." It galls her to admit that she owes her information to Steel, but she's not so imperceptive that she can't recognise jealousy when she feels it.

Gruber shuffles in his seat. "I see. Well, then, you will understand that they simply would not have taken your friend."

"I do *not* understand. They are powerful and they are dangerous—Why hasn't the Gendarmerie removed them?"

"Remove them?" he gasps. "Count von Tier is a confidant of the Emperor himself, his family have lived in Austria for generations! *Remove* them? Do you hear yourself, fr—agent?"

"You're telling me that not only do you know they're there, but you're happy to let them *stay*?"

He stands, putting his hands behind his back and going stiff with indignation. "I have already explained the situation," he says. "You are not to visit Schönbrunn again."

Eve releases the chair with a muttered expletive.

They're interrupted by the young man from earlier, who catches himself on the door frame before he tumbles into the room. "Agent Gruber, there are demons gathering on the Ringstrasse," he says, in German so rapid she struggles to keep up. "I think they may be rioting."

"Summon the guards," Gruber replies and sits down. "Have everyone stay inside until they are dealt with."

The young man bobs his head and runs off again.

"Aren't you going out there?" Eve demands. "Someone could get hurt!"

The man collects the papers on his desk, taps them together, avoids her eyes. "The guards will deal with it."

Eve whirls and hurries back down the stairs. "If there are enough to start a riot," she says to Cassius in English, "then how can this place be doing its job?"

"Evidently it's not." The demon keeps pace with her, his dark brown coat fluttering. "Not if it's taking bribes."

"You think they're taking bribes?"

"It's either bribes or blackmail, and given the fancy decorations—" He flicks one of the gold-framed paintings. "—I suspect it's the former."

They reach the lobby and she eyes him. "You're not usually this forthcoming."

He spares her one of those smiles that isn't really a smile. "It's always better to be on the side that can pay for your bread."

They emerge into such an overcast sky that it might as well be night. Eve pauses outside the station and peers down the street. There are knots of people in flat caps and mufflers grouped together along the Ringstrasse, but men in blue jackets are already marching towards them.

Eve jogs down the wide street to reach them, but by the time she gets close, the knots have dispersed like ink in water and there are only guards left behind. Guards and a few torn pieces of paper trodden underfoot. She plucks one from where it's wrapped around the trunk of a thin tree and huddles under an awning to read it.

Most of the print is smudged or blurred, but a few lines stand out clearly from the off-white paper:

They tarnish Copper, hammer Silver,

even melt Gold! No more!

Social Order!

Equality For All!

"Workers' rights," says Cassius, disparaging. She shoots him a look that makes him put distance between them and he adds, defensively, "They're Unionists, not demons."

"They're both," she points out. "Copper, silver, gold—these aren't words for political pamphlets. They're demons. And they're inciting rebellion." She considers the guards, now patrolling the street. "I don't think I blame them, if they're being controlled by a group of fire-wielding aristocrats."

He snorts. "Is that a chip on your shoulder?"

"It's common sense." She folds the pamphlet and puts it in her coat pocket. "And if the Gendarmerie won't help us, perhaps these Unionists will."

AGENT J. HORNER

Even in the darkness of an early winter's night, men flit among the spines of half-built ships and scurry between the docks and the town. The hammer of construction is a continuous drone that Jacob struggles to tune out. He trails Khurana along the pier, dodging sailors and builders and the blast of a frigid wind. Buttery yellow lamplight illuminates the crashing waves, but everything beyond its reach is pitch black.

"Here," Isis says, pulling them to a halt.

Salt stings his face and he squints at the crooked wooden sign she points out. "Are you sure? It doesn't look much like an inn." It could have been an inn two hundred years ago, but the wind and the years have worn it to a husk of weathered stone.

Cooper squirms past them to examine the sign. "This is it. The agency sent word in advance; we should have rooms booked." He pushes open the door—it creaks almost as loudly as the wind—and vanishes into the dimness inside. His demon doesn't hesitate to go in after him.

"Well?" Blythe demands. "Let's get out of this god-forsaken cold." He and his Reaper stand behind them, one on either side.

Jacob catches the look that Khurana and Isis exchange but can't decipher what it means.

The women enter and it's not as though he can abandon them (he hears the professor's order at the back of his head, *Ensure Khurana stays by your side*) so he ducks into the inn. It's dark and dingy and almost as cold as the pier. There seems to be an upper floor, if the stairs in the corner actually lead somewhere, and an attempt at a fire smoulders in a hearth at one side.

"There should be four rooms," Khurana says to an old man behind a counter who looks as though he's rolled straight off a ship after months of sailing; his body is a collection of bones held together by stretched, weathered skin.

The innkeeper's beady gaze drags down and up over Khurana's travelling dress, and he doesn't bother to hide a sneer. "Got two rooms," he says. His eyes glint when he looks at the rest of them and he sucks his teeth. "You want any more, you go elsewhere."

"Max and I can share," Jacob interjects, as Khurana's mouth goes tight. "We don't mind." He checks on the demon to be sure, and Max drops his head in the simple nod he uses.

Blythe manoeuvres himself to the counter and plants both hands on the surface, looming over the skeletal old man. "You've got four keys," he says, and Jacob sees them hung up behind the man; he hadn't noticed in the dark. "We'll take them all, and you'll get paid at the end of the week."

"Why—"

"If you've got a problem with that," Blythe continues, "we can call a police officer. There are some on patrol along the docks."

Are there? He hadn't noticed that, either. Jacob feels his face go hot, his brows dip into a worried funnel. He needs to pay more attention. Who knows what else he's missed.

The innkeeper chews on his lower lip, then plucks the keys off their hooks, one by one, and drops them onto the counter, ignoring Blythe's outstretched hand. Then he turns his back to them.

"Cooper, you're with me." The Reaper agent tosses two keys at Jacob, who catches one and fumbles the other. As he stoops to pick it off the floor, the new agents head up the stairs with their demons.

"It doesn't matter," he hears Isis whisper. "Alia. We won't be here long."

No one calls Khurana by her first name, to the point that he'd long ago forgotten she had one. He straightens and sees that Isis has stepped in close, her hand at Khurana's hip, her shoulders and rib cage tilted towards the woman in a way that makes him think, *Oh*. A way that makes a tiny seed of yearning sprout under his sternum.

"Is this all right?" he asks, bouncing the keys in his palm, overly conscious of the muscles in his face. "We can go somewhere else if—"

"It's late." Khurana snatches a key, her brows crowding each other in a fight for supremacy, almost as expressive as his own. "You should go to sleep."

He thinks of the professor's order, says, "I'll carry your luggage. Help you get settled in."

Isis lifts the portmanteau before he can reach for it. "We do not need your help." There is a pointed weight to the word *your*.

"Did I do something?" he blurts out and they look at him in surprise. "If I offended you somehow…" he says, groping for words, wondering if he'd looked oddly at them and they'd taken it as disgust.

"Not at all." Khurana is her usual self, cool and distant. "We will wake you in the morning."

They float away, climbing the stairs with a quick economic step that flicks their skirts out of the way, leaving him with the innkeeper, who peeps over the counter at him.

Jacob holds tightly to the remaining key. "Let's go up then, I suppose."

Max already has the trunk and Jacob follows him up the stairs, avoiding a couple of protruding nails. The demon has to put his shoulder to their door to open it. It groans as he does, revealing a room not much bigger than a closet that smells faintly of mould. When Max drops the trunk on the bed, a cloud of dust puffs into the air.

"And I thought the place in Scotland was bad." Jacob sidesteps a suspicious stain on the floorboards and shoves open the window. A cold wind nips at his cheeks. "This might be the worse one yet."

It earns a lessening of the grim look on Max's face, but not by much. "Perhaps the agency is struggling with funds."

"Probably because that new French chef cooks nothing but duck a l'orange and beef whatever."

"Bourguignon," Max corrects.

"Dominic hated French cooking." He doesn't mean to bring him up, but that's the way it is with Dominic; the man lingers in his memories like a rancid smell.

"Agent Rayne hated most things."

Jacob can't argue with that. He's the only one who grieves Dominic's death, and a quiet voice tells him he probably shouldn't, but if he listens to that voice he'll have to take a harder look at those memories, pull the man from the pedestal he'd put him on. He isn't quite ready for that.

"What do you think could be attacking these Catholics? More Blood Drinkers?" After a few moments of silence, he looks over. Max is staring at their trunk, and something about his expression makes Jacob peel away from the fresh air. "What's the matter?"

The demon looks sideways at him. His amber eyes and the profile of his nose are all Jacob can see in the darkness. "Más vale holgar, que mal trabajar," the man murmurs, with the familiarity of repetition.

"You couldn't do anything wrong," Jacob replies immediately. "Even if you did, it would be my fault, not yours."

Max hums.

"Is there something you're worried about? The case?" He waves a hand to encompass the rooms on either side. "There are eight of us, and Khurana misses nothing. We'll be fine."

"Eight," Max repeats, toying with the worn leather buckles on their trunk. "Why..." He stops and Jacob waits patiently. "Why would he not send a regional agent?" Max asks, slowly.

"The professor? Well, we don't have any agents in Ireland. I suppose there's Williamson in Bristol, but—" Bristol *is* closer. Why didn't Monaghan send him instead? "We don't have enough Hound agents," he says. "Not 'til Hazel comes back." Which will be soon, he hopes. And then they can clear up this nonsense about Hazel being involved in the Ripper murders.

"Eight people on one case."

"Those will come off if you keep worrying at them," Jacob says, seeking some levity, but the demon doesn't even look up.

"I..." Max stops again, and in the silence that follows they hear the complaint of an old door being pushed against its hinges.

Jacob touches Max on the shoulder, sliding his other hand to the short dagger he keeps in a strap under his jacket. Without speaking, the demon takes up position by the door, hand on the knob.

Reapers don't have the best hearing, so when Max glances back and shrugs a shoulder he isn't surprised. He holds the dagger loosely—weapons never sit right in his hand, nothing really does except a brush—and nods. Max twists the knob and pushes. The door grumbles an objection as it swings open.

He lets the demon dart out in front of him, ready to take the brunt of an attack, and slips into the corridor after him. Khurana and Isis stand at the top of the stairs, portmanteau in hand and coats buttoned. Jacob blinks at them.

"It's late," he says, his mind blank and struggling to catch up. "Where are you going?" A shuttered glance passes between the two women. Jacob tightens his grip on the dagger.

"You should go to sleep," Khurana replies. "The case will need you."

"It needs a Hound more than a second Reaper." Is this what the professor had been trying to warn him about? "Why are you leaving?"

"Horner—"

Another door opens behind him and Jacob has the bizarre thought to tell the innkeeper to oil his hinges. The two new agents emerge with their demons. They don't wear coats, but their boots are still on and they don't seem surprised at the sight of the four of them standing in the corridor in the dark. They don't look at Jacob. They don't pay attention to him at all; their focus is on Khurana. Their expressions, oddly, seem pleased.

"Good," says Blythe. "At least we can get this done quickly."

CHAPTER SEVEN

A parlour next to Steel's bedroom had been granted our use, filled with a round table and three chairs along with a small chaise longue and a few bookcases. These are populated only with religious texts, which seems ironic given the room's occupants.

Whatever cook is ruling the palace kitchen has the skill to deliver an excellent facsimile of a British tea. It's strong and served without milk, perfectly bitter for my taste, but Steel wrinkles his nose at it. The cake, though, can't be sneered at: dense chocolate sponge split with apricot jam and smothered in a rich chocolate glaze. Still, he only takes three bites and then puts it down.

Over the rim of my cup, I raise an eyebrow at him. "Are you dying?" I say, teasing. It earns half a smile, one that pulls up the side of his mouth in a devilish smirk.

I immediately scratch that adjective from my mind.

"I'm fine," he replies, his knees bouncing, hands clasped together between them.

Debating the rationality of the decision for a second, I shelve my caution and touch his arm—carefully, just the pads of my fingers. "All will be well."

"You can't promise that."

"If it's not, I'll let you kill him."

His laugh is more of a breath. "That's a promise I'll make sure you keep."

Then he twitches and stands, and a moment later the door opens. A servant—the same servant who'd been lingering outside our new rooms—bows.

"Lord Luciel of House Lucifer," he announces, and steps aside to let Luka in. The demon enters as the servant bows himself out, closing the door, and the two demons examine each other with furrowed brows, cataloguing the little differences between them.

Seeing them together is like looking into a warped mirror; the reflection similar in the broad strokes, but the details altered to something new and strange.

"Will you have some tea?" I offer, to break the silence.

Luka shakes himself and gazes down at the spread of crockery and cake. "I see they have blessed you with Vienna's favourite dessert," he says, taking a seat. Nothing in his bearing indicates that he's uncomfortable under Steel's piercing glare. "Von Tier must be courting your favour, son of Leviathan."

"My name is Steel."

"Is it?"

Steel doesn't so much as flicker an eyelid in response.

"Tea?" I ask, a little desperately.

"No, thank you," Luka demurs. "Too bitter for my taste."

It's only with an exertion of control that I do not look at Steel. "Cake, then." I cut him a slice with determination, handing it to him on a small gold-rimmed plate.

"Thank you," he says, polite, if distant. I wonder if he's used to speaking with humans, or if House Lucifer keeps them only as servants, like Asmodeus. Or worse.

"Well?" Steel bursts out. "Are you going to sit there and eat cake or are you going to tell me who you are? Why you look like me?"

"You were the one who brought cake to this soirée."

Steel's presence in my head turns incandescent with rage.

"Perhaps we could start with something simple," I interject. "You are not Austrian, Herr Luciel, are you?"

His eyes narrow a fraction, either at my guess or at the title. He remains still—he's very still, no wasted movement in his bearing—and replies, "I am not."

"Are you Russian?"

"Why would you assume that?"

"House Lucifer is the most powerful of the demonic Houses, isn't it? Russia is one of the great powers of the world." Alexander III sits in his palace playing political games with Queen Victoria, their pawns the conquered countries in their grasp.

His gaze passes over the array of silverware the servants have laid out. "It is possible to be too close to power."

"Oh?"

"Some would consider it foolish. Dangerous, even."

My skin prickles. "I could not imagine that House Lucifer makes foolish decisions."

"Nor I."

"Then your country...?" I probe.

"Wallachia. They call it Romania, now."

"What is our connection?" Steel cuts in. "Don't tell me every demon in Lucifer's House looks the same."

Luka sets the plate on his lap. "We share the same father."

"We don't," he protests, although there's not much force in the words.

"My father is no longer spoken of in House Lucifer, but my mother once told me that he called himself Lyr."

Steel sits heavily in the chair opposite. "It's a lie."

The demon looks at him. "What reason would I have to lie? Or do you think I somehow disguised myself thus to, what, appeal to your rage?"

"How do I know the dark ways you think?"

"Your mother told you?" I ask, watching him. "You didn't know him by that name?"

"I did not know him at all. By the time I was born, he was gone. He never knew I existed." The demon cuts off a piece of cake with the side of his fork and we stare at him. "What?" he asks, a smirk twisting his mouth into a grimace. "You thought I was his love child, conceived in secret? No. He could not fulfill his duty to his House, and so he fled. Evidently he had not expected my mother to take so quickly."

Steel is silent, digesting this.

"Then it was a political match?" I say. "Lyr and your mother."

He inclines his head. "As the firstborn son, he was required to produce heirs."

"Firstborn." Steel clutches at the arms of his chair. The fabric tears under his claws. "You're saying I'm the heir to House Lucifer."

"I am saying nothing of the sort," Luka says, with a brief tightening of his hand on the fork. "When Lyr fled, the marriage was declared illegitimate. We are *both* bastards."

"Speak for yourself," Steel mutters.

"Then the House has no heirs?" I ask.

"It has two perfect heirs." Luka has dissected the cake into tiny morsels, and he spears one with the fork. "After I was born healthy, my mother married Lyr's younger brother. They had two sons. So, no need for either of us," he adds, to Steel. "I am a spare and you are... Well, you are a Leviathan, are you not?"

"What I am is none of your business."

Luka seems to be dancing around something, some core at the heart of this drama that will tell me whether or not his House is to be our enemy. "Why did Lyr flee?"

"He was weak," the demon says, without hesitation. "You see it in the eyes." He gestures to his own, to the irises of liquid gold. "Luckily, my mother's blood was strong enough to overcome the deficiency."

The cake is on the floor and Steel's hands are around his neck before I can do more than inhale.

"Take that back," Steel orders. "Take it back, or I will choke the life from you myself."

"Steel—"

"And face Asmodeus after murdering me?" Luka asks, remarkably cool considering the clawed hands squeezing the breath from him. "How will your pet human fare when they come after you?"

Growling, Steel throws him away and stalks over to the window. Luka flicks back a stray hair that has fallen over his forehead and scoops up the fallen plate. The cake is a lost cause.

"Pet?" I ask, quietly.

Luka's gaze is veiled. "How else am I to take your presence? Bastard or not, demons of our class do not fraternise with humans, however tall or durable or pretty their hair." In the corner of my eye, Steel twitches.

"I have never been described as durable, before," I say, dryly.

"Demons usually prefer to take lovers that will not shatter in their arms. Not literally, at any rate." he adds, in a way that must raise the pulse of most women and more than a few men. Perhaps it would have done the same for me, if I were five years younger and had not known Steel. As it is, I'm left cold.

"Are you quite finished?" I ask and he blinks. By the window, Steel huffs a laugh and leans both hands on the windowpane.

"Then what is your purpose here?" Luka asks, discarding the flattery. "You are not blooded, and you do not carry yourself like a warlock."

How on earth do warlocks carry themselves? "I thought you said demons don't take human partners."

"They should not, but...mistakes happen. Von Tier's twin daughters are proof enough of the result—no magic, no affinities, nothing to them but hollow shells."

"Skilled enough to create an antidote to Bellemeure's poison," I counter.

His gaze sharpens. "And now we reach the point of *my* interest. My House desires knowledge of this Bellemeure."

"No doubt they do." I take a sip of my tea, waiting, and am gratified when he clicks his jaw in annoyance.

"Very well," he says, "What do you want?"

"Why exactly are you here?" Irritating the person who can help us may not be my best idea, but it is amusing. Perhaps Steel isn't the only one I should be reining in.

He examines me with a thin smile, as though I've performed a trick for him. "Leviathan marks the second noble House to fall in thirty years, with no one the wiser as to how, or by whose hand. My grandfather finds this...concerning."

"Your grandfather still lives?" Steel asks, raising his head.

"*Our* grandfather still lives," Luka corrects. "And he will continue to do so for another century at least, if no one kills him first."

Steel had told me that demons had long lives, but a century...

"We can live at least that long," Luka says, seeing my surprise. "Once we've reached maturity, our body's ageing slows to a crawl. Ours will begin soon," he says, to Steel.

My partner doesn't look surprised, but he says nothing.

"So, he sent you here?" I ask, trying to focus on the pertinent issue. "Why?"

He shrugs. "He sent each of us: my youngest brother to Mammon, the older to Beelzebub, and me to Asmodeus, the last and least favoured House."

Steel stirs. "I thought Mammon was the last House."

"It was, until the Count's brother divided Asmodeus by trying to establish his own. But you'd know more about that than me, I'd wager."

Steel and I share a look. "You know about the Marquis?"

"The Count does not care to track the whereabouts of his younger brother, but my House sees all. All except the reason behind his recent disappearance."

I answer the unspoken question. "Bellemeure."

His expression is remote. "I see."

"Why the concern?" I ask. "Wouldn't Lucifer be able to consolidate power, if the other Houses fall?"

"If the other Houses fall, then so, too, could we. The lower castes cannot rule themselves," he says. "Without structure, they will turn feral."

Caste, again. All the magic in the world can't disguise the fact that this is only a struggle for power. And we're helping.

I swallow another sip of tea, but it does little to calm the sense of unrest uncoiling in me.

"So," he says, "now that I have given you what information I have, tell me what you know."

Steel turns from the window, propping his elbows on the sill in a display of nonchalance. "You assume that we'd trust you after that?"

"I assume that you are smart enough not to make enemies of a powerful family," Luka replies. "Am I wrong?"

I glance at Steel. He sighs, flicks his fingers in a *go ahead* gesture.

"Bellemeure is the woman behind the attacks on the Houses," I begin. "That's the name she used in Paris, at least. She was working with von Tier, helping him to establish a new House in exchange for production of a drug that suppresses magic."

He watches me with those unnerving gold eyes. "Even without magic, they could not have been defeated by a single woman."

"In Florence, the servants handed out drugged wine," Steel says, quietly. "When I came back to find everyone dead, House Leviathan was gone."

"What is she?"

"I don't know," Steel replies. "I didn't recognise her scent."

"There's more," I add. "She has a companion, a Chinese woman called Chang Mei. She moves…" I don't know how to describe it. "She's incredibly fast. Faster than Steel."

"An unknown Asian breed, then," Luka says. "They have their own quarrels, they are nothing to do with us."

I recall what Chang Mei had said, in the catacombs. "She wants revenge. Bellemeure's helping her get it."

"Two demons, no more? No House, no affiliation?"

"She's resourceful," I warn. "And if the servants who helped destroy Leviathan are any indication, she may already have allies in Vienna."

"I will make enquiries." He rises, then glances at Steel, hesitates. "Regarding your magic," he begins and Steel stiffens. "I will be in the garden rooms tomorrow morning with the Count's daughters. Their antidote should cure whatever Bellemeure's poison has done to you." He leaves after that, not commenting on the conflicting emotions twisting Steel's features.

I wait for a few moments, until Luka must be out of earshot, and ask, "What do you think?"

Steel's smirk seems directed at nothing, a combination of cynicism and self-deprecation. "I don't know. If he's telling the truth... I always assumed they were married," he says. "My mother wore a ring and they never told me different. If this is true, then my father was married to someone else all along. Did she even know?"

"Do you think he would have kept it a secret?"

"No. Maybe. I don't know." His smirk dissolves under the weight of his frown. "I don't think he would have left if he'd known there was a child," he adds, very quietly.

If what Luka had said about Lyr's eyes was grounded in common superstition, then perhaps Lyr didn't have much to stay for. "He fell in love with your mother."

Steel sighs. "I don't know what to think. I just want to find Bellemeure and be done with this. Go home."

I wonder if Luka or the Count will let him, now that they know who and what he is. "Then let's concentrate on finding her. Everything else can wait."

CHAPTER EIGHT

When the servant had summoned us for dinner not long after nightfall, Steel had refused to leave his suite. An array of cold dishes had arrived at the parlour not long after and, after a cautious inspection of some questionable sausages, we'd cleared the plates. At the servant's return and his offer to show me to my room on the other side of the palace, Steel had launched into a long, impassioned argument and demanded they give me the room next door.

The result is a neat blue bedroom just down the corridor from Steel's, with a bed that could hold four people and a rug that my toes get lost in. Far more than I need, but when I protest Steel becomes suddenly deaf and leaves me with an overly-loud, "Good night."

I allow myself a moment to appreciate the thick damask curtains hanging over the bed and then I get to work. Count von Tier hasn't shown any reason to mistrust him yet, but he's still a Revenant demon. It would be foolish to take him at his word.

I start by stripping the bed. The sheets are made of expensive cotton and the pillows are stuffed with feathers. Squeezing them results in a ripped seam and a burst of fluffy down. No sign of hidden daggers or needles, or anything that could cause damage. The curtains hide nothing but a missed stitch or two, and the spaces under the bed and the grandiose wardrobe have been swept clean.

Taking a breath, I stand to one side and fling open the wardrobe door. I feel like an idiot doing it, as if something's going to come screaming out at me, but Jacob told me too many stories of assassins hiding in royal bedrooms for me not to be cautious.

But the wardrobe is empty of assassins, of enemies of any kind. It's *not* empty of clothes: dresses spill out in every conceivable shade, silks and satins and even a heavy velvet lined with muslin. At least I won't be in need of something to wear.

Having satisfied myself that there's nothing in the room that might attempt to kill me or, worse, interrupt my sleep, I dig the box of spare cartridges out of my coat pocket and stuff it in the bedside drawer. Then I fall into the cloud of a bed and let myself relax.

Perhaps it's the feathery pillows, or the soft as butter sheets, but I fall asleep almost instantly. I wake to a slate-grey sky that prevents any reading of the time. Hoping I'm not stealing someone's clothes, I choose the least eye-catching gown in the wardrobe that I can dress in without aid. The white bodice has a round collar and is embroidered with gold and silver willow branches. Once my hair is pinned back in a simple bun, I don my coat—the revolver knocking against my thigh—and go looking for Steel.

I don't go far. He's in the corridor, waiting for me.

"You're awake early," I greet him and the bridge of his nose wrinkles.

"Couldn't sleep," he explains. His wardrobe must have been full, too, because he's wearing a dark navy suit that I haven't seen before. No tie or cravat, though; his collar is undone. He doesn't intend to make an impression.

"The library?"

He shoots me a guilty look. "You don't have to come with me, if you'd rather not."

"I'd like to meet the Count's daughters," I reply, as we fall into step with each other. "Not to mention this antidote that they've been brewing."

His stride takes on a spring and the part of my mind that houses my sense of him reverberates with hope. "If it works, I'll be able to use magic again. Maybe even..." He wriggles his fingers.

"The lightning?" Unease crawls out from a dark corner of my mind, a spider catching the vibration in its web. "Just be careful," I say, trying to keep that feeling from the connection we share. I don't want to taint the meeting with his brother, not when the demon offered his help.

A servant waits at the bottom of the stairs and leads us through the palace and to a bright open room. Parrots and peach trees cover the walls, painted beside green ferns and pink melons. Branches stretch out over the ceiling towards an intricate candelabra. Two glass doors lead onto a garden. One is open, letting in sporadic gusts of wintry air. Luka stands in front of it.

Next to him, a young woman sits reading. Her brown hair is pinned back in a bun not unlike my own, and in lieu of a dress, she wears a striped shirt tucked into a blue silk skirt. On the other side of the room, a second young woman—the image of the first, but in vivid yellow silk over a full bustle—argues with a servant. Their German makes the exchange impenetrable, but by the way the woman flings her hand towards a closed door, she desires entry, and by the way the servant shakes his head stonily, he's denying it.

"Ignore my sister," the woman with the book says in English, without lifting her head. "She cannot comprehend the word *no*."

"Good morning." I curtsy, though the woman stays engrossed in whatever she's reading. "I'm Hazel," I offer, "and this is Steel." The demon holds himself rigid, his gaze flickering between the two women before returning to Luka.

"You came," says the latter, turning to regard us. "I assume you're here to take up my offer?"

Before Steel can answer, the second woman flounces across the lacquered floor. "They said I can't go in!" she exclaims, though I'm not sure if she's using English for our benefit or so the servant can't understand her. "It is not as though Prince Rudolf is here *now*. Why *can't* I look at his rooms?" Both sisters have the same carriage and colouring as von Tier, but where his eyes are the black pits of a Revenant demon, these women have simple brown eyes. Human eyes.

"Katharina," Luka says, "this is Steel."

"Who? Oh, yes, the other Dragon." The woman in yellow regards Steel with finely arched brows. "How do you do?"

"This is the mixed breed?" the other woman asks, finally abandoning her book. She stands and circles Steel, making me take a few steps back to stay out of her way. She lifts up his arm and examines his talons, then plants her thumb on his chin to tilt it down and gaze into his eyes. "Fascinating."

Steel has the same expression I imagine a wolf would if attacked by a mouse. He twitches out of her grip. "Madam—Fräulein—you have the advantage of me," he says, with polite indignation.

"Luciel said you drank Bellemeure's poison," she continues. "And you haven't been able to use magic since?"

Luka steps in. "This is Johanna. They are the Count's daughters."

"Hanna. Only Father calls her Johanna," Katharina adds. "You can use magic?" she asks Steel. "What kind?"

Steel's eyes roll helplessly in my direction.

"Before the drug, he could manipulate water and perform some magic," I say, thinking of the binding ritual that had altered our connection. "Since he drank it, he hasn't been able to do the former. We haven't tested the latter."

"Fascinating," Hanna says, again. "So you do not possess Lucifer's gift of the skies?"

"If by that you mean the lightning he used," Steel answers, nodding at the other male demon, "then no, I don't think so."

Luka's gaze had switched to me as I spoke, and only now does it leave my face. "That may be a failure impossible to correct, but first we should rectify the issue of the drug. Can it be done?"

Hanna nods slowly. "I believe so, though I will need to prepare an appropriate dose. We should test the rest of his magic, first. I don't often have the opportunity to examine a Dragon breed." She shoots Luka a look.

"And this will be the only opportunity you get," he replies, firmly, then adds to me, "You will need to step outside. Our magic is not for human eyes."

"What?"

"No," Steel responds. "Hazel stays."

Luka lifts one shoulder, spreading his fingers. "Then we cannot help you."

I stare at him. He doesn't care if I see his magic; he's already used it in front of me. He just wants to send me away.

The demon's expression doesn't change and the two Revenants remain silent, obviously taking their cue from him.

Steel sighs, then says, "Fine."

It takes me a moment to understand that he's asking me to leave. "You want me to go?"

He meets my gaze, earnest and serious. "I can't face Bellemeure without my magic."

My face warms underneath the stares of the other three demons. "But—are you sure you'll be all right?"

Luka murmurs something that must be either a Romanian insult or a nonsense exclamation. I assume the former. "He is a demon," he adds, in English. "He will survive your absence."

I send him an acidic glance.

"I'll be fine," says Steel, even as Hanna creeps closer to peer into his ears. "You'll know if something happens. And if they wanted to kill me, they would have done it already."

Burying my hurt so it doesn't bleed into our connection, I nod. "Then I'll explore the gardens," I suggest and Luka takes a wide step away from the glass door. With a last glance over my shoulder, I step out into the cold air.

Behind me, Hanna says, "I need to take your measurements, first, to ensure the appropriate dose. How much do you weigh?"

CHAPTER NINE

G ravel crunches under my boots. The park behind the palace forms a series of manicured lawns intersected by a wide path. Overturned earth makes patterns in the grass, flower beds waiting for spring. Beyond them, more green lawn stretches to a pale structure at the top of a sloping hill. Trees border either side, and I head for them, slipping my hand inside my pocket to grip the gun.

Climbing the hill warms my muscles and makes my breath come in quick foggy pants. Frost coats the grass with tiny particles of ice which disappear under my feet. As I step into the dense mass of trees, I alter my path to lead away from the palace, listening for the crunch of footsteps behind me.

None come. Good.

I work my way deeper into the forest, until I'm surrounded by birdsong and the hiss of branches in the wind. When I think I've covered enough distance to be mostly out of earshot, I take out my revolver and drop my cloak to the ground. Even if the demons can hear a shot from here—at least, Steel and Luka probably will—Steel will be able to tell I'm not in any danger.

"It's most likely that your target will be at close range," Dumont had told me, when he'd handed me the new revolver. "Still, you should take the opportunity to practice your shot, if you can. Familiarity with the gun will help if you are taken by surprise."

If only he and René had come with us. I could use a few more allies.

Using one hand to anchor the other and steady my aim, I raise the gun. There's a tree some sixty or seventy yards from my spot. I aim at a knot on the trunk and fire.

The retort shocks a flock of birds into the air. Their dark shapes wheel above the tangle of trees, their wings fluttering so quickly they look like butterflies. I peer at the trunk. Not even close.

I take aim once more, fire. Twigs shower the ground and the birds let out a fresh flurry of protests. That one nicked the trunk. The next two shots do a little better, scoring pale lines across the bark. The fifth hits the trunk dead on and I repress the urge to shout in triumph, focusing on the concentric circles of the knot. My last bullet hits the trunk at about shoulder height, carving a dent just outside the knot.

I lower the gun to my side. The last shot might have been mostly luck, but at least I know I can hit a target. I bend to grab my coat and a twig snaps.

I freeze with my fingertips grazing wool. Taking a deep breath, I pick up my coat and stand, scanning the trees around me for any sign of what caused the noise. The trees are still, save for a faint rustle of their branches in the wind. The spaces between their trunks are empty.

I shake out my coat and brush pine needles off it. With a quick spin, I throw the coat behind me and settle it on my shoulders, searching the forest for any unusual indications.

Nothing. Nothing but the birds in the sky rolling back and force, not settling. Still not settling. As I slide my revolver into the pocket, I turn my face towards it, as if the action takes all of my focus.

There, in my peripheral. Something behind a tree near the one I've been shooting at; the movement of something small peeking out and back again. I crouch and make a show of tightening the laces of my boots, peering up as I watch for it and—There. Something small and...leathery.

I whirl towards the tree, one hand in my pocket, on the handle of my gun. "Come out where I can see you."

Nothing happens.

I take a step towards it. "Come out," I repeat. If only I'd asked for a few lessons in German. "Come out, or I'll shoot." Whatever it is doesn't need to know that I'm out of bullets.

There's a long pause filled only with the squawks of the birds. Then the thing I'd seen clambers around the side of the trunk into view. It has eyes, big and dark, and a body that reminds me of a bat; small, furry and incongruous with the leather of the wings draped over its back. It clings to the bark with tiny claws, the whole thing no bigger than my hand from wrist to fingertip—perhaps bigger with the wings.

I stare at it for nearly two whole minutes without speaking. It stares back, motionless, prey caught in the gaze of a hunter. "What *are* you?"

Its tufted ears pivot towards the sound of my voice, but it makes no noise, not even the scraping demonic language that I'd heard from Steel. My hands itch for my notebook, for a pen to attempt a sketch of the thing. Its claws are so small they only just sink into the bark. It seems to have no other way of causing harm, yet I can't be sure. Steel never mentioned a demon like this.

Cautiously, I approach the thing. Its image reminds me of the way that imps are depicted in folklore or religious paintings, just in miniature. As I near, it hunches closer to the tree. I'm not stupid enough to take my hand from my gun; even without bullets, I can still use it as a club.

"Do you understand me?" I ask.

A twitch and the fur at its neck stands on end. I stop, watching it for signs of aggression. This close, I can see that the fur of its upper body ends abruptly at the roots of its wings, at vivid red wounds that have been stitched together with black thread. Its lower legs hold the same scars at its pelvis, and something about the legs themselves seems familiar. They're thinner than its body, covered in very short rough fur—rather like a tarantula—and they sprout in an odd direction, inorganic, like whatever devil created this monster put it together wrong.

It lets out a pained wheeze. Perhaps I'm only imagining that it's in pain, though looking at its scars, it can't not be. The thing scrambles away, using its tiny claws and odd legs to scuttle around to the other side of the tree. I follow it, and it loses its grip and falls. On instinct I reach out to grab it, but I miss, and the shriek it makes when it hits the ground makes me wince.

The beast scurries away from me, fast enough that I have to jog to keep up. My brain is quick to point out the flaws in following an unknown demonic creature through an unfamiliar forest, and I slow my pace, sticking close to the trees.

Its path is unerring and I stay on its tail. Just as the fear of going too far from the palace starts to pluck at my courage, the trees end in a clearing. The creature doesn't hesitate; it scampers across the sparse frozen ground towards a wooden structure with a slanted roof at the centre. A small building with no adornments or decorations; a hunting lodge, perhaps.

The creature scampers across the clearing and disappears behind the lodge. I stay within the cover of the trees. Most of the windows are shuttered, and the two on the ground floor that aren't are dark. It could well be abandoned; the timber is dark with age.

It's on palace grounds, though, so there should be no reason why I can't knock. I can pretend to be lost, if necessary, and ask for directions back to the palace.

A flock of crows fly up from behind the building, squawking. They circle, shouting at something below them. I move through the trees around the lodge towards them. As I get nearer, I hear a low crunching sound, like ground ice, and the squeak of a small animal. The noise isn't loud, made obvious only by the silence of the forest. I follow it away from the building, deeper among the trees until the sound grows loud enough it must be only feet away. Hiding behind a tree, I peek around it. Immediately I forget the imp; a body lies on the forest floor.

CHAPTER TEN

The sound I'd heard comes from a small animal with a striped tail and black marks over its eyes. It scampers off as I step closer. When the rustle of its escape fades, I'm left with only the birds for company.

I crouch next to the corpse. Only some of it is fully intact—a shoulder, the thighs, the meatier part of an arm—the rest has been mutilated or mauled. I wrap the wool of my coat around my hand and gently prod it. The flesh is cold, even through my coat, and barely gives under pressure. Decomposition doesn't seem to have set in yet, but that could be because the cold is preserving it, not necessarily an indication of the time of death.

Its head is damaged by a large wound that has carved off its nose and its lips, and destroyed any chance of recognising it. Other wounds litter its torso, shaped oddly like bites, though the flesh seems to have torn, exposing red muscle and white bone. One calf is entirely missing.

I circle the body to stand at its surviving foot. The corpse has both arms—what's left of them—splayed out to either side, its legs relatively close together, foot turned up. It must have fallen backwards, or been pushed. Scraps of clothing still cling to parts; simple wool trousers and a cotton shirt, no identifying marks or livery. No coat. The fingers that have not been scavenged are tipped with black talons.

It's male, at least twenty years if it was human, but I guess between twenty and fifty, with the talons. I examine the bites and the smaller nibbling marks of scavengers. My gaze catches on its wrist and I lean closer. About two inches above the joint is a line of stitches. Carefully, I turn the man's arm. The black thread circles the limb, covering a recent scar, as if the hand was severed and reattached. I check the other arm, find remnants of the same thread in the flesh that remains. The shade of skin does not match; it's paler below the join, where the sun would normally bronze the hands, and patterned with freckles that end at the scar.

I drop the hand with a flinch. It's not that the hand was reattached; these are the hands of someone else.

At the sight of the thread, my brain had begun digging for references to cases with surgical amputations, but at this realisation it fumbles, and gives me instead a mental image of Lavender's tattoo, the ink marred by scars. Monaghan and his demon had tortured her by cutting her into pieces, seeing how quickly she would heal, learning how her powers worked.

I sit on my heels for a moment, considering why my brain had fixated on that memory. The stitches are precise, but not small or unobtrusive; the thread is thick and black, stark against the man's skin. Judging by the colour of the scar, it's a recent injury, only partially healed. It wasn't the cause of death.

I look closer at the man's other wounds. Signs of bleeding from his ruined face and the bites in his torso tell me he was either alive or newly dead when they were inflicted. Possibly the cause of death. I need an autopsy to be sure.

A couple of indentations remain around his abdominal cavity, visible enough that I can measure them between forefinger and thumb. I'd need calipers for a precise measurement, but I estimate about thirty millimetres between what I gauge are the imprint of canines. A medium sized dog, perhaps.

Thirty millimetres is also the distance between canines for a human—or a demon.

I look again at the wound on its face, trying to ignore the empty eye sockets where the crows have been at work. There are indentations, but the distance is too wide to be another bite. I spread my fingers in the air above the wound; claws. This close, the scent of rot curls up from the corpse, and I straighten, cant my head away to clear my lungs.

A demon would have the strength for this kind of attack, but I can't think of a demon that has talons long enough. Or a motivation. This kind of mutilation feels...savage, bestial. Nothing like La Sorelli's injuries, back in Paris.

I'm struggling to put together a picture of the culprit when a wave of searing pain slices through my brain.

My vision goes black for a moment, then returns in a blurry wave. I'm on my knees, clutching handfuls of dead leaves, gasping for breath. Conscious of the risk of descending into shock, I run my hands over my body, searching for the wound.

But there isn't one. It's not me who's hurt.

I race back to the palace, branches scraping at my face as I push through the trees. The pain in my head fades, replaced by fogginess. I can't read anything from it, but it's there. Steel is still there.

I burst through the door into the peach tree room. Luka's figure blocks my view and I push past him, knocking him off-balance.

"How dare—"

Steel crouches on the ground, both hands flat on the floor, his head bowed. I drop to my knees beside him and find his pupils blown wide, elongated ovals oscillating wildly.

"What happened?" I ask, reaching for his shoulder. Static electricity crackles between his body and my palm. I jerk back.

"You see?" Hanna's voice is smug. "I told you it would work."

Standing, I stay close to Steel, avoiding the flickers of light that his body emits. "What did you do?"

"She administered the drug." Luka tilts his head as he regards Steel. "It does seem to be working," he says, to the other woman. "Although he's not emitting any other magic."

"It will need testing."

"If it worked, then why is he like *this*?" I demand. "He's not responding!"

Hanna nods a few times, her pale lips a straight line. "The influx of magic will require some adjustment," she says. "But he is responding well. If he weren't, he would have lost consciousness by now."

"He's doing much better than the others," Katharina pipes up. She stands against the far wall, distant from the thin trails of scarlet that mark the floor in familiar glyphs.

"Others? What others?" I look at Luka and Hanna. They meet my gaze, Luka with cool disdain, Hanna with faint surprise.

"We did not have a sample of the drug to use, so I had to recreate the formula through experimentation." She puts her hands on her hips, staring down at Steel, something avaricious in her gaze. "This version seems to have unlocked his latent abilities. I will have to make some notes." She walks out without another word.

"I'm fine," Steel mutters, hoarsely. He uses his knee to push himself into a standing position. His eyes are heavy-lidded. "I can…feel it again."

"You need to rest."

"I'm fine," he repeats.

"She is right. You should give it time." Luka nods at the sparks that drip from Steel's hands. "That will need to settle, and I would suggest you avoid the more flammable furnishings for the time being."

"I need to talk to you," I whisper.

Luka sets a hand on his shoulder, apparently unaffected by the sparks. "Come," he says. "They have a glass house heated by steam. We can test your Leviathan's abilities there." He steers the demon through the door into the garden, where I just came from. Neither look back.

"What did you say your name was?"

Startled, I glance over at Katharina. "It's Hazel, my lady." The title slips out without my intent. In her dress and with her painted lips, she looks like royalty. My shoulders curve inward to make myself smaller.

"Pretty."

"Are the woods safe?" I ask steering my mind from Steel's departure.

She gazes at me in surprise. "Why, of course."

A wolf could have made the bites on its body, but the claw marks look like they came from a bear, or a lynx. "What about wolves? Bears?"

"You have been listening to fairy tales," she replies. "There are too many people here to attract such animals, though you may see a rabid dog or two in the city. You are perfectly safe while you are with us. Do you not feel so?"

I can't read her. She might mean it simply as a question, or she might already know about the corpse. "I come from London. I'm not used to...all of this." I wave my hand vaguely. The cold will preserve the body. I can find a lamp and investigate after dark, when the palace is quiet.

"Do not worry about your friend," she says. "Luciel's primary interest is in his own bloodline. He would never harm Steel."

That does little to reassure me. "You call him Luciel? Not Luka?"

"He has not offered me the use of a diminutive. But I have not lost hope yet." She wags a slender finger at me. "I may not have Hanna's affinity with the sciences, but even half-bloods like me can become warlocks."

"It's that easy, is it?"

The humour in my tone either escapes her or is too insulting to grace with a response. "It is not something we have much experience of," she admits. "It is not my House's speciality. But it can be learnt. Humans have been able to, after all."

That peaks my interest. "Oh? I didn't know that."

"How else would they be able to retain so many of their...what do you call them? Polizei?"

"Agents," I respond.

"Their magic may have been created with the unwilling support of my Wraith cousins," she continues. "But you must continue to feed it, to ensure that it works, otherwise the magic will fade. All things fade, in time."

"Even Houses?" I ask, keeping my voice light.

She stiffens, her scarlet lips pursing. "Well," she says, "I am sure that the prince and your companion will return shortly." She turns to go and I regret the irritation that had prompted the gibe.

"Prince?" I call after her.

"Luciel is a son of our First House," she says, without pausing. "Even if he is not an heir, he is still royalty."

AGENT E. WILSON

Favoriten seems much like Vienna's other districts, except that the buildings press tightly against each other and the shops that line the ground floor are boarded up, their painted signs faded. Bits of card and discarded paper linger in odd corners, and men dressed in rags take refuge in empty doorways. The icy wind steals away any foul scents that might be polluting the air.

It hadn't taken long to catch up with some of the rioters, their caps and mufflers making them easy to spot. Eve tails them with her chin tucked into her collar, a stolen bonnet pulled over her hair.

"This is a waste of time," mutters Cassius, taking long strides beside her to match her quick march.

"Thank you for your opinion." The rioters stop by a shopkeeper's stall to exchange a few words. She pauses with them. "Can you smell them, yet?"

"I'm a Phantom, not a dog."

Eve prays for patience. Being the first female Phantom agent carries less and less glamour the more time she spends with an actual Phantom. If only she'd been given permission to summon a Hound.

The workers move on again, disappearing down an alley. She follows, hands in her pockets, coat collar propped up around her ears. There must be a group working together to create these pamphlets and organise these riots. It'll be the first time demons have been known to work together at this level, at this magnitude. If they succeed, demons of other countries might follow. How long, then, before the secrets that keep their world hidden are stripped away? And what will the demonic Houses do to prevent that from happening?

She turns the corner and comes up against the two workers, who stand facing her, waiting. "Hello," she says into the tense silence as they face each other.

"Why are you following us?" The demon who asked keeps his fists balled, his wool jacket too thin to keep out this cold. "Who are you?"

A warrant card probably won't help her, here. Instead, she shows them the pamphlet. "We're looking for the people who printed this."

An exchanged glance. She can't tell what kind of demon they are, but their bearing indicates they know their own strength. She shifts her weight onto her heels, bringing her body slightly further back, behind Cassius.

"You're not one of us," the man replies. His glance lingers on Cassius. "And you're not Austrian."

"What happened to 'equality for all'?" is the Phantom's snide response. "Or are you a nationalist party in disguise?"

One of them spits on the ground, making Eve flinch and put her hand to her chest, feeling for her dagger. They don't make any move to attack, though.

"Our friend was taken by the ones in Schönbrunn," she says, ignoring the way Cassius' lip curls at the word 'friend'. "The Gendarmerie won't help us. I was hoping you might."

A ripple goes through both men. "If your friend has already been taken," one says, "then it's probably too late."

"What does that mean?"

The other man throws a furtive glance over his shoulder. "Not here," he mutters. "They're patrolling."

"Come." The first man beckons at her. "This way."

He stalks off without waiting to see if she'll follow, but she does, tugging Cassius along by the edge of his sleeve. The second worker falls in behind them, a guard for their back or a barrier to keep them from running, she's not sure which. She keeps her hand under her coat, fingers on the hilt of her dagger.

They're led through the district's smaller streets to a place where two roads meet at an angle. A tavern nestles in the corner of their joining, its wooden sign proclaiming it a bar. The first man ducks inside without hesitation. Turning slightly so that any attacker would strike her shoulder before her head, Eve slides through the door.

It's not a trap. Or at least, she's not immediately met by one. The interior is lit by oil lamps and candles. No windows break up the bare wattle and daub walls, and the furniture is old wood, worn smooth. Behind the square bar at the centre stands a man with greying hair and a thick beard, the only other person here.

The door closes behind them. Eve turns, finds the worker who'd followed them standing against it, preventing any means of escape. Wonderful.

The man at the bar exchanges a few words with the other worker, and after a moment they look at her. "You've had dealings with Asmodeus?" the man behind the bar says, in a rasp of a voice that hints at vocal chord damage.

Eve steps closer and sees the scars winding around his throat. "A friend of mine was abducted. Two friends, actually," she corrects, reluctantly. "They were taken into the palace. I don't know how to get them out."

"Your name?"

"Eve. This is Cassius." She jerks her thumb at the demon, who glares sullenly at them all.

The man bobs his head. "Noah," he says, and nods at the other two. "This is Benjamin and Elias." They watch, as if now that they've brought her here, their work is done.

"Can you help us?" asks Eve, cutting to the point. If they can't, then her time here is wasted.

Noah leans on the bar, his sleeves rolled up to his forearms, his skin pale against the dark wood. "What exactly happened to your friends?" His dark eyes are narrowed, assessing, the colour of tree sap. A Reaper. No wonder there's no trap—they have no need of one when this demon can crush her head in one hand without breaking a sweat.

She steps up to the bar, mirroring his pose. "We were investigating Asmodeus for a case," she says, watching him for a reaction. His expression remains impassive. "My friend, Hazel, and her partner were caught by their guards."

"Are your friends human?"

"She is."

He leans back. "Then it is likely too late. She'll be dead by now."

Eve catches the omission. "And her partner?"

"They are not human?"

"No." He pauses and dread winds tight in her stomach. "Well?"

The man steps out from behind the bar. "It is easier if I show you."

Surprised, she lets him take her to the back of the tavern, where a narrow staircase leads to the upper floors until something tugs at her chest. She stops, looking over her shoulder. Cassius hasn't moved.

He lifts his red brows at her. *Bad idea*, she reads in the expression. Or, more likely, *Don't be an idiot.*

She frowns at him. *Don't give me any trouble.*

His eyes flick to the ceiling and back in a very clear non-verbal curse, but he picks up his feet and follows her.

The upper floor isn't empty. The corridor that they emerge in is packed with crates and suitcases and even a few people, propped against the wall or sleeping curled up against it. Noah picks his way between them to an open door at the far end. From it comes a groaning sound.

Eve tries to avoid stepping on anyone's fingers as she gets close enough to peer around the Reaper. Straw mattresses lie in rows in the room, each occupied with sleeping figures. One is making a low, continuous moan. His shoulder is wrapped in bandages stained scarlet, and the veins around the wound are black in the dim light, pulsing alarmingly. His arm seems intact, but as she watches, it flickers and disappears. The rest of him stays visible.

"What's wrong with him?"

A woman in an apron kneeling in the room throws her a harsh glance. Eve clicks her teeth together to keep from making another sound.

"How is he?" Noah asks, his rough voice barely disturbing the air.

"No change," the woman replies in curt, accented German.

They stay for a moment, listening to the man's painful groans, and then Eve backs away. She gestures to the Reaper and he precedes her downstairs with a steady, unhurried gait. Cassius, who'd stayed behind her, leans around to peek into the room. His already light skin turns the shade of new paper and he hurries after her, sticking so close that she can practically feel his breath on the back of her neck.

Downstairs, she folds onto a bench, resting her wrists on her knees and clasping her hands together. "That wasn't a natural wound," she says, piecing together the injury, thinking of the arm she and Khurana had found in Whitehall a few months ago. That demon—Lavender—had been taken apart to see how her body worked. The demon upstairs seems to have been taken apart and then put back together. "The arm isn't his, is it?"

Noah folds his arms, though the action doesn't seem defensive, more of a way to keep himself warm in a draught. "No," he answers. "We think the arm belonged to a Phantom demon, though it could have been a Wraith. We're not sure."

Cassius stands behind her on the bench, his coat brushing her side. "Who did that to him?" His voice is almost as hoarse as Noah's.

"Asmodeus. And he was one of the lucky ones," says the Reaper.

"Lucky," mutters Cassius. "How is that lucky?"

"He made it out."

She exhales slowly. "And you're certain it was Asmodeus?"

He nods. "He escaped through the woods. If it wasn't for one of our poachers, he would have died there. The arm is killing him."

A rejected transplant. Even demons can't heal through that, it seems. "One of the lucky ones, you said," she says. "It's not the first time this has happened, is it?"

He returns her gaze. "It is not."

"The Gendarmerie won't help you," she thinks aloud, "not if it means going up against the Empire's friends. Is that why you organised a riot? The pamphlets?"

He shifts his weight. "I did not organise them."

She waits and, when he says nothing further, asks, "Who did?"

"You are an agent." Noah regards her expressionlessly. "Why should we trust you?"

"Because my friend is in danger." She stands, facing him with squared shoulders, even if hers are a fraction of the width of his. "Because I don't care about your quarrels with the Gendarmerie. I became an agent to help people, not to play politics."

He tilts his head in acknowledgement. "We sent one of our people in as a servant, to spy, but he has not reported back in three days. If we help you get into Schönbrunn, you must find and free him."

"They have more guards than I have hair on my head," Eve says, tugging at a wayward curl. "How am I supposed to find one demon?"

"Your friend is there. You can free them both."

She inhales through her teeth, uncaring if the hiss annoys him. "Fine," she says, eventually. "But then I want to meet this leader of yours."

"If you succeed, I am sure she will want to meet you," the Reaper replies, unsmiling.

Agent J. Horner

"Running away?" asks Blythe.

"Returning to London," Khurana says. She holds her cane-sword in both hands, one on the hilt, ready to unsheathe it. "Is that a problem?"

Jacob does his best to melt into the wall. Beside him, Max has gone tense and compact, his thickly muscled body drawn tight in anticipation of a fight. He just wishes he knew who they were supposed to be fighting.

"The professor would prefer that you remain here," Blythe says.

Khurana scoffs. "As a corpse, perhaps. Is that not why you were sent? To dispose of me?"

Silence, and Jacob stares blankly at the other Reaper agent. Flickering candlelight comes from the man's room, illuminating enough of the corridor that he can see their expressions—attentive, calculating—as well as the mould creeping along the ceiling. The whole place is derelict. He'd disappoint his mother if he died here.

What a strange thought. You can't disappoint a ghost.

"Will you swear your loyalty to the Agency?" the agent asks.

"Loyalty." Khurana's blade comes free with a gentle *shush*. "The only thing Monaghan is loyal to is his own ambition. I refuse to be part of the world he envisions."

"Then you won't be." The agent looks at Jacob and the candlelight glances off his eyes. "Horner. You heard her. She is an enemy of the Agency. Tell your demon to attack."

"Attack?" Jacob sways, finds he's clutching the dagger to his chest as though it's a toy. Max is looking at him, too, his gentle mouth gone taught and unhappy. If Jacob ordered him to do it, he would.

Más vale holgar, que mal trabajar. But he cannot do nothing.

He draws a shaky breath and takes a step backwards, a step towards Khurana and Isis. "We should discuss this calmly," he says. His demon shifts, turning to face the new agents and their demons.

Cooper flicks back the corner of his jacket, revealing a pistol holstered at his hip. The man's Phantom demon is smirking. "What a shame," the agent drawls, "that you sneaked into our room and tried to attack us. Couldn't stand being the only other Reaper agent, eh? Such a pity I had to shoot you."

Dominic would do this, weave in false stories so Jacob would lose sight of the truth. Only little things, like who saw the clue first, who really caught the culprit. All things to make sure that Rayne won, and Jacob had only realised it was a game when it was too late.

It's the first time he's admitted it, acknowledged that Rayne could be anything other than handsome and brilliant, and anger at being forced to makes his words trip over each other. "You don't know anything about the Agency. It was made to protect people. *We were made* to protect people. Not murder each other in some quest for glory." It might be the loudest he's spoken in days and he gasps in a breath afterwards.

"A pretty speech." The agent reaches for his pistol and Max lunges.

Jacob's seen his demon fight a few times before, but each time feels like the first. The Reaper's strength is beyond inhuman; he slams into the agent, hurling his body into the wall and the next few moments blur. Jacob ducks low, balancing with one hand on the floor, and slashes at the Phantom demon's legs with his dagger. Someone goes for Max—he feels the growl of his demon reverberate in his own chest—and a man shouts. As the Phantom stumbles, Jacob yanks him down and stabs the blade through the demon's side, twisting to see what's going on. Khurana fights Blythe, her sword against the man's fists. Her face is rigid with determination. He won't last long.

In his hands, the Phantom demon disappears. He lets go in surprise and a fist socks his jaw. Jacob falls with the weight of impact, letting his back hit the floor. He'd trained like this with Rayne and Cassius, once. The Phantom had leaned over him, grabbed his throat. Jacob pulls his legs up, kicks out. His feet slam into something solid and the demon yelps.

Then Max is there, grabbing the air, wrenching, and the Phantom's body shimmers into view, Jacob's blade protruding from between his ribs. Max drops the demon, heaving for breath. Scrambling to his feet, Jacob yanks the dagger free. The blood on the blade looks black in the darkness.

Blythe is falling, bleeding from a dozen cuts and harried by Isis, who darts around Khurana's sword, her fists bristling with tiny blades. The last demon is nowhere to be seen.

"Where's the Reaper?" Jacob struggles to remember his name. "Valerian. Is he dead?"

His partner rubs his face, leaves a dark smear across his cheek. "I…"

"He escaped."

Jacob pivots to face Khurana, avoids looking at the body now at her feet. "He left?"

The agent levels a hard look at Max. "Your demon let him go."

"He ran," Max says, staring at the floor. "I did not—I thought I should stay."

"You did not consider the chance that he would run back to Monaghan to report on what happened here?" Khurana wipes her sword clean on a fistful of her skirt and slides it back into her cane. "Nor the reception that we will get on returning, if he does?"

Max looks miserable. Someone has torn rents in his jacket and it dangles from pathetically from his broad shoulders.

"It's all right," Jacob finds himself saying. He clumsily wipes the dagger on his trousers. "Word would have reached him, no matter what we did. These bodies are not going to just disappear."

"Throw them in the water," Khurana orders. "Take out their warrant cards, first."

He stops part way through sheathing his blade, gapes at her. "Throw him in the…? These are agents. We can't just toss their bodies into the ocean. The police must be told. We must arrange the burial—I don't even know if they worship God," he says, and distantly realises that his hand is shaking. "Someone will know. They may have family. Arrangements—arrangements need to be made—"

His face stings with impact of a slap. Jacob touches his cheek. Khurana is in front of him. Khurana had slapped him.

"Qué estás—"

"He needs to see reason," Khurana cuts through Max's burst of startled Spanish. "And we do not have time for discussion. We must leave. Now. Grab the bodies." She and Isis bend to pick up the Phantom demon. They haul him down the stairs, his body slung between them like a paschal lamb.

"Jacob." Max's touch on his shoulder is hesitant, fearful.

He thinks of the moment downstairs when Isis had called the woman Alia, thinks of the professor telling him, *Ensure Khurana stays by your side*. He shakes himself. "Can you handle this one?" he asks, gesturing at the bigger corpse.

"I—Yes."

"Good. Let's go." It takes him a couple of tries to get a good enough grip to throw Cooper's body over his shoulder. The cadaver is bony and he wonders where the man came from, whether he'd grown up on scraps in the slums of London like the rest of them or if his childhood was spent in green fields and muddy forests.

He navigates the stairs carefully, ignoring the thump of the body's arms against his back. The innkeeper is gone. In Monaghan's service, or just scared by the sound of the fight? Either way, it won't be long until the police arrive. Khurana was right. They don't have time for a debate.

Outside, night has cast its shadow over the docks. Sailors and workers still linger, but they huddle in puddles of lamplight, smoking or seeking illicit trysts. One or two look their way, but a sharp curse from Khurana has them scurrying away.

There is no one on patrol. Blythe had been lying.

Khurana and Isis toss their body into the dark water. It makes barely a splash. Jacob walks to the edge of the dock and shrugs his shoulder. The waves swallow the corpse in an instant, washing over the ripples it left in their surface.

Max follows, and as the third body hits the water, Isis says, "They are not weighted. The beach will find them by morning."

"Then we should be away."

"The trains won't run until dawn," Jacob says, watching the pulse of the ocean as it moves back and forth. No stars alleviate the black of the sky, giving the water nothing to reflect. "We'll have to hire a private carriage. Or walk."

Khurana looks at him for a moment, then says, a little stiff, "Forgive me. I had thought that you would be with them."

He touches his cheek again. The sting is already fading. "I'm with Max," he says, and the demon lifts his head. "Whatever path keeps us safe, I'm for it."

"Even if it means turning against the Agency?" Isis asks. Her ivory skin and hair make her a ghost in the darkness.

"The Agency is not one man." Is this why Hazel had left? And Eve? "I have questions," he adds.

"Not here. We must find that carriage, first, and then to London. And then," Khurana says, "then I will answer your questions."

CHAPTER ELEVEN

The maid they send me doesn't speak a word of English. Undaunted by my incomprehension, she communicates in cheerful German with a rolling, fluid accent I'm starting to identify as purely Austrian. She strips me down to my small-clothes and clucks over my figure.

"Hopeless, I take it?" I ask, with a self-deprecating smile.

The maid clearly understands my tone, and I expect I'm not the first strange guest she's had to deal with. "Nein, nein. Alles wird gut."

She spends a few minutes strategising, then rifles through a selection of outfits in the wardrobe. She chooses one that comes in segments: a bodice, laced at the back, which she spends a good minute loosening before tugging over my head; a bustle with an underskirt of embroidered cotton; a second bodice with elbow-length sleeves which she leaves laced to just under my bust, somehow making the choice feel like a decision to show-case the fabric underneath rather than a difficulty in lacing the thing around my ribs; and finally, a thick overskirt that might as well be armour for how much it weighs. I'm excessively grateful when the maid stops and steps away, blowing her fringe out of her face as though she just delivered a calf.

I shake out the heavy skirt. The outfit has clearly seen better days, and the dark shade of blue looks like it would be at home at a funeral. Still, it's better than the worn out red dress I've been dragging with me since Paris.

Next, the maid tackles my hair, and I let her wind and twist and braid as much as she desires, which seems to be a great deal. I concentrate on the nimble movement of her fingers, trying to keep my mind from straying. Unsuccessfully.

I'd waited for Steel in the garden rooms for another hour to see if he'd come back, but he and Luka had disappeared for the rest of the day. The faint presence at the back of my head hadn't erupted in pain again, and it had grown close not long after I'd been summoned to dress for dinner, brimming with exhausted satisfaction. He must have made progress.

A tap on my shoulder and I realise the maid has been trying to speak to me. "Forgive me," I say. "It looks lovely."

She beams and bows herself out of the room. With one quick look in the mirror to check that the end result is presentable, I leave the room and knock on Steel's door. The rest of the corridor is quiet, lit by two sconces set at long intervals apart. The sun has long since set, and the black windows only show the freckles dotting my cheeks and the bluish skin under my eyes.

The door opens and a servant slips out of Steel's room with a bow and hurries down the corridor. Steel looms into view a moment later. "I thought that would never end," he grumbles.

"Where were you?"

"I was with Luka. You were the one who suggested I spend more time with him." He shuts the door behind him and turns to face me fully, giving me a view of his borrowed clothes.

The servant is retreating down the corridor, but still in ear shot. I search for something to say. "The suit fits you well."

The trousers are black with an odd sheen that shines like the reflection of stars on water. The jacket is cut from the same material, decorated with gold buttons down the lapel. Gold feathered epaulettes perch on his shoulders in imitation of real ones. Black and gold, the same colours Luka had been wearing.

"It should, it took thirty minutes to pour me into it." His gaze flits over my dress. "You look—" He stops, as if he'd tripped on a word and was looking for another.

"Thank you," I say, when it's clear he can't find one. "Did it work? With Luka?"

In answer, he holds out his hand. A thread of white light crackles over his palm. It's faint and it disappears almost immediately, but his grin stretches to his ears. The knot in my chest slips loose.

"Luka says I'll be able to do more with practice," he says. "And the rest is nearly back to normal. Whatever they gave me, it worked."

"Good." I glance down the corridor. The servant has gone. "When I was outside—"

Somewhere, a clock strikes the sixth hour and Steel clicks his tongue. "Luka says they have dinner early. We'd better find where we're supposed to be before we're unfashionably late." He walks off, and before I can hurry after him to tell him about the body, another servant appears at the end of the corridor.

The man bows, as if he's used to strangers roaming around the palace after dark. He says something in German, ignores our blank faces, and turns with a clip of his shoes to stalk away. After a shared, incomprehensible glance, we follow him.

He takes us through wide corridors and large rooms with painted ceilings until he opens a door onto what I at first think is a jungle. Tall palms vie for space with orange trees, green leaves dotted with scarlet buds froth from every direction. It takes me a moment to see the pots at their base, the windows behind them. The glass is foggy with steam and even the floor seems to be warm, heated by some kind of plumbing system to keep the plants alive.

Steel strides through first, ducking under an aggressive plant with large leaves and white bark. As I make my way through the foliage, catching the damp, earthy smell of freshly watered soil, the plants retreat, revealing a long table set for dinner. Around it stand a group of gentlemen and a few ladies, their eyes unnaturally large, unnaturally black.

There's a dip in sound as we enter. One woman detaches from the group and comes towards us, her blonde hair shining in the light of a dangling chandelier.

"You're here, finally," Katherina says, with a smile that takes the sting out of the words. "I'm so glad the dress fit. Herr Steel, let me introduce you to my cousins." She takes his arm as she speaks and steers him over to the nearest demon. Steel baulks, but he's dragged into conversation too quickly for him to get a word in, leaving me alone at the edge of the room.

I breathe a sigh of relief. At least it's not me having to make awkward conversation with strangers. I creep closer to the plants, examining the demons. They all wear the blue military jackets von Tier had favoured, and while some have gleaming blond hair and others tawny brown, all have the same flat black eyes. All save Katharina.

I circle the room and pass two demons deep in conversation. Their German is incomprehensible, a stream of harsh consonants and liquid vowels that blur in my mind; I'm not going to learn much tonight beyond what they choose to tell me.

Katharina flits among the crowd, a server at her elbow. She smiles prettily at the Revenants, offering them more wine. They barely acknowledge her presence. Over against the wall stands Hanna, her arms folded under her breasts and a faint sneer twisting her face.

Turning, I see Luka alone by the glass walls and, after a moment's thought, I alter my path to greet him. His gaze flicks down to me when I stop beside him, then back to the glass. To me, there's nothing to see in it but darkness.

"Having a pleasant evening?" I ask.

Another glance, this time with narrowed eyes. "As pleasant as can be, with such company." His tone is quelling. In case I hadn't been able to recognise the insult, I suppose.

"Yours is an improvement over mine, I fear."

"Many of low birth struggle to recognise when they have been elevated beyond their capability."

Interesting. I'd expect him to take aim at my intelligence or my appearance, not my ancestry. "I'm sure they're exceptionally grateful for the condescension."

"Let us dispense with the pleasantries," he says, abruptly. "Is he fucking you?"

"I beg your pardon?"

"I can think of no other reason why he chooses to keep you."

The easy answer would be to say, *No, of course not*, but I don't want to give him the satisfaction. "Our relationship is none of your business."

"He shares my blood," Luka says, "so, it is my business."

"You were awfully quick to disown him, earlier." On the other side of the plant-filled room, Katharina stares at us with a dark frown. "What changed your mind?"

"What he does reflects on my reputation. I will not be mistaken for some indigent lout who cannot keep his cock clean."

I blow out a breath. This is not the kind of conversation I am prepared for. Divert, divert. "We'll be out of your hair soon enough. As soon as we find Bellemeure."

"*I* will find Bellemeure," he replies, cold and even. "Leviathan's son should focus on regaining his magic."

"So, teach him," I reply, meeting his flinty gaze head on. "Or are you afraid he'll show you up?"

"I do not fear anything he could do."

"If you're so confident, then what do you have to lose?"

He glares at me, too controlled to scowl but clearly wanting to.

"Katharina is looking for you," Steel interrupts us. He holds two flutes filled with something pale and sparkling. He offers one to me, but I decline with a shake of my head. If my conversation with Luka is any indication, I'll need a sober mind tonight.

Luka takes the second glass, sighing. "I cannot avoid her all night, it seems." He heads off to where the woman is still watching us from over the brim of her glass.

I struggle to calm my irritated heart and think back over the conversation dispassionately. Luka revealed one thing; he cares about his reputation. Even unwittingly, Steel is a threat to that.

"Sorry if I interrupted," adds Steel, an odd stiffness in his voice.

"Just as well," I reply. "I think Katherina would have murdered me if I'd taken up any more of his attention." The woman had stopped glaring daggers as soon as Luka had drifted away, and now her smile looks relieved.

"Apparently she's been attempting to court him ever since he arrived."

"She's welcome to him."

"You don't think he's attractive, then?" His attention is fixed on his glass.

"Not particularly," I say, which is partly true. Beauty withers under scorn, and while Luka has plenty of the former, he has more of the latter.

Steel knocks back the dregs of his champagne. "I suppose there are some who don't find extremely beautiful people attractive." It's uttered in the general direction of a nearby palm tree and loaded with sarcasm.

"I wouldn't describe him as *extremely* beautiful."

That seems to ruffle his feathers even more. "I see," he says, crisply. "You have very particular taste, then?"

Does he *want* me to be attracted to his brother? "A face is a mask for mind and heart," I say, bemused. These aren't words that I've spoken aloud before, have barely given much thought to myself, but they feel true as I say them. "It is those that interest me."

"Oh." This is said with more than a little confusion, as though I've given him a puzzle he doesn't know how to begin, let alone solve.

A voice cuts across the room, and I turn to see a line of servants trailing in carrying covered trays.

"Dinner," Steel says. "Finally."

He heads for the nearest chair, but a servant cuts him off, gesturing to one further down the table. I'm shown to the last chair at the opposite end. It's a small table for a palace, twelve seats in total, but the distance feels insurmountable. It takes a few minutes to arrange ourselves and almost immediately the servants jump to attend us. They're all human, the servants, dressed in black suits and white gloves. While they're not serving, they stand against the wall like living statues.

A course is served: soup, presented with individual covers that the servants lift with a flourish, all at the same time. I expect the demons to exclaim at the reveal, to praise the chef, but they ignore the display, turning to each other to begin a conversation. The servants retreat to the wall, silent.

Following their example, I say nothing. Diced beef, carrots and onion float in the golden soup, hot and steaming and full of savoury flavour. I eat slowly, watching the rest of the table from under my lashes. Katharina is speaking quietly to Luka. The male demon seems focused on his soup, his replies short.

I turn to the Revenant demon on my left. "Guten abend," I offer and he jerks, inhaling his spoonful. "Are you all right?" I ask, as he coughs. He nods, shooting a glance down the table to where the Count sits at the far end. "I didn't catch your name," I offer.

"It's Leitner."

"Herr Leitner." Perhaps I can make my own allies. "Do you work here, or are you related to the Count?"

He casts another glance up at the head of the House. "Um. Yes. The Count's second cousin."

"I see."

"But of course we must throw a ball," Katharina says in English, drawing my attention. She smiles over at Steel while the rest of the table goes silent. "Prince Rudolf will be starved for entertainment until the season begins, and we must show off our guest."

"Don't put yourself out on my account," Steel replies, a dry twist to his mouth

"Nonsense," she says. "We are in dire need of a ball. And why not make it a masquerade, just for some fun?"

Steel winces.

The Count looks thoughtful. "Perhaps it is not a bad idea. If we invite the Crown Prince to attend, we may persuade the Emperor to grant us the use of his palace for a little longer."

"I will send a personal invitation. It will be fun, ja?" Katharina looks at Steel again, who wrinkles his nose. "Ah, your friend is also invited, of course," she adds, without a change in tone. Even I can't tell if she's being sincere.

"I don't think—"

"It sounds delightful," I interrupt, glancing down the table at him. A large party would be the perfect time to attack. If I can get Eve and Cassius here, in disguise, we might be able to lure Bellemeure into a trap.

Katharina claps her hands. "Then I will send out the invitations." She smiles again at Steel.

The servants clear our plates and serve a second course, thin cutlets of meat coated in breadcrumbs. They don't look at me as they serve, treating me with the same professional courtesy as they treat the demons, and retreat again to the wall when they're done. I take a gulp of the rich red wine that I haven't touched until now, using the gesture to glance surreptitiously at the Revenants.

They give me the same sideways look; some with scorn, the way Rayne used to look at me, and some with an unnerving hunger that makes me think of caged wolves. I place my glass down, rolling the rim so it doesn't make a noise. My fork, when I pick it up, trembles.

They're not Drinkers; they have no appetite for my blood. They're just demons.

Just demons, descended of the most distilled evil ever known, with experiences and appetites as inhuman as a beast's. The only thing keeping them in line is Steel's presence. I don't even have an agency to protect me anymore.

I tighten my grip until the fork steadies. I will have to be my own protection.

CHAPTER TWELVE

The demons lose interest in me by the time the table is cleared. In fact, they lose interest in the dinner altogether, scorning coffee and cigars to disperse to wherever in the palace they're staying. Katharina occupies Luka's attention with talk of magic, keeping him seated, and Steel gets caught up in their conversation, leaving only the four of us and the Count. With the three demons occupied by the discussion, the Count turns to me.

"Do you enjoy the orangery, Fräulein?" he asks.

"It's lovely." In the low light of the lamps, the man looks so much like the Marquis that my breath catches. "How long have you been staying at the palace?" I manage, filling the weighted pause with words. If he's speaking to me, if he can see me as a person, he may be more likely to consider me an ally.

Looking into his eyes, blacker than the darkness outside the glass walls, I swallow my doubt.

"A month, only," he says. "The Emperor granted us the use of it while he is in Habsburg."

"That is generous." I scrape for something to say that would be of interest to someone living in a palace and a memory surfaces, one night when Jacob had a little too much to drink and tried to persuade Maia to let him paint a mural in the lobby. "The frescoes are very beautiful."

"They are. The palace contains some of the most beautiful paintings in Austria. I look forward to showing them to Herr Leviathan." His gaze transfers to Steel as he speaks, then it returns to me. "Now, however, I think it is time to retire. Fräulein." He indicates the door, holding his arm out for me to precede him.

I glance over my shoulder, but Steel is engrossed in whatever Luka is telling Katharina. Unwilling to cause a scene, I glide past the Count and out of the orangery, back into the dark corridors. The servant who had met us earlier is waiting.

"Bring sie auf ihr Zimmer," the Count tells him and then gives me a crisp nod. "Good night, Fräulein." He marches away, dispersing my suspicion that he might be waiting for Steel.

The servant minces closer, clearly eager to take me away, but I wait until the Count has disappeared before I let him shepherd me back to the upper wing of the palace.

It's silent as we walk and the man offers nothing, not even a change in expression. The glass rattles in a strong wind and our reflections blur in the dark windows. Steel won't stay downstairs for long. I'll wait up for him, make sure he's all right.

When we reach my room, the servant opens the door for me, and I wonder if he'll report back to the Count to confirm that I've been secured. With a cold curtsy, I slip inside and wait for him to shut the door. After a moment, I hear retreating footsteps. No lock, and no guard, either. Something to be grateful for.

A low fire crackles in the room's hearth, though it does little to chase the cold from the room. I pull the heavy drapes beside the window closed and then get to work stripping off the heavy brocaded dress and stuffing it back into the wardrobe. There are a handful of simpler dresses squashed to one side, as well as a mink stole in a box on the shelf above. I choose a high-necked damask gown that's easy enough to button alone, and sit on a chair by the window to think.

There's a possibility that the corpse could have been mauled by an animal, the beast chased away by Revenants or guards. The park is not a wild place, though. A bear or wolf would not go unnoticed.

Something cracks against the glass by my head, making me jump. I duck instinctively, then stare around the empty room, feeling foolish. Probably a bird, mistaking the firelight behind the curtains for day.

Then another crack. That doesn't sound like a bird. I stand to the side, lift the drapes enough to peer outside. The light from the fire obscures most of the view, so I tug at the latch to open it.

It doesn't open. I pull back the drapes entirely; the window is nailed shut. The nails have been painted over so they're almost impossible to see, but I confirm their presence with the tips of my fingers.

The sound comes a third time and, staring at the window, I see a tiny chip in the glass. Someone is throwing stones.

I flip the drapes around me, shielding the light of the fire so I can see better. My room looks over the rear garden and the forest, but if I hadn't seen it earlier I wouldn't have known;

the view is almost completely dark. Except for a tiny glimmer below me. As I watch, the glimmer widens into a glow, then disappears. Then again. Then a third time. Then it stays hidden.

A signal. Eve.

I mirror the signal with the drapes, then hurry to grab the fur stole and wrap it around my shoulders. Taking my gun, I crack the door open. Still no guard. I close the bedroom door quietly and creep down the corridor. My brain helpfully maps the route I took earlier, and I tighten a clammy hand on the revolver.

But the palace is deserted. Only one lamp out of three is lit, as if the servants had moved through the palace after dinner, dousing any lights but those that were absolutely necessary, and the vast rooms swallow any noise that might be coming from elsewhere in the building. Only the light click of my heels on the stone floor keeps me company, and I tread as lightly as I can.

Through the glass panelled doors of the peach tree room, I glimpse the light again. With my hand on the door, a doubt hits me, a sudden fear that I might be being misled, that the light isn't Eve at all, but someone intent on luring me outside.

If it *is* Eve...

I press the gun to my ribs, keeping my finger close to the trigger, and open the door. This one isn't locked, either. The Count doesn't fear Bellemeure at all.

The stars are hidden by a veil of thick clouds. Warily, I approach the light, the frosted grass crunching under my boots. As I grow closer, the shadows coalesce into two familiar figures; Eve and Cassius.

Relief momentarily obscures the realisation that I'd barely thought of them at all since we'd parted. "Are you all right?" I ask, coming into the shelter of the trees.

"I should be asking you that question." Eve shifts her weight, keeping her coat between the small lantern she holds and the palace. "Why are you still here?"

"Steel has a half-brother," I explain, "and they look alike."

A cold breeze tugs at my dress and the tail of Eve's coat as she stares at me. Eventually, she lets out a huff. "Of all the things you could have said."

"He has a what?" demands Cassius.

"A half-brother. The Ambassador to House Lucifer, apparently."

The Phantom demon swears, which does nothing to reassure me. I refrain from mentioning Steel's magic. Eve had little affection for my partner in London and I doubt that's changed since.

"I thought you might be hurt," Eve says, and I can't tell if I'm imagining the reproach in her voice, or if she means it.

"They're watching us. And Steel—They're a little *too* interested in Steel." Eve opens her mouth and I cut in, "I'm not leaving him here."

She exhales through her teeth. "Fine. We'll have to think of something else, then."

"Besides," I add, "I found a body in the woods."

"Murdered?"

"Or an animal attack. I'm not sure. What have *you* been up to?" I add, trying to add a glimmer of humour.

Eve jerks her head at the demon, and Cassius rolls his eyes and produces a slip of paper. I take it and unfold it. A pamphlet.

My brows arch. "Someone's inciting riots?"

"Not some*one*, some demons," Eve says. "We ran into a few, but they won't let us meet their leader until we prove we're not allied with the Gendarmerie."

"You think it's Bellemeure."

"I think a group of angry demons could become a nasty weapon and people are going to get hurt, regardless of who's wielding it."

I tilt the paper towards the sparse light. "A few of the letters are faded," I say, "and there's bleeding in the ink. They're using an old press, probably second or third-hand. By the gradient, I'd say it's manual, not steam-powered."

"Not bad," says Eve, making me smile wryly. Then she adds, "Sometimes I think the only difference between you and Monaghan is a formal education," and the smile slips off my face.

"I'm not like him." My voice comes out low and hard, colder than the wind kissing my cheeks.

"I didn't mean—Never mind." Eve tweaks the pamphlet out of my hands. "That's useful, thank you."

"Great, now we know what kind of *printing press* they used," mutters Cassius. "It's only a matter of hours before we find her."

We ignore him. "They sent a spy into the palace, but they've lost contact," Eve continues. "They asked us to find him." She waits, her gaze heavy and expectant.

"I'll need more information than that," I answer.

"That's all I have. That and—they said another demon escaped from the forest near here, wounded."

"Wounded?"

"His arm was stitched on."

"He's a Sentinel demon," Cassius interjects, "with the arm of a Phantom."

Immediately I think of the corpse. "A transplant."

"An unwilling one," adds Eve, grimly.

"The body I found—its hands had been stitched on. And I saw something else; a creature with grafted wings."

"The spy?"

"If they use imps as spies."

Eve's face is blank, uncomprehending. "Imps?"

"Little demons." Cassius puts his thumb and forefinger together with a narrow gap between them. "Very rare, nowadays, and they don't speak, so I doubt it's what we're looking for."

"But there might be others," I add. "The body is..." I orient myself to the paved gardens and point into the forest further south. "...that way."

"Then let's go."

Cassius harrumphs. "Now?"

"No time like the present. Where's Steel?"

"Inside." I teeter on the point of calling for him, or heading back to find him. But if he's inside, with Luka and Katharina, he can keep them occupied.

I don't like the thought that follows; that with Luka, talking about magic, Steel might not want to come.

"Let's go. We don't have time to wait."

CHAPTER THIRTEEN

The wind makes playthings of the trees, sending their boughs into a whispering frenzy over our heads. I take the lead, pushing branches out of the way for Eve, who follows, and ignoring Cassius' low grumbles at the rear. In the dark, the forest looks different than it had in the day. Spaces between the trunks become yawning holes that could hide any number of dangers. I compulsively thumb the barrel of my revolver, suppressing the urge to press my finger to the trigger. Dumont would have had conniptions if I did. *Never touch the trigger unless you intend to pull it*, my brain says in his voice.

"I saw it near here," I say, as we pass the tree I'd used as target practice. My whisper blends into the hiss of the wind, but Eve hears me.

"Hide," she murmurs, and at first I think she's talking to me.

Then Cassius makes a snorting sound and says, "I don't take orders." But when I glance over my shoulder, he's out of sight. Eve grimaces at me and I huff, my breath bursting out in a white cloud.

We stop talking as I search for any sign of the lodge, or the flicker of a wing behind a trunk. The trees end abruptly before I pick out the hulking black building at the centre of the clearing. No light from a window beckons us onward; there's nothing but darkness and silence.

Eve and I exchange a glance. I point two fingers at the side of the lodge, then one in the other direction, meaning for us to split up. Eve knocks my hand down, grabs my elbow, and pulls me with her around the side of the building, sinking that plan.

Cassius leaves crunching footsteps behind us, flattening patches of snow. He keeps pace as we angle around the furthest wall. I take Eve to the back of the building and then through the trees to where I'd found the body. The ground is disturbed, the body gone.

"It was here," I whisper, gesturing. "On its back, its face torn off."

"Someone moved it." Eve raises her lantern to look at the building. "Let's get inside."

The lodge's door is closed but askew, not quite flat to its frame. The windows that flank it are dark, and on second glance I see they're curtained. I slip into the space between the door and the right hand window. Eve does the same on the other side. She gestures at the door.

A puff of steam accompanies Cassius' sarcastic, "Do you think I have a key?"

"Pull it down, then," Eve commands.

Invisible hands lift up the small circular knocker, and pull. The door jerks open with an audible judder. We go still.

Nothing emerges from the dark open doorway, and no outcry goes up from elsewhere in the building. Perhaps it really is deserted.

Before I can check myself, I'm gesturing at the air where I think Cassius is, asking him to go first. I stop, but Eve nods and she stabs a hand towards the door. If the Phantom demon is reluctant, he keeps any protests to himself. Faint thuds of boots on wood indicate he's stepped inside. Eve follows, a blade in her hand, though from where I can't guess. I cup one hand in the other to steady my aim and bring up the rear with the pistol.

It's impossible to see. I get the impression of a small space, and grope into the darkness at my side, bracing myself. Wood. The door leads into a corridor. The flanking windows must be in rooms on either side, so there should be doors ahead.

Eve's fingers brush my hand, and I make sure to keep the gun tilted towards the floor. We continue forward slowly, keeping that tenuous connection. On the left, my fingers meet empty air—the first door.

Ahead, Cassius makes a sound. "A fireplace," he murmurs. We move left through the open gap, Cassius, then Eve, then me, trailing them. The ground under my feet softens; a rug. Someone was here long enough to make this place comfortable.

There's a scratching sound, flint on steel, as Cassius tries to light the fire. By the weight of the air, the room can't be much larger than ten feet or so, which leaves space for a second behind it, judging by the size of the building as it appeared from the outside. Four rooms, laid out in a square.

My brain puts up a valiant effort to distract me from the unguarded space at my back, but my neck prickles nonetheless. With his keen vision, Steel would have swept through all four rooms by now.

A spark flares and dies just as quickly. A second catches, and widens into an ember that reflects enough of a glow to see the edge of a rug and the worn wooden boards underneath it. At the sight of the logs and dried pine cones in the hearth moving of their own volition, and a surge of instinctive animal fear saps the strength from my legs.

It's only Cassius. He's nothing to be frightened of.

After a few moments, the ember blossoms into a small fire and a crisp fresh scent seeps through the room with the light. The room itself has little that stands out; a desk against the wall, the rug I'd felt earlier and a lone wooden chair by the fire. Ragged, moth eaten curtains shield the window. I touch the wooden planks that make up the wall and ice bites at my fingers.

Eve stands next to me, regarding the curtains. "No one's been here for a long time," she whispers.

"The fire hasn't been lit for a long time," I correct. "There are other rooms."

"I can smell blood," Cassius adds, slowly, as if he'd been planning not to mention it, "though I'm not sure where it's coming from." His voice moves past us as he speaks.

Eve flips her dagger into a reverse grip, the blade parallel to her forearm. "Be careful."

"Oh, are you concerned for me? How sweet."

"Only so you won't alert someone to our presence," she hisses back.

I find a stack of candles tucked next to the hearth and light one from the fire. The wax coats my palm in a slickness that stinks of fat. Old-fashioned tallow candles.

Eve has moved into the room opposite, exploring in the glow of the fire that stretches across the corridor. I take my candle and start down the passage. Two more empty doorways open into other rooms, as I'd thought, and a wooden staircase leads to a second floor. Half the steps have shattered, leaving a wide gap in the middle that's too far to jump—for humans, at any rate. I raise the candle, wincing as a drip of wax seeps down to scald my thumb. The upstairs is completely dark.

Turning, I try to peer through the shadows to see further, and the wood under my boot rings hollow. A hidden space?

I press my back to the wall to better examine the floor. Set into the floorboards is a square cellar door. At its centre lies a rope handle.

"Eve," I whisper and she's there in a moment, examining the door with a tilt to her head. I aim my gun at the floor, nod at her to lift it.

She grasps the rope knot and yanks on it. The cellar door opens without a sound, revealing a faint warm glow. We pause, and Eve holds the door half open as we strain to hear whatever might be below us.

Still nothing. The glow could be a banked fire, or a lantern left alight.

Eve hefts the door open, leaving it propped ajar. She looks over her shoulder, waggles her knife, and a steamy breath fogs the air beside her.

"Here I go, then," mutters Cassius. A faint rustle, then the stairs leading into the cellar creak. I listen to the soft thud of his footsteps move away. Then stop.

Crouched next to me, Eve puts her hand on the rim of the opening and her fingers grow pale under her nails. Until Cassius' whisper drifts up, "You'd better come down."

As Eve's grip relaxes, I clamber over the edge. The steps are narrow but clean-cut, and the wood shines with polish. Wooden struts hold up the roof, obscuring my view. Only when I reach the bottom can I see the sawdust floor, the rows of wooden tables, the off-white sheets covering the bodies on top.

CHAPTER FOURTEEN

"A morgue?" I say, before an uncovered object on the table nearest me registers; a body, lifeless, its limbs stitched to its torso with thick black thread.

My head swims for a moment and the faint golden light scatters over the sawdust. I'm in London again, talking to Eve about the severed arm she found in Whitehall.

No, this isn't that. This isn't Lavender. I take a deep breath, make myself look at the room clinically. A small coal stove in the corner is the source of the light. The ceiling is shallow, like the kind of cellar used for wine storage. But in this one, six wooden tables line the wall, three of them covered in sheets draped over misshapen lumps. A fourth holds the corpse. The last two are empty. Metal rings dangle from the wall and rust-coloured blood stains the straw and sawdust underneath. At the far end of the room is another door, but this one is closed.

"Jesus," mutters Eve, under her breath.

I step up to the uncovered body and examine the corpse. "This is the same kind of procedure I saw on the imp."

The corpse's claws are black and blunted, its body unmarked save for the scars of the surgery. Scarlet streaks on the wood under the shoulders and hips indicate the demon was alive when the surgery was performed. The stove sheds little warmth; that at least is something to be grateful for, as the smell rising from the bodies hasn't yet bloomed into the stench of rot.

Eve circles to the other table and lifts a corner of the sheet. Another body, this one badly contorted, its pieces replaced with monstrous, bestial limbs.

"Been dead for a while," Eve says, dropping the sheet. Her dark skin has taken on a greyish hue.

"Are one of these the spy?"

She blows out a breath, her cheeks puffing. "I don't know. I'll have to go back and describe the bodies to them." All the corpses are male, but that tells us little.

Something clinks; metal on metal. Both of us whirl towards the sound. One of the rings on the wall sways to the side. It's attached to a chain, the other end hidden behind one of the tables.

"Cassius—"

"I don't think so."

"Get over there!" Eve snaps.

Placing my gun on the table, I drop into a crouch, peering between the legs of the tables. Half buried in sawdust shavings is a black wing.

I snap my fingers. "Come out. We won't hurt you." Eve makes a frustrated sound and I cut in, "Not if you're good."

The imp's large dark eyes peep up out of the sawdust. White rings its irises and its tufted ears swivel, one pointing in my direction, the second pivoting to capture the sound of the others breathing. It crawls out of the sawdust, two of its odd spidery legs perched against the wall like a cat ready to launch itself across the room. A leather collar sits snug around its neck, attached to the chain.

"Someone locked you away after you got out," I realise. "Were you the only one who survived?"

Its eyes flicker off to the side, to the stairs and back. It's so small, how could it live through this kind of operation?

"So, what," says Cassius, "someone's cutting up demons and sewing them back together? For Lucifer's sake, why?"

"To see what their weaknesses are." Eve's voice is thin. She had seen Lavender's destroyed body first hand.

I keep still. The imp eases its way over the sawdust towards me, coming out from under the table. "Easy," I whisper. "Why don't we take that chain off, hm?"

There's a gust of air and the imp shrieks, its shrill cry piercing through my head and making my ears throb. It flaps its wings, struggling against an invisible grip.

"Got it," Cassius says, grimly.

"What are you doing? Let it go!"

I hear his snarl in his voice. "It's chained to the damn wall, do you think it's going to welcome you with a kiss?"

"Not if you *hurt* it." I had promised. "Eve, tell him to let it go."

Eve hesitates.

"Eve. *Look* at it."

The thing cuts a pathetic image, flapping against Cassius' hold, emitting small cries that have grown softer and weaker.

"Eve, please."

"Cassius, let it go."

The Phantom demon throws a derogatory curse in my direction and the imp tumbles to the ground. It lies in the sawdust, its sides heaving, its front legs curled up close to its body.

"Not like that!"

"You *just said*—"

"Now is not the time," Eve interrupts. "And if that thing bites you, Hazel, it's your own fault."

I don't want to admit that she's right, but I cover my hands in my borrowed stole, just in case. "See if you can find any clues."

When I reach the imp, I find that the collar has been buckled so tightly that the skin of its neck bulges on either side. It watches me, the white sliver at the edge of its eyes widening.

"Easy," I say, again. "I'm not going to hurt you." I unintentionally emphasise the first word and earn another curse from Cassius. My whole lineage must be damned by now, with the amount of vitriol he's thrown at me.

Keeping the stole wrapped around the meat of my hands, I tug at the buckle. It's stiff, the leather stained, and it refuses at first to come undone. The imp whimpers, and despite the furred spindly legs jutting from its torso, something in my chest pangs.

My family never had a pet, as a child. I'd never thought twice about the bedraggled cats that stalked the workhouse looking for rats, or the three-legged dog that would sit outside the Ten Bells and beg for scraps until the owner got fed up and chased it off. No one could afford to feed another mouth. No one could afford to feed the mouths they already had.

Not that this monstrous creation is a pet, or should be thought of as one. Its teeth are sharper than any London street hound.

"There's nothing else down here," Eve announces. She drops a sheet that she'd been looking under, her lip curling. "Just more bodies. We can try the other rooms upstairs." She gives me a doubtful look, but I nod.

"I won't be long. It'll be faster if you make a start." Clearly this place isn't deserted; whoever owns it could be back at any moment.

Two sets of footsteps march upstairs, and I breathe a little easier now that I'm alone. Eventually, I manage to work the buckle open and pull the leather apart, loosening the collar. The imp inhales deeply, its sides puffing out until the skin stretches over its ribs. It continues to lie there, breathing, its eyes fixed on my hands.

After a moment's hesitation, I wrap the fur stole around its body. The legs are awkward and the tips jut out once I'm finished, but it seems content to let me swaddle it until only its head is visible.

What on earth I'm supposed to do with it now, I don't know. I could leave it here, but if its captor returns, it'll end up back in the collar. Sighing, I scoop the creature up and tuck it under one arm, so if it does take it into its head to try and bite me, I'll be able to drop it before it can strike.

I navigate the narrow steps carefully, one eye on the imp, but it peers out from its fur cocoon as if it's never seen the world before. Its wings and legs must have come from juvenile Stalker and Scout demons and Eve had said that the demon she'd seen had a Phantom's arm grafted onto it. The perpetrator isn't trying to learn how demons work. They know what demons can do; they've made very particular selections to choose specific talents. They're trying to create something different, something new.

The building is close enough to the palace that any activity wouldn't go unnoticed by House Asmodeus. If I'm right, and those demons were operated on while alive, then at the very least, they would have screamed. The Revenants must know.

One-handed, I let the trap door fall softly shut, replacing the rope handle where it had lain before we touched it. The sound of a heavy exhale makes me look up. A small cloud of steam puffs into the corridor and disperses under the breeze from the open door. The imp under my arm squeaks and starts to struggle.

"Cassius won't hurt you again," I tell it, though that seems to do nothing to calm it. "Where's Eve?" I ask the demon.

He doesn't reply. My gaze darts from the rug to the walls, trying to place him in the otherwise empty corridor. A second misty cloud floats into the air, closer than before.

My patience for games has long since run out. "Did you find anything, or not?"

Still nothing. Indents appear in the rug; the shapes look like bare feet. But Cassius was wearing boots.

"What did you say?" Eve appears in the doorway of a room down the corridor.

"I—"

Cassius appears behind her, hovering at her shoulder, visible.

The breath comes again, close enough that I hear the hiss of an exhale. It isn't Cassius.

CHAPTER FIFTEEN

I clench my hand and the emptiness of my palm quickens my heart into a deafening drumbeat. I left my gun in the cellar. "Eve!"

The indents in the rug vanish and I throw myself sideways. Something crashes past me and slams into the far wall.

"What the hell?" I hear and shout back, "It's a Phantom demon!"

Hugging the wriggling imp to my chest, I push myself off the the wall with my other hand. We have to find a way to make it visible. If I can't see it, I can't shoot it.

But first, I need my gun.

"Distract it!"

"What do you mean, *distract it*?"

But I'm hurtling towards her before Eve can finish the sentence. Scrabbling sounds come from behind me, and the rug jerks under my feet, throwing me off balance. I stumble to one knee still clutching the damned imp, and it shrieks at the sudden shift.

"God damn it." Eve widens her stance and flicks out her hand. A dagger shoots past me in a silver flash. It thuds dully against the wall. "*Damn* it!"

I catch the frame of one of the doors, spin around it and throw myself into the room. The small fire we lit earlier crackles.

"Get down," Cassius snaps out, countered by Eve's, "Watch the rug!" The Phantom shouts and something heavy thuds against the door frame. The wood splinters.

One of the logs in the fireplace has only half caught, its end lying on the stone hearth. I grab it, wince at the heat that sears my fingers, and hurl it at the doorway. It hits the air and tumbles to the ground, rolling across the floor. A spark from the lit end jumps to the wooden floorboards and smoulders. Ash makes a smudge in middle of the empty air.

A strange growl throbs through my chest. The unknown demon's fingers grip the frame and I pause for a single breath, my eyes so wide they hurt, waiting for my moment. The frame cracks, the floor creaks under a footstep, and I spin to the left. Claws scrape blistering trails over my ribs.

The gun, the *gun*.

I race out of the room and shove the imp at Eve, who scrambles to get around me at the demon. "Take this," I demand and run towards the cellar door.

"What are you doing—"

The rope, the door, the stairs. I grab the handle and yank, flinging the cellar door open with a crash. The demon is making a growling, savage sound, and down the corridor Cassius yells, "Get out, woman! The building's on fucking fire!"

I miss half the stairs and hit the sawdust with a bone-jarring thud. Where did I put it, where *is it*—

A distant corner of my mind surges with fear, like part of me has been suddenly drenched in ice.

I scramble between the bodies to the table. The stairs groan under a heavy weight. God, I should've brought more bullets. I slam into the table, too fast to stop myself, and knock the breath out of my lungs. The revolver's there, lying parallel to the corpse, right where I'd left it. I snatch it up, spin, thumb the safety back.

The last stair quivers. I take aim at the smudge of ash, throwing a desperate prayer to whatever god is listening, and shoot. Dirt sprays from the back wall of the cellar. The growling doesn't stop, a constant low rumble that blends with the distant crackle of flames. A table near the stairs topples over. Its corpse flops onto the floor.

Again. I pull the safety, squeeze the trigger. The bang masks the sound of its impact and I scour the wall, trying to find where it hit.

Then the creature groans. The air shimmers and starts to blur, revealing a hulking figure. The thing might have the power of a Phantom demon, but it's not wholly Phantom. One of its arms is huge and furred and ends in a paw like a bear's. Other, unrecognisable limbs are stitched to it, and its face ends where it shouldn't; the bottom half of its jaw is gone. Instead, three rows of teeth sprout from its upper gums. Its eyes are little more than slits, scrunched up in pain and rage that has carved deep furrows into its upper face.

I hesitate, and in that moment it launches forward. Choking on a cry, I dodge, earning another lance of pain across my side. I grasp at the stairs, use them to propel myself so I can jump three at a time. Behind me, another table topples to the ground.

All my breath goes to fuelling my body, none left to shout a warning. When I reach the top of the stairs, I grab the cellar door and slam it back into place. It won't hold for long.

I turn for the door. Fire climbs the wall on my right, licking at the wooden ceiling. The log. Stupid. I stumble past it, my back burning and my arm crawling with pain. Heat presses against my face. A crash behind me and a rush of air whips my skirt against my legs. It's broken out of the cellar.

Clutching my revolver, I break into a run. The fire leaps for me as I pass and I slap my dress out of the way. I burst out of the building, catching a glimpse of Eve, struggling in Cassius' hold. The thing is still behind me.

I drop to the ground, feel the gust of air as it rushes past me. Someone is shouting, though I can't make out the words. The demon recovers, sinking its claws into the ground to steady it. Its panting breaths are harsh and wet. I pivot onto one knee, take aim and fire. The bullet whizzes past it, thudding into a tree and showering pine needles onto the grass.

With a throaty growl and a flash of those hideous teeth, the demon surges towards me. I jerk up my arm. My back hits the ground, sending a flash of agony through me. My revolver is caught in its half-mouth and its teeth scrape against the metal nozzle.

"*Hazel!*"

Claws sink into my shoulder and a grunt escapes through my gritted teeth. I struggle to pull back the safety, my grip slippery with its saliva. The thing makes a throttled, moaning sound that could have once been a word. The safety clicks. I squeeze my eyes shut and pull the trigger.

Hot liquid splatters my face. The growling cuts off, and the sudden silence makes me think for a moment that I've lost my hearing. I open my eyes. The bullet went straight through its head. The rest of the thing's skull is still attached to its spine and as it slumps over, brains spill onto my chest, onto the ground, turning the white snow red.

CHAPTER SIXTEEN

"Hazel." Steel's there, suddenly, wresting the demon's carcass off me and shoving it to one side. Then he's pulling me to me feet, plucking at my torn shirt to see the scratches on my arm. "You're hurt."

I have to crack my jaw to speak. "It's not bad." Fire crackles from the building, eating its way through the wood.

"Did it bite you?" he asks. "Hazel, did it bite you?"

"No," I manage. My fingers ache where they grip the revolver. I consciously loosen my hold.

His hands cup the sides of my neck. His face looks gaunt in the light of the fire, cavernous. "You were nearly—" He stops again, his gaze searching my face as if there's something there he's desperate to find.

"What happened here?"

Steel yanks his hands back as if he'd scalded them. Luka stands under the trees, regarding the burning building.

"Did you do this?" he asks, his expression otherwise impassive.

Eve wrenches free of Cassius' hold and levels a dark look at him. "Of course not."

"Technically..." the Phantom demon starts.

Eve cuts across him. "Who are you, anyway?" Her eyes abruptly widen and she glances from him to Steel and back.

Cassius regards the new demon for a moment, then looks at me. "My, you look a state," he drawls, wrinkling his nose. "Is any of that blood and brain on your face actually yours?"

Everyone's attention turns to me. "Thank you for the concern," I mutter, under my breath. "What do we do about the fire?" It's worked its way through one room and is devouring the second, the light throwing the trees into sharp relief. "It'll burn the evidence."

"What did you find in there?" Steel nudges the dead monster with the toe of his boot. "Not more of these?"

"Something like that." If the fire gets any larger, it'll be visible from the palace. "We need water."

Steel lifts his hands, palm up. "Luckily," he says, "it's a cloudy night."

A drop lands on the crown of my head, then another, then rain falls from the sky in a steady downpour. The flames hiss where they flicker at the door and the windows, but the fire still rages inside.

Luka sighs heavily. "You can't stop it. The building has a roof." His short black hair is still somehow perfect even under the raindrops pouring down his face. He flicks his fingers and a spear of jagged light cracks through the sky and strikes the building. The light is gone a second later, leaving a vivid imprint streaked across my vision and filling the air with the crisp scent of a storm. The fire bursts through the second floor.

"That made it worse!"

"And now they'll think it was because of a storm," he says, slowly, as if I'm an imbecile, "not because of whatever you did in there that set an entire building on fire. You are welcome."

Eve makes an outraged sound, her chin going up the way it does when she's winding up for an argument.

"Did you know what's in there?" I ask him, before she can let loose. "Did you know what they were doing?"

"What I know is that the Count will not be happy that you've destroyed a building on the Emperor's estate. Nor, for that matter, will the Emperor." Scorn permeates his expression so deeply that I can't tell if he's lying.

A faint squeak catches my attention. My fur stole—mud-stained and singed—lies at the foot of a tree, wriggling. I cast Eve a reproachful look.

She rocks onto her heels. "What? I kept it alive."

I scoop up the bundle and the creature goes still. As I turn back to the building it keens, and I step away from the fire.

Steel reaches for the stole in my arms. "Why do you have a—*What the hell is that*?" He recoils and then, recovering, attempts to look as though he'd done nothing of the sort.

"One of the victims."

"Victims?"

"Look," Eve cuts in, "we should go before they send guards to investigate. And in case you hadn't noticed, we're surrounded by trees." The rain seems to be keeping the fire from spreading too rapidly, soaking the wood and cutting it back as it tries to escape, but that might not last long.

Luka strides across the clearing, grabs hold of the monster's bear-like arm, and throws its body through the doorway into the burning building. The casual display of strength awes me for a moment, until the reality of what he did clicks.

"That was *evidence*," I hiss. "You just destroyed evidence!"

He brushes his hands. "Evidence of what? That some lunatic had taken over an abandoned shack and used it for his ungodly experiments?" His tone cuts. "Are you saying you think that thing should be released to the public?"

"You know that's not what I'm saying—"

Cassius hooks his fingers around Eve's elbow. "If you're all going to stay here, that's your choice, but I am not going to stick around to explain why their forest is on fire. Eve." He starts pulling her backwards, towards the trees, and she raises her shoulders at me as if to say, *He has a point.*

"I still want to know what the hell happened," mutters Steel. He creeps closer to my side, eyeing the imp warily. It eyes him back.

Distantly, a bell starts ringing. Someone's seen the fire. Eve and Cassius are already making their way through the trees at a swift jog.

"Not here." I follow them, tilting my head back and letting the rain wash over my face. If I start to think too much about the warmth on my cheeks, or the small fragments I can feel at my hairline, I won't be able to get through the rest of the night without vomiting.

Luka matches stride with us on Steel's other side, silent. Both he and Steel wear the suits they'd worn at dinner, and the tips of Luka's fingers carry the smudge of tobacco. He rubs them together as we walk.

The sound of shouting and running footsteps echoes behind us. I twist to see a few shadowy figures outlined by the fire. Then the orange glow starts to dim, the flames recede. We follow Eve and Cassius until the sounds dim and the remaining fire is hidden by thick trunks.

Eve stops first, putting one hand to the nearest tree and leaning over, catching her breath. "I should have brought more daggers," she mutters.

"You shouldn't have been there in the first place," Cassius replies, his voice sharp. "Your professor will have me slaughtered if you get yourself killed."

"Why were you there?" asks Steel.

"I think we can do away with the rain, now." Luka leans against a pine tree, arms crossed, as casual as if he's at a family outing waiting for the games to start.

"Oh." Steel sheepishly raises his hand and a moment later the rain lessens to a few recalcitrant drops.

I peel back the fur stole and the imp's skin crawls with a shiver. "This is why we were there." In my peripheral vision I see Steel's look of horror, but my gaze is on Luka. His lashes flicker, but that's all his expression. "Someone has been experimenting on demons."

"Who?"

"I was hoping you could tell us that."

Luka's brows arch upwards. "Oh? You think I make it a habit of practising my sewing technique on hapless idiots, do you?"

"I think House Asmodeus does little without your knowledge."

His mouth twists at the corner. "Then I fear you would be surprised. I was sent here precisely because Asmodeus was *not* informing anyone of its actions."

"These things are the results of experiments?" asks Steel. He points at the imp as he says it, and the thing snaps at him. He jerks his finger back, frowning.

"There were others, in the cellar," Eve adds. "All demons, all with some kind of transplant—limbs, wings, that kind of thing."

"But why?"

"Magic?" I ask and Luka shakes his head.

"There are no rituals that require this kind of work. Blood and organs can help focus spells, but this is...illogical." It's odd, hearing that word from a demon's mouth, but I don't disagree.

"Then we need to talk to the Count," Steel says. "Find out who's behind this."

Cassius' voice is cuttingly sarcastic. "And make yourselves a target? By all means. See how far that will get you."

"I think one of them may have been a spy," Eve says, and Luka's head snaps up.

"A what?"

"There are copper class demons in the city who've been trying to find a way to bring Asmodeus down. One of them must have escaped from that building and reached home, so they sent in another to find out what happened."

"If the first failed, I don't see how a second would succeed," murmurs Steel.

"At any rate," continues Eve, "I'll need to go back and tell them what happened." She shoots me a meaningful look.

"I'll go with you." I need to get away from the palace, talk to Eve about Bellemeure somewhere Luka or Asmodeus's demons won't hear us.

"If you're going, then so am I." Steel meets my exasperated gaze with a stubborn shift of his jaw. "You could get hurt again. I only knew you were in trouble because—" He cuts off, clearly remembering our audience. "Because I was outside and smelt the smoke," he finishes, and Luka's head tilts towards him. Steel hurries on. "It's not safe to go with them."

"The Count may not notice her missing," Luka says, a cool tone to his voice that almost disguises the disgust in the word *her*, "but he *will* notice if you leave."

"Luka's right," I say.

"They're both right." I glance at Eve in surprise and she shrugs a little. "I doubt these demons will be happy to give up a demon of his class, if this is the kind of fancy magic he can do. Besides, you're covered in..." She makes an eloquent gesture that takes in the filth staining my hair and most of my face. "Cassius and I will go."

"Alone? It could be dangerous."

A wry smile. "Not as dangerous as taking a gang of people with us, some of them demons."

Luka pushes off the tree, giving Eve a curt, dismissive nod. "That sounds sensible. In the meantime, we can attempt to get to the bottom of whatever misguided soul created that monstrosity." The imp peels its lips back from its teeth in a tiny snarl.

I sigh, sensing the edge of fatigue like a cliff in the dark. Steel's gaze is a heavy weight on my face. "Very well. But you'll come back, right?"

"As soon as I have more information," Eve confirms. "And, preferably, more daggers."

Her attempt at humour isn't quite enough to make me smile, but it lifts some of the tension dogging my heels.

"You should exit by the stables," Luka says. "The ostlers will be asleep at this time of night, and they're human. It should not be hard to sneak past them."

"Thanks," Eve replies, shortly. She gives me a look—*be careful*—and I send her one back, then she drags Cassius into the forest and disappears into the dark.

"Come, then." Luka puts a hand on Steel's shoulder and steers him around to face the palace. "A bath, I think, before someone catches sight of her like that."

I tuck the imp back into its fur wrap, hoping I haven't made the wrong decision.

CHAPTER SEVENTEEN

A bath in Whitechapel was a quick wipe with an old rag and icy water. A bath in Schönbrunn palace is a deep, claw-footed tub filled almost to the brim, the water so hot it steams, the towel soft and thick and set to warm by the fire, the soap redolent with the scent of orchids and lilies. Luka had ordered me to hide in my room while he pulled servants from their beds to fill the bath. Though I'd resented his high-handedness at the time, now, gazing at the whorls of steam rising lazily though the air, I have to smother gratitude.

Silence blankets all but the low crackle of the fire as I ease out of my clothing. The sleeve of my dress drags harshly over my wounded arm and a pained noise escapes me.

"Are you all right?"

Steel's voice makes me jump and I clutch my clothes to my chest a moment, scanning the empty room.

"Should I call for a doctor?" The words are muffled and I realise he's outside the door.

"Why are you here? I thought you'd gone to bed." The pain has softened to a dull, throbbing ache and the wet sensation of blood, which is probably not a good sign.

"How could I go to bed after you wander off and nearly get yourself killed?"

Tired, struggling to ignore the pain in my arm and my side, I reply, "What, are you my father now?"

"Am I your—You do realise that this house is filled with demons who could kill you in an instant?" he snaps. "That Bellemeure could be Lucifer-knows-where, waiting to attack? I come back and find you gone, with no one the wiser as to *where*—" His voice cuts off and I ease myself into the bath, wincing when the hot water reaches my wounds. "I was...concerned," he says, more quietly, though tension still simmers under the words.

"I'm sorry," I reply, in the same tone. "I should have realised how it would look. Did anyone notice?"

"I don't care if anyone *noticed*, I care that you walked into obvious danger without *calling for me*. You know you can, don't you?"

Sighing a little, I sink deeper into the water, letting the heat ease through my muscles. "I know."

"Then why the hell didn't you?" he demands.

Part of me—*all* of me—is glad he's behind the door, so I don't have to meet his eyes. I'm not sure I could. "I didn't think I needed to."

"That's a lie."

I huff, blowing ripples in the water. "I am not overly fond of this connection," I say, dryly. A soft noise makes me picture Steel leaning against the door.

"I am not overly fond of being lied to." His voice hasn't lost that tension.

Luckily the light is too dim to make out my reflection in the water. I take the jug set thoughtfully on a table beside the tub, and use it to rinse the blood out of my hair. Steel says nothing, stubborn as an old goat, and I put the jug down with a harder click than I mean to.

"I lean on you too much," I say, wetting the soap, concentrating on the tiny bubbles in the lather. "If I can't handle myself, what good am I as an age—as someone pursuing a murder case?"

"I could say the same about myself," he points out and I snort. "What, you disagree? Tell me honestly, how far would I have gotten in Paris without you?"

Modesty battles honesty, and the latter wins. "Not far."

"Exactly."

"That's different."

"How?"

"You're..." Damn this man, why don't I have an answer? I always have an answer.

"Exactly," he says, again, smug.

I twist to glare at the door but as I do I pull at the scratch on my side and yelp.

"What is it? What happened? Did you fall?" The door handle twists.

"Steel, if you open that door," I say, gritting my teeth against the pain, "I swear I'll make you regret it."

"I struggle to imagine that," he says, but the door remains shut. A heavy exhale follows. "The Phantom should have protected you. When I see that bastard—"

"It wasn't his fault. That...thing...was too fast. And he had Eve to take care of. Besides, I had my revolver." The pain fades to a manageable level and I start working the lather through the lengths of my hair.

"Thank Lucifer for that." Something scratches at the door and I hear a small squeak. "Oi, get away."

Pausing, I look at the line of shifting shadow under the door. "Is that the imp?"

"It is a pest," he says, in overly articulated tones, as if he's directing the words to a child. The imp squeaks again.

"It's a victim, just as much as the others. What is it, anyway? I mean, what was it?"

"A lesser demon. The kind you only think you see in the darker parts of the forest, the kind that breeds myths and folktales. I've only heard rumours about them myself, I didn't think they actually—Stop that," he interrupts himself as the scratching begins again.

"How many are there?" I ask, thinking of my journal. Another entry I'll have to add later.

"Can't be many, given how little we've seen of them. I expect most have been hunted to extinction. Or kept as pets by foolish nobles," he adds, pointedly.

"Lucky that I'm not a noble."

"Hmm."

I rinse the soap from my hair, avoiding looking at the murky water too closely. When I'm as clean as I'm going to get, I grip the sides of the tub and pull myself to my feet. I have to hold onto the porcelain tightly as I step out, the flames blurring at the edges of my vision.

"Are you out? We need to wrap your wounds."

"Just a moment." I'd do it myself, but the thought of binding my aching arm makes me shudder, and I'm not such a fool as to leave it untreated.

Some attentive soul has left a nightgown with cap sleeves draped over a wooden lattice screen. I squeeze as much water out of my hair as I can and pull it on, perching on a lonely chair by the fire.

"All right," I call. "You can come in, now."

The door opens and a dark shape dashes across the floor towards me. I yank my feet away just as it veers to a stop and I recognise the imp. Its huge eyes glimmer in the light of the fire and it makes a soft, inquiring noise.

"What," I say, flatly, my heart beating somewhere in my ears, "are you doing?"

Its ears droop. Sighing, I let my legs drop from where I'd hunched them up protectively and it scurries to my feet, curling up there and glaring at Steel, who follows less frenziedly.

"I still think you should have left it in the forest," he says, returning its glower with one of his own. The creature lifts its lip to bare a single fang.

"Perhaps I should have." I have no idea what I'm supposed to do with it, or how I'll hide it. But all I want right now is to stop thinking, so I incline my head towards the strips of cloth in his hand. "Bandages?"

"Of a sort. I repurposed one of the nightgowns in your closet." He kneels beside me, putting him on a slightly lower plane. The imp gives a warning growl.

I shunt it to the side gently with one foot. "Steel is a friend," I tell it.

"We'll see about that," the demon mutters. He lifts my arm, examining the scratch. "This doesn't look poisoned and the bleeding seems to have stopped, but we should wrap it."

"I'm so glad to have you around to tell me these things."

Steel's mouth barely lifts. He wraps the first strip tight around my upper arm and I hold myself still, breathing shallowly. "Don't leave without me again. Please," he adds, as I glance at him. "You could have been hurt, seriously hurt, and I wouldn't have—" He cuts himself off again.

He probably would have known, through the ritual. Known that I was hurt and roughly where I was, but unable to get there in time. I imagine if it had been the other way around, then have to stop before Steel notices the uptick in my pulse.

After a moment, he sits back on his heels and frowns at my arm, wrapped tightly if unevenly in white cotton. "That will have to do."

"Thank you."

"Is that it?" His gaze flits over my body, hovering at my waist. I glance down. A scarlet drop stains the white cotton.

"I can wrap that one," I say, softly.

He stands, yanking at his sleeves to pull them over his hands. "Katharina is planning some kind of party tomorrow," he says. "We can investigate then. I assume you want to start straight away."

"I do. Whoever performed those experiments won't be pleased that we destroyed them. They might have trouble masking their anger. And they might be looking for a new location, more victims."

"They can't see that." He gestures at the imp with his boot. "They'll know it was you. They may suspect you already."

"He'll hide in my room." I reach down to touch the soft fur of its back and it goes still, tense for a moment, then when I make no other move, it relaxes.

"He," breathes Steel, shaking his head. "Can you walk?"

Our rooms are only down the hall. "I'll be fine."

"All right." He goes to leave and then stops, pivots instead to stand behind my chair and put a hand on its back. I tilt my head to look up at him, a lock of damp hair spooling loose and falling across my forehead. "Promise me," he says, "that you won't do anything dangerous without me."

I blink. "I don't make promises lightly."

"I know. That's why I'm asking."

"I promise I won't take on anything dangerous without telling you."

"That's not what I asked," he says, lightly, although his expression as he looks down at me is serious.

I offer a diversion. "Promise *me* you'll be careful."

"I promise I'll be *extremely* careful," he replies, a smile hovering somewhere in the vicinity of his mouth. "Although my promises aren't as good as yours."

"They're good enough for me." My throat is a little stretched by the position, and the words come out lower than I mean them to.

His gaze flits over my face. He lifts his hand, hesitates, then gently moves the lock of hair from my forehead. "Then I'll make you as many as you like," he murmurs and with that, he's gone.

Agent E. Wilson

As the night wears on, the air only grows colder. They're lucky Steel can only summon rain and not snow.

Cassius is a silent, grumpy figure at her side. "What?" she asks, dreading the answer. "Why aren't you happy now?"

"I would be happy if we weren't wading through sludge in the middle of the night."

Sludge is an exaggeration; the streets of the Favoriten district are lined with old crates and torn paper, but the cobbles are slick with rainwater, freshly washed by Steel's little trick. Even the clouds above her have thinned, sapped of their moisture.

His magic reached all the way to this part of the city. No wonder Monaghan wants him brought back to London.

"And I'd be happy," Cassius goes on, clearly warming to his subject, "if we hadn't spent the last hour trudging through filthy city streets. *And*," he adds, and Eve wishes she'd never asked, "I'd be happy if we hadn't just fought off some kind of laboratory creation and had to flee through a burning building."

"We didn't have to *flee*," she replies, because that is too much. "That was your fault—you dragged us out."

"If I'd let you, you would have stayed there fighting until the roof collapsed and buried you alive."

"It would have been better than running like a coward."

"Lucifer spare me." He casts his gaze skyward. "At least cowards get to live."

"Not all of them," she reminds him.

"Neither will you, not if you're going to throw yourself into these ridiculous situations."

They lapse into silence. Most of the tenement buildings on either side of the narrow street are dark, but a few windows hold a lit candle, or the faint glow of a fire. From somewhere comes the bark of a laugh, and, later, the sound of an argument. Their boots thump on the uneven cobbles.

The tavern, when they reach it, emanates the low murmur of many voices. Thin yellow light seeps through the cracks in the wooden door. Eve greets the guard with a nod.

"You again," he says.

"I went to the palace. Is he in?"

Wordlessly, the demon stands aside, letting her open the door herself, like a gentleman. Scowling, she uses her shoulder to shove it wide, halting at the throng of people within.

Demons are packed into the pub. Some of them carry glasses—beer, mostly—and all of them face away from the door. A few give her a curious glance as she shuts it, their gazes landing on her, then Cassius, then flicking away.

Resonant German reaches over the crowd. She pushes onto her toes to get a better look, sees the Reaper demon standing on a crate at the back, giving a speech. His throaty voice rises and falls with the skill of a master orator, and the scratch in some of his words only makes the crowd hold their breath to listen.

"This looks not at all like a place we should be," Cassius mutters, in her ear.

She grasps his sleeve and starts edging around the demons to make her way to the side. The air in the room practically vibrates, on the edge of erupting into raucous applause—or, if the speaker chooses, into something more deadly. Cassius is right; they shouldn't be here. Eve puts her shoulders to the wall and lets the words wash over her.

"We have lived in fear for too long," the speaker calls, earning a murmur of agreement from the crowd, "kept under the heel of the so-called diamond class—but who was it that called them diamond?"

"They did!" someone shouts.

"And who are they to bestow that title on themselves, at the expense of the rest of us? What have they done to earn the right to lead?"

"Nothing!" another man calls, from the back of the room. He's echoed by a few others.

"Nothing," the speaker repeats. "Nothing but reap the rewards of our labour! Our sweat, our blood! Our own *children*, even!" He gestures to the ceiling and the crowd stirs, getting aggravated. Cassius shifts uncomfortably at her side.

The speaker raises his hands. "Our time will be soon," he says, soothing, a circus master holding back a lion. "For now, remember this: we have power. Together, we outnumber them. Together, we are stronger than they could ever be."

There are nods, shouts of agreement. The man hops off the crate without ceremony, heading towards the bar, and the noise of the crowd disperses into low whispers that might be just as dangerous as the shouts if given enough time.

Eve pushes off from the wall and intercepts him. "Can we have a word?"

His gaze flicks to her hands first, oddly, then to Cassius, then he searches the empty space behind them. "You did not find him?"

"We did."

A crease forms between his brows as his eyes return to her face, then the realisation hits and a mask of indifference descends over his expression. "We had best speak upstairs."

As she follows him up, away from the crowd, Cassius tugs at her coat. "There aren't any doors upstairs," he mutters.

No escape, he means, but she's not going to turn around now, not when they're sitting on a powder keg. Exploit enough poor, downtrodden folk for too long, and they'll rise up to take back their power, regardless of the consequences. And that kind of revolution never ends peacefully.

Though she can't deny the lick of fire that had ignited in her at the speaker's words. Even she isn't immune to their tactics. She just has to remember that they're ultimately only that—tactics. All leaders are practised manipulators.

Someone has swept the first floor corridor clean and the moans that had disturbed the peace before are silent. Eve follows the Reaper—Noah, she reminds herself—into the sick room. The mattress where the injured demon was lying is empty of all but stains.

"Where is he?"

"He did not survive." She has to strain to hear Noah's rasp of a voice. The speech must have taken a toll. "The arm would have killed him, eventually, and he was in agony."

Staring at the streaks of blood, she pieces those sentences together. "You ended his life."

"I ended his misery."

"You won't see any judgement from me," she replies. "It's none of my business what you do with your injured."

He eyes her like he doubts her word, sinking his chin until his mouth almost disappears into his beard. "What did you find?" he asks and if there's a tension to his voice that hints of desperation, it doesn't appear in his face.

"Five victims," she begins, watching him, "all of which showed some form of experimentation. Most of them were dead."

"Most?"

"One attacked us." Her skin twitches at the memory, at the jagged cluster of teeth sprouting from its jaw. "We had to fight—it didn't survive."

A long breath escapes him and his posture shrinks. If there was a chair in the room, he would have sunk into it. "None at all?" He doesn't seem to expect an answer, so she doesn't give one. "Why would they do this? What possible purpose could this serve?"

"You think it's Asmodeus?"

"Who else could it be?" he demands. "Who else would have the power or the twisted desire to perform such acts?"

"Humans are capable of terrible things," Cassius replies, but the remark only draws a snort.

"If humans had the strength to tear off the arm of a Phantom demon, we would have been destroyed long ago."

"It wasn't only demons they were using," Eve says, "they used animal parts, as well."

"Savagery," Noah mutters.

Eve folds one arm against her waist and props up her other, touching her fingertips to her sternum, where her dagger used to sit. Damned monster. She should have brought two. "Why did you bring us up here?" she asks. "If those friends of yours downstairs knew that Asmodeus had built a laboratory, using their fellow demons as subjects, you'd already have the rebellion you're planning."

"We are not ready," he answers, though his attention seems to be on the stained and empty mattress.

"Oh?" Eve keeps her voice casual, hoping to draw him out while his mind is preoccupied. "What are you waiting for? Are there others?"

"So many questions," comes a voice in accented German. "Are you thinking of joining us?"

Eve spins around, barely hearing Cassius' whispered curse. A young woman in a black dress and bonnet stands in the doorway, her hands tucked under an apron. Her features speak of Asian ancestry. "Who are you?" Eve replies.

"*What* are you?" Cassius asks. He's tucked himself close to Eve's side, as if she's going to protect him, and she'd laugh if not for the cold calculation in the stranger's gaze.

"Is she here?" asks Noah, his brows snapping close together, his voice gone deep with urgency.

"Not yet," the woman replies. "But soon."

A Chinese woman served Bellemeure, Hazel had told her, *and she was exceptionally fast...* "If I threw my dagger," Eve says, pressing her hand to the empty space in her bodice, "would you catch it?"

"Before it left your hand," the woman promises.

"Chang Mei," Eve says and curtsies. "A pleasure. I've heard much about you."

CHAPTER EIGHTEEN

S now clouds the windows on the day of the ball, coating the gardens in luxurious white sheets. Not the soft slush that falls in London—real, proper snow, thick enough to vanish in. I watch flurries whirl past as my maid completes the final touches on tonight's ensemble. Although the dress she's chosen has been designed to drag over the floor, on me the hem brushes the carpet, negating the need for a proper bustle. The bodice is low cut at the centre, arrowing up to my shoulders and ending with a loop of silk around each arm, a gesture towards keeping me warm.

"Danke schön," I tell the woman, smoothing the damask over my hips. Under the insipid light of the gas lamps, the crimson fabric looks as dark as blood.

She bobs her head with a small, pleased smile and reaches for my hair. From under the bed comes a scrabbling sound. I cough into my fist, loudly, to cover the noise.

"I will do the rest myself," I tell her, propelling her out of the room. She protests, the German far too complex for me to attempt to understand and I smile blankly, closing the door on her.

Crouching by the bed, I peer underneath. Two glimmers of reflected light peer at me from the darkness. "I told you to be quiet. You can't be seen, remember?"

A mournful whine.

"I won't be gone for long. It's only dinner." I'd taken my breakfast and afternoon meal in my room, and the imp had seemed happy with the cured meat and boiled vegetables, nibbling from my hand. It had scurried under the bed at the maid's knock an hour ago, and now it edges closer to me. "Stay here," I tell it, wondering how much it can understand. "Stay."

Another knock comes and the imp shrinks back. "Come in," I call, recognising Steel's presence.

"I don't think they'll be serving dinner under the bed," he says, as he enters.

"I'm not sure I can get him to stay hidden." I sit back on my heels and my hair, still loose, tumbles over my shoulders.

Steel pauses, his gaze flickering over me, then he comes to my side and drops to one knee. "Oi," he says, in a flat voice that makes the imp flinch away. "Hide and don't come out." Then he stands, holds a hand out for me. "There. Done."

"There's no need to be mean."

"It's been here for less than a day and it's already causing problems."

It's difficult not to look at him and think of last night, how softly he'd said, *Then I'll make you as many as you'd like.* Swallowing, I take his hand and pull myself to his feet. "He's a witness."

One imperious eyebrow rises. "Good luck getting him to testify."

Throwing him an exasperated look, I take advantage of the imp's silence and step outside, shutting the door. No outraged scratching follows, so perhaps it had understood after all.

I tug at the long black gloves I'd found in the wardrobe, making sure they cover the bandage on my arm. "Where is this dinner?"

"One of the receiving rooms. Seems like only Revenants so far, which should be fun." He rolls his eyes, but the way his shoulders twitch tells me his levity is a front.

"I'd be interested to know how many of them spend their time in the woods."

"And I."

Any further conversation is cut short as we descend the stairs into a low bubble of noise. Music floats through the lower rooms; violins and cellos, even a harpsichord. We trace the sound to a vast ballroom with a shining parquet floor filled with men in black suits and women in red or yellow dresses. I count fifteen in total, hardly enough to fill a quarter of the space. Yet the musicians on one side of the room work at their instruments as if the Emperor himself is in attendance.

I'm reminded of the ministers' party that we'd attended in London, the way the politicians had courted favour with pretty compliments and pointed barbs.

We take a step inside. No one visibly reacts, save for a few discreet glances thrown our way. Most pass over me and linger on Steel; assessing, covetous. He falters.

"We should be on our guard," I murmur, turning to start a circuit around the edge of the room, the way two young women at their first ball might. "With so many Revenants here, *she* might take the opportunity to introduce herself." The warning seems to help; he turns his attention to the dark, frosted windows.

"It's warm," he says, and at first I think it's an odd comment, but then I realise he's watching the scarlet and gold reflections in the glass. The Revenant demons emit a heat that makes the room simmer.

My own dress is a streak of flame next to him. "Not particularly subtle, are they?"

He sends me a sideways glance as we walk and says, stilted, "You look...nice."

"Thank you." My fingers twitch self-consciously. "So do you." He wears a sharp black tailcoat with a yellow flower in the pocket and a cream waistcoat and shirt. It makes the line of his shoulders exceptionally broad, emphasises the length of his legs.

"I always look good." He says it with a kind of bleak, self-directed scorn that takes some of the arrogance out of the words.

"Well, that's not true," I reply, seeking to redirect whatever brought on that tone.

"Excuse me?"

"You look terrible in the morning. And at night. Did you know you snore?"

The edge of his mouth curls up. "I drool, too."

"Disgusting," I say, mildly. "You're a hopeless case."

He laughs, drawing more glances from around him. His ease bolsters my confidence and I examine the room more closely. Count von Tier stands among a small cluster of other demons and I spy Katharina with another young woman, not her sister. Servants holding trays of glasses line the wall in strategic positions, blank-faced. None of the Revenants appear to be drinking.

"Hanna isn't here," I say. It was Hanna who'd cured Steel, Hanna who'd developed the antidote to Bellemeure's drug. Hanna who understood the science of it.

"Perhaps she's enjoying a stroll in the woods," Steel replies.

My attention goes back to the servants. If this has been going on for as long as those bodies would suggest, then they must know about it, too. Must fear it.

"Good evening, my prince." Katharina halts our slow progress around the ballroom. She wears a floor length gown the colour of afternoon sunlight and white silk gloves that stretch to her elbow. "Allow me to introduce you to someone."

As Steel is muttering, "Prince?" under his breath, she loops her arm into his and steers him off my circular path and into the centre of the room. I consider following, but with the way the room's attention clings to Steel, I'll be less noticeable on my own. I fold my hands together and keep walking.

German dominates the conversation, but as I walk a strain of French catches my ear. I slow, making a pretence of watching the snow fall in the gardens outside, though I can barely see it beyond the reflection.

"I thought Prince Rudolf was going to be in attendance." The speaker is an older woman with black Revenant eyes and a rust-coloured gown.

"He declined the invitation," her partner replies, a man in top hat and tails. The links at his cuff are dull, plain metal, and the sleeves of his coat don't quite reach his wrists. "Rumour has it he's off with that Vetsera woman."

"The Turf Angel? I thought that was merely hearsay."

"The Count had better hurry up and nail him to one of his daughters, or the Habsburgs will throw us out."

"Surely not!"

"The Emperor's growing older," the man replies. "My spies tell me he wants to make Schönbrunn his permanent residence."

"Then what is causing von Tier's delay?"

"Lady Katharina has her eyes on a far more valuable prize."

I trace their gazes in the reflection of the window. Katharina is talking to a man with grey hair and an intimidating moustache, Steel on one side and Luka on the other.

"House Lucifer?" The woman makes a contemplative noise. "Neither are true sons, though."

"The heirs will not take a wife with no power," the man replies. "That's what you get, for breeding outside the House. It'll be a miracle if either girl is fertile."

"But if these males are not true sons, the whole game may be pointless. The Count should test them with a quickening first, make sure they'll provide good stock."

Anger boils low in my stomach. Steel has lost everything; everyone he considered family is dead. He doesn't deserve to become a pawn in the political manoeuvring of the wealthy, demon or not.

Sickened, not wanting to hear more, I turn away. The heat in the room has me breathing shallowly and my steps are unsteady. A door leads off the main ballroom into a small resting room and I head for it. That was why the Count was so keen to bring Steel into his House; a groom for one of his daughters.

No, not a groom; that would imply a measure of respect. The Count wants a stud, a stallion to bring power back into his line.

He's not going to let us leave. The thought silences every other ripple in my mind, then I amend it: he's not going to let *Steel* leave.

"Hiding?"

I turn at the sound of Luka's voice. The demon enters the room without so much as a by-your-leave and goes straight to a window. They're smaller here than the ones in the ballroom, and he pushes one open with ease. The memory of our recent dinner conversation rises and I do my best to smother a frown. I can't afford to alienate this demon.

Yet I can't quite resist the urge to say, "You do know it's snowing outside."

"A welcome relief from all that hot air."

A biting breeze sweeps in through the open window, clearing the haze that had been clinging to my skin. Annoyed at the need, I step a little closer, into the path of the wind. Luka ignores me, lighting a thin cigarette, and I examine his appearance: his clothes are all black, even the shirt and gloves, and his short hair is slicked back.

"Are you going to a funeral?" I ask.

"I am already at a funeral." Luka's voice is so dry and condescending that I'm surprised his expression doesn't flicker as he says it.

"Who died?"

"Good taste."

I allow myself a breath of a laugh. "Then you're not a fan of parties? That's something you and Steel have in common."

"One of very few things."

I take in the snow-laden fields outside. A figure crosses in the distance, the line of a rifle jutting up from his back. A guard. So, the Count is not so casual about Bellemeure's presence as he appears.

"How long do you intend to stay here?" I ask.

"That depends."

"On Bellemeure?"

"On Bellemeure." The breeze drops as he exhales and a thin curl of smoke drifts into the night sky. Stars shimmer at us through a slit in the clouds.

"Are we safe, tonight?" I ask, glancing sideways at him, looking for a shadow or a twitch in his expression that might give me a clue. Turned away from me, I can only see the line of his nose and the unnatural gleam of one golden eye.

"*I* have no concerns," he says, with delicate emphasis on the first word. That's easy enough to comprehend.

"I'm not concerned for myself, surrounded by so many demons," I say. "I'm not her target, after all." There, a flicker in his countenance.

"You should not be so cavalier. Anyone under this roof is a target."

"Including you?" He doesn't reply and I change tack. "Your lessons will help, I imagine. Steel could talk of little else, afterwards. And Katharina seems to be very...dedicated to your needs."

A short exhale that could have been a snort if it had more breath behind it.

"I am surprised that Prince Rudolf did not attend," I continue, as casual as he is. "Is Katharina disappointed?"

"I doubt it," Luka says, flicking ash onto the white snow. "It's the Count who wants a throne. His daughters only care about their power. I should never have—" He stops and looks down at me, thumbing the cigarette. "So, you're not entirely useless, I see," he muses.

"In England we have a saying," I reply, coolly. "Give a man enough rope and he will hang himself."

"I am not a man."

"But that's your secret. You are just as much a man as any of the servants in there." I tip my head towards the light and music behind us.

"Careful," he says, his mouth gone hard. "My brother might be wrapped around your finger, but I am not so easily manipulated."

"I suppose we'll see."

"Now that he and I are family," he says, as I'm turning to leave, "that makes his connections my own. How is your friend getting along? Eve, was it?"

I turn back unwillingly.

"Perhaps I should invite her to return to the palace as a guest." His mouth is still hard, his eyes cold. "Revenants have such powerful urges."

I remember von Tier's fighting pit, the burnt and broken body of La Sorelli. "You wouldn't."

"Do not presume to know what I would or would not do," he says, evenly. "I am House Lucifer. Asmodeus may own this city, but I own *them*."

"You do not own Steel," I reply and he exhales more smoke, dragon-like.

"I suppose we'll see."

CHAPTER NINETEEN

I flee from Luka, not caring how weak it makes me look. His eerie golden gaze seems to see straight through my carefully assembled defences and I have none left to use against him.

At the door, I almost collide with the Count. The demon raises his glass at me in greeting. "Good evening, Fräulein."

How long has he been standing there? "Good evening, my lord. Are you enjoying the ball?"

"Oh, very much. I am finding it quite enlightening." He takes a sip, holding my gaze. He wears a crimson shirt under his tailcoat and gloves the same colour. "And you, miss Locke?" he asks and although he doesn't smile I can hear the amusement in his tone.

A twist of unease pulls at my stomach. With the Count in the way, I can't see Steel. "As you say; enlightening." He's nearby, the connection tells me, still in the room.

"Not as eventful as I had hoped, unfortunately."

I glance at him. "You were hoping for something else?"

"Well, I did wonder if your demon-hunting witch might appear tonight. I am keen to meet our enemy face to face." He taps at his flute's stem with one gloved finger. "Then again, perhaps

I have already met my enemy. What is that saying—give a man enough rope...? How much rope does one need, I wonder, to make a noose?"

My breath freezes in my lungs. "Perhaps you also have the saying, here," I reply, with effort, "the enemy of my enemy is my friend?"

"A Sanskrit proverb, if I am not mistaken. We have something similar: Wenn zwei sich streiten, freut sich der Dritte. We should not argue amongst ourselves. I would certainly prefer not to," he says, with a magnanimous tilt of his glass. "Not if it can be avoided."

"And if it can't?"

"Then it will prove an unfortunate waste. I do so despise waste." He bows low and says, "Good night, Fräulein." Faced with such a clear dismissal, there's nothing else I can do but walk away.

The musicians have struck up a slow waltz and some of the demons are circling the ballroom in pairs. Steel stands by the wall, craning his chin to scan the room, looking for something. Katharina talks at him, gesturing towards the dancing couples.

As if my attention had drawn his notice, Steel's gaze finds mine. He shifts as if he's about to head in my direction but I hold up my hand, subtly gesturing at him to wait as I make my way to him.

"—so long for a dance," Katharina is saying when I reach them. She touches Steel's elbow. "Will you not oblige me, Herr Steel?"

"I am not fond of dancing."

"Lady Katharina," I interject. A more direct approach may have better results. "I had hoped to greet your sister this evening, but I do not see her. Is she well?"

The woman drops her hand from Steel's arm. "Oh, she does not enjoy these kinds of gatherings. She would much rather attend a seminar than take a turn with one of us. Even if she did come, all she would do is sit with her nose in a book."

"Does she study?"

"No, Papa would never allow such a thing." Katharina glances over to where the Count stands, now speaking to the French couple I'd overheard earlier. "But there have been a few open seminars that she managed to sneak into—do not ask me how." She tilts her head towards the musicians as the tune changes. "Ah, this is Mozart. I love Mozart. He lived in Vienna for a time, you know."

Steel prompts her. "I can't imagine a Revenant demon would have much interest in the sciences."

Katharina sighs, waves her hand dismissively. "There was a human professor she saw, years ago, who fired an obsession in her. What was his name? Franzen—Franken-something. She came back from his lecture convinced that she could control death itself."

"Fascinating," I say, through a dry mouth.

"You should be grateful." She smiles at Steel. "Without her expertise, we would not have been able to cure you of Belle-meure's poison."

"Or protect yourselves from it," answers Steel, expressionless.

Her smile wanes. "Well, yes, I suppose, if the woman is even in Austria. I expect she has long since given up on whatever strange ambitions she had."

A young man who looks fresh out of the schoolroom wanders past us. I snag his arm. "Lady Katharina was just saying how much she would like to dance," I tell him, pulling him gently to her. "Would you oblige her?"

He looks blank, but when I gesture to the dancers he seems to comprehend my request and bows to Katharina. Her eyes go tight at the corners. "Oh, I—"

"Do not curb your enjoyment on my account," Steel adds, ushering her forward. "I am sure we will find time to speak later."

"Yes, of course." She waggles a finger at him as the young man escorts her away. "Do not go far."

When she's absorbed in the dance alongside the other couples, Steel turns to me. "That seems like a pretty damning account," he says, under his breath.

"I agree." I glance once more at the assembled demons, a shiver going through me whenever I catch their black-as-pitch eyes. "Perhaps we should go and find some proof."

Steel huffs a breath. "Is that a suggestion or are you going regardless of what I say?"

"If it's the latter?"

"Then I suppose we should go and find some proof," he says, exhaling as though I'm dragging him away from a fairground.

"I could go alone."

"Absolutely not," he answers, almost before I finish speaking, and his gaze drops to my arm, to the bandage hidden under my borrowed gloves.

A curl of warmth unfurls pleasantly in my stomach, which is such a ridiculous reaction to the possibility of being wounded that I ignore it. "Shall we, then?"

He accompanies me to the door, walking slowly so as not to draw too much attention. But when we reach it, a servant steps into our path. I halt, speechless. Are they truly going to keep us prisoner?

"She is not feeling well," Steel says and my chest rumbles with the low vibration of his voice, a growl poorly hidden among the words. "I will return once I have accompanied her to her room."

The servant bows shallowly and says, in heavily accented English, "We will inform the Count." A wrist motion sends a second servant stalking across the room towards the man. "Good evening, Fräulein," he adds, stepping out of the way.

Steel's hand had gone to my back the moment we were confronted, and now it flexes, urging me forward. We step through the door into the corridor and I wait for his fingers to loosen their grip on the back of my bodice before I say, "You didn't seem surprised."

He grimaces. "It's not the first time they've kept track of my whereabouts."

"What?"

"They don't like me going anywhere alone."

"Why didn't you tell me?"

He looks affronted. "I can take care of myself." I put enough heat into my glare to boil water and he adds, ducking his head,

"That's different. I'm descended from two archdemons. You have a revolver."

Annoyingly, I can find no grounds to argue with him. "I still wish you'd told me."

"I didn't think there was any malice in it."

"Not yet, perhaps, but that might change when we decide to leave."

He has no rejoinder to that and we proceed in silence. The corridors of this part of the palace are wood panelled and painted white, the floors made of brown and cream tiles, placed to form a pattern like a rug. Sprigs of holly and mistletoe have been spread about the palace by servants, tucked into vases and draped over antlers.

"We need to find out where her rooms are."

"That, I already know." Steel sends me a sideways glance, his mouth curled up at one corner in a smirk. Then he blinks and his hand falls from my back. He clears his throat, staring forward. "Luka wasn't happy about being placed in the east wing," he goes on. "He complained—at length—about being woken up by the dawn sunlight."

I refrain from making the obvious comparison. Steel probably isn't ready to acknowledge the demon as his family. Nor am I, for that matter.

"He asked the Count for a room in the west wing, where the Empress stays, but von Tier said Katharina and Hanna have the apartments there."

To have the kind of power that grants you the rooms of an Empress...and what have they done with it? Throw balls while the people around them suffer. "And you know the way, I assume?"

"You assume correctly."

We move quietly through the palace and our brief moment of levity fades away. The opulence of the walls and the intricacy of the portraits grows as we reach the first floor of the west wing. A strong wind whistles through a loose windowpane, making an eerie groaning sound. We pass a glass door that opens onto a terrace and enter a dark corridor carpeted in red. I take my cue from Steel, whose brows are tightly knitted, eyes unfocused. Listening.

No one emerges to stop us or chases us down, and we reach a set of double doors. There he pauses, not going quite so far as to press his ear to the wood, but standing sideways and tilting his head towards it.

"I hear nothing," he murmurs. "Not even breathing." He rests his hand on the ornate gold handle and, at his quick glance, I nod. He cracks the door open, waits, then edges it open a fraction more, just enough of a gap for him to put an eye to.

I wait, trying not to hold my own breath, glancing over my shoulder at the empty corridor behind us.

"It seems empty." He opens the door, slow enough to stop it if it creaks. But the hinges are well-oiled.

My first impression as I step into the room is of light and greenery, and I have to blink a few times before I realise that we are not outside. The windows are large and airy, built to capture as much light as possible. Now they're dark and the light comes instead from a handful of pretty wall sconces. Leaves froth from shelves on the wall and dangle from planters, spiny and round and serrated, some with flowers, some without. They fill the air with a strong, sweet smell, although something about it turns my stomach. The room itself is built with a rounded mezzanine balcony that oversees a second room below.

Steel creeps forward to the balustrade that splits this level from the one beneath it and peeks over. "Empty," he confirms.

Careful not to touch anything, I move further into the room. Books are interspersed among the plants, all with worn covers, if they have covers at all. I pull out a few until I find one in English; a manual on domestic medical recipes. The plant beside it has thin, jagged leaves. Further along, the shelves hold a collection of jars and vials. Creams and oils, largely, but some hold things inside, too misshapen to be recognisable. The skin along the back of my neck prickles, sending a discomforting tingle over my scalp.

"This must be how she created the antidote."

Steel is already descending the circular stairs to the other room. I hurry to follow him. Verdant ivy winds over the banister, along with a hairy brown vine without leaves. I am careful to graze neither, hugging my torso as I descend. The light in the lower room comes from a large electric bulb connected to a wooden base. The filaments inside it glow so brightly I have to blink away their after image.

"There's something on the floor," Steel says, kneeling.

"Oh?" I peek over his shoulder. Stones lie in chevron shapes of white and brown. There's another pattern on top, a complicated series of lines and glyphs. My hands itch for my journal, or pen and paper. I've seen something like it before, but where—?

"A ritual," I say, just as Steel says, "A spell."

"So, she's using magic as well as science." I scratch along one of the glyphs and bring up a line of dried blood under my fingernail. Grimacing, I scrape it out, rub my hands on my skirt. The plants obscure any scent that might have lingered. "Neither Hanna or Katharina have magic, though." I recall the conversation I'd overheard earlier and relay it to Steel.

"The Count said they were blooded," he agrees. "I suppose their mother was human."

"I wonder what happened to her."

"I'd rather not know." Steel stands, examining the room. "Warlocks can study to perform spells like this, but they're usually human, and the process takes decades."

"Who told you that?"

"...Luka."

"Ah."

"But why science? How would science help them with a spell like this?"

The surgical procedures performed on the demons in the woods don't seem to have much connection with this ritual. Those had been about combining body parts of different demons, seeing if the whole would survive.

Still, just because I can't see the connection yet does not mean it isn't there.

I pick absently at a stray cuticle. The daughter of a powerful group of demons with no ability to cast magic, no ability to use fire, reduced to nothing more than chattel to be sold. There is no future in this palace for those without power.

"We should go," Steel says, disrupting my thought process. "Before she comes back."

I nod and we move back up the stairs and slip through the corridors. The lack of guards or even servants astounds me. For a moment, I almost *want* Bellemeure to attack the place, if only to punish them for their arrogance and conceit.

We keep quiet until we reach my room and Steel follows me inside, closing the door behind us. I go to my knees beside the bed. The imp peeks out from underneath and, seeing me, crawls out to snuffle at my legs. "We should talk to someone, see if we can find out what the magic was being used for."

"Who?" The bleakness in his voice makes me look up. "Eve said the agency are in their pocket and they even call the Emperor a friend. Who's going to stop them?"

My mouth purses. Everything in me recoils at the thought of my response, but I force myself to give it. "Luka."

The wrinkle that forms at the bridge of Steel's nose tells me what he thinks of that.

"Our other options are...limited." Our other option, my brain takes this chance to tell me, is out there somewhere preparing an army to attack.

Sighing, he rubs his nose, smoothing out the wrinkle. "All right, I don't see what else we could do. Tomorrow, we'll tell him."

I scratch the imp behind its ears and it flops onto its side like a cat. Steel watches it for a moment, and then his gaze lifts to mine. My breath catches, my mind immediately bringing up the ghost sensation of when he touched my hair.

He ducks his head, breaking the connection, and says, "Good night, Hazel."

"Good night, Steel."

When I'm alone, I focus on ruffling the fur on the imp's belly.
Not on the way my name had sounded in his voice.

AGENT E. WILSON

"I would return the compliment," says Chang Mei, "but I have heard nothing of you." With her large, liquid eyes and narrow pointed chin, Eve's first impression is vulnerability, but the way the woman holds herself speaks of someone who'd be at home with a blade in her hand. Her own itches with the urge to test that theory.

Eve bows shallowly, not lowering her gaze. "Agent Eve Wilson. Cassius," she adds, introducing him with a tilt of her head. "I see you and Noah already know each other."

The Reaper demon hovers between them, his hands half-raised as if he had gone to intervene and then thought better of it.

"Agent?" Chang says. "You're not one of theirs, though. British, I'd say, by your accent." The last sentence is in English, forcing Eve to take a breath as her mind catches up.

"You're proficient with languages."

"Not by choice."

That implies a history that in a different life Eve might have shared, and she steers the conversation away. "You work for Bellemeure."

Chang makes a *tch* sound, glancing away, her lip curling. Her teeth are small, the canines duller than other demons. Her strength must be in her speed. "You are allied with the Leviathan."

"You know of him?" This comes from Cassius, apparently growing confident enough to join the conversation.

"I know he still lives when he should not."

"Because you let him go," Eve says, "didn't you?"

Chang's not bad at hiding her emotions, but she's not as practised as Hazel, and Eve sees the twitch in her fingers and the tightening around her mouth that the words provoke. "A mistake," she replies. "I should have killed him then, and anyone allied with him. A mistake I will correct now."

"Wait," Eve says, throwing up one hand in a pathetic defence, and at her side Noah makes a wordless protest, drawing Chang's attention.

He eyes Eve's hand and the way Chang has shifted onto the balls of her feet, picking up the context of the situation even if he doesn't understand English. "They are not our enemies," the Reaper says, in German. "They've seen the palace. She was right—Asmodeus is experimenting on our people."

There's a weighty pause as the woman internalises that information.

Eve needs to get to the bottom of this *she*. "We found bodies in the forest," she continues, in German so Noah can follow her. "Someone is performing surgery on demons, amputating their limbs and grafting new ones in their place." It's barely noticeable, but Chang winces. "One of them attacked us."

"Survivors?" she asks, quickly.

"Only one. He didn't *seem* to understand us. I don't know if he was drugged, or driven mad by pain. We were forced to kill him to escape."

"When we tell the others," says Noah, his amber eyes glinting with a dangerous fire, "they will act. They will not let this stand."

"Are you ready for that?" asks Eve. "A revolution?"

"Some revolution," adds Cassius, "if it's only one family being targeted."

She shoots him a warning look. What is he doing?

"It would be more effective," he continues, ignoring her, keeping his blue-eyed gaze on Chang, "to bring down the structures that would stop you."

There's no way that Eve's going to let him attack an agency. He's close enough that she can touch his arm with only a twist of her hand, so she pinches him. He twitches and flashes a canine at her.

Chang focuses on him. "You speak of the Gendarmerie."

"Asmodeus own them." Cassius grabs Eve's hand when she goes to pinch him again and squeezes. Battling her better instincts, she stays quiet. "They'll fight on the Count's command. And what will you do if the whole of Vienna is turned against your little outfit?" He jerks his head at Noah. He'd spoken in English, so the Reaper demon stares back blankly.

"You're suggesting that we destroy one of the city's largest police forces in order to *avoid* attention?" Chang Mei drawls. For some reason, the sarcastic tone in her voice fills Eve with the urge to say, *Ignore him, he's always like this.*

"I'm suggesting that you think strategically," the Phantom says. "We could help you." Another squeeze. Eve squeezes back, digging her nails into the back of his hand.

"Oh?" Chang looks amused.

"But we'd need to meet your mistress," Cassius finishes and Eve's so shocked she can't even return the triumphant look he shoots her.

The woman regards them searchingly, looking for the trap in his words.

"Hazel can help you get into the palace," Eve adds, letting her reluctance show in her voice. "She'll know the guards, their movements. She can let you in. Take them by surprise."

"And if some of your people distract the agency, it will leave the rest free to attack the palace," Cassius adds.

Eve repeats a succinct version of the idea in German for Noah, and the Reaper takes a half step forward. "It might work." He looks at Chang. "If we can get in while they don't suspect us, we can stop them. Pay them back for what they've done to us."

Eve hesitates, then says, "We destroyed one of their laboratories, but there might be others. This way, we can find out." It feels manipulative, like she's using defenceless victims as a tool for her own ends, and it makes her skin feel too tight for her body.

But it sways Chang. "Bellemeure will decide if you are worth keeping alive," she says. "Have your agent friend meet us at—"

"Kaffeehaus Herzog," Eve interjects. "Hazel knows it. We can meet you there."

"Very well. Midday tomorrow. *Without* her demon." Her gaze goes to Cassius, as if she wants to say the same for him, but her eyes fall to their still-clasped hands and all she says is, "If you betray us, your death will be slow and painful."

"Noted," mutters Cassius as she leaves.

Eve shakes free of his grip, scowling. She was only supposed to stay for a week. Now, she's involved with some kind of serial murderer and a revolutionary plot. She has to put an end to this, and quickly. Monaghan isn't going to wait forever.

AGENT J. HORNER

The skeleton of the district's gasometer looms over Whiston Street, its cast-iron girders black against the clouded sky. Jacob finds himself glancing over his shoulder at it, as though the second he removes his gaze it'll start crawling over the rooftops toward him.

He shifts, touches the dagger now safe against his ribs. "We're a little far from the agency."

"That is the point," Khurana replies. She knocks on the door of the tenement building in front of them. To the side a curtain swishes, someone there and gone before Jacob can get a good look. Then the door cracks open.

"It is not safe to be here," says Maia from the doorway, her hair tucked behind her scarf, her apron neat and clean.

"Maia," he blurts out, just as Khurana steers him inside with a hard prod of her cane. "Where have you been? Didn't you go back to India?"

"Come inside, child, before you wake up the whole street." It's said with Maia's usual fond exasperation and Jacob swallows back the rest of his questions.

It's dark in the apartment that Maia leads them to. She busies herself lighting some candles, going to the window and tweaking the curtains so they hide the light. His demon goes at once to the fireplace, raking out the ashes. Burning with curiosity, Jacob hands him two of the logs beside it and waits as he starts a small but healthy fire.

"Has there been any trouble?" Khurana asks and the cook replies, "Nothing unusual, no. I have seen no demons."

"You would not see them—"

"Peace. I stay inside; the girl on the corner fetches for me." Maia sits in one of the spindly wooden chairs by the fire, pulling a fringed shawl around her shoulders. Her gaze hasn't dulled at all and she levels it at Jacob first, then Khurana. "You told me you would not return for some days. What has happened?"

"Monaghan attempted to murder us."

Jacob jerks and makes a wordless sound of protest. "We don't know that for certain," he says, when they look at him. "All we have are the words of two men who've barely been here a month. They could have been acting independently and blaming the professor for it."

"The agents and their demons," the Hound agent replies. "Or did you forget their existence?"

"He does not know," says Maia, making him blink.

"Know what?"

"Did you truly believe that Locke committed those murders?" Khurana asks, instead of letting her answer.

"I—Of course not." Jacob goes to cross his arms, realises how closed off that will make him look, and drops them. "I didn't know what to think."

Khurana mutters something that sounds like, "All men are fools," and then adds, louder, "It was the professor. He was behind the Ripper case. He was behind Agent Turner's murder. Locke fled him and he sent Eve to bring her back."

He searches for humour in her face, a sign that he has missed the punchline of this joke. "Are you saying Professor Monaghan murdered all those women?"

"His demon performed the actual murders." Isis' voice is so quiet he can barely hear her over the crackle of the fire.

"Tiberius?"

"You said you would choose whatever path would keep us safe," Khurana reminds him.

The fire has eaten away the worst of the cold, but he burrows into his coat regardless, hiding in the collar. "Yes, but—When you said turn away from the Agency, I thought you were speaking metaphorically. I didn't think—I didn't think you meant *treason*."

The woman plants her cane on the floor with a click. "You have spent the last three years trailing at Rayne's heels," she says. "You cannot remain in his shadow for the rest of your life."

"That's not—" He huffs, looking to Max for support, but the demon has stayed on his knees by the hearth and merely watches him. "Dominic saved me," he ends up saying, though he didn't intend to. It was Dominic who'd pulled him from the fight with his fellow ostlers—not a fight; that implies it was an even match. They'd corralled him at the back of the stables and had been a hair's breadth from beating the life out of him. All for a kiss with some boy he barely remembered. "I owe him a debt."

"Owed," Khurana corrects. "Or do you intend to follow him into the grave?"

"Do not needle him, Khurana," interrupts Maia. "You were as aimless as Jacob once. It was only your demon who taught you to look beyond the end of your sword."

Isis slides up to Khurana's side and slips her hand into the other woman's. "Tell him," the demon says. "Tell him what Lavender gave us." The agent sighs, but she doesn't let go of Isis' hand.

"What?" Jacob prompts, when the silence makes him itch.

"There is a way to separate agent from demon," Isis begins, when Khurana still does not speak. "The ritual can be amended to break the chain that binds you to each other."

The first thing Jacob feels is a searing lance of fear. To have no demon, to be *alone*— "Wh-what do you mean?" he stutters.

"It undoes the part of the ritual that acts as a chain," Isis continues. "Lavender knew the magic that created it, understood it. She gave us a way to change it. We are no longer confined to a twenty foot distance."

"Who else knows about this?" The professor couldn't know, surely. "Does Hazel know? Eve?"

"Agent Locke and her demon made the change before they fled," Isis confirmed. "Eve..." She trails off, glances at Khurana.

"We did not get the chance to confide in Eve before Monaghan sent her away." The woman says it with a heavy voice.

"We should have been told about this," Jacob says. "We *all* should have been told."

"Now you have."

He shakes his head, pulling the collar up so its sits against his cheeks. The walls of the apartment seem to press in on him, stealing the air away. "This is foolish," he murmurs. "First you speak of treason, now you advocate disobeying the core tenets of the Agency. Come on, Max. We're leaving." He needs to get out. He needs to breathe in the icy smog of his city and figure out what it all means, what he's supposed to do. He makes it to the door before he realises Max isn't following. "Max?"

The Reaper demon gets to his feet. "I cannot," he says.

The words do not at first register, as though he'd spoken in Spanish and Jacob could not translate them. "What do you mean? What can't you do?"

"I cannot go with you."

"Why not? We can just leave. Max, let's go, please. Nothing has to change."

The demon wraps his long arms around himself, stares at the floor. "He will send us out again," he whispers. "He will send us out to kill again. Are you not tired of it?"

"I don't know what you mean." He makes the words short and level, clings to them to stay steady. The others are silent and he wishes they would speak, would slice through this moment and end it.

"You will have to use this ritual to separate us," Max continues, his voice calm as though he doesn't know what he's doing to Jacob, doesn't know the depth of the hole he's working open inside him, "because I cannot follow any longer. I cannot be bound to you and be ordered to kill." The demon looks up, looks at him. The corner of his lip is raw and bleeding where he's been gnawing at it.

Abruptly Jacob sees them as if from outside the window, caught in a moment of stillness. The demon, all his strength sapped, tearing at his own flesh in his anguish. Himself, desperate to cleave to this last bastion, ordering Max to obey him regardless of what it will cost them. He had once sworn to protect his demon, his partner. What is his vow to the Agency compared to his oath to Max?

"I'm so sorry," he breathes in a rush of self-loathing. Hurt lingers underneath, the hurt that Max could so easily turn away from him. He hates himself even more.

"You'll stay, then?" Max asks, with an edge of cautious hope that undoes him; it hadn't been easy for Max. It hadn't be easy at all.

"Yes." His body relaxes as he says it, as if it had known the truth before he had, and in that moment his duty becomes clear; he must protect Max. "I'll stay. I'm with you."

"Well," says Khurana, brusque and impersonal, granting him a moment to rally, "now that the matter of your allegiance is settled, we should plan our attack."

"Attack?" he and Maia repeat at the same time.

"You did not think we would end this without blood?" The woman taps her cane decisively. "First, we dispose of the demon. Then Monaghan. You will need to take his place, Horner—Pemberton will never accept me in that role—then we get to work on unravelling his policies."

"Wait, wait." This is going too fast. And what does she mean, he'll need to take Monaghan's place?

"We will not kill Tiberius." The Reaper's jaw juts out in the way it does when Jacob has to coax him into trying whatever unusual dish Maia has set before them.

Khurana's brows furrow. She seems genuinely perplexed at Max's refusal. "Tiberius is a pawn of the professor and a murderer himself. He contravened those same tenets of the Agency that your partner is desperate to uphold. It is your duty to dispatch him."

"It is my duty to deliver justice," Max replies. "Tiberius cannot be doing this willingly. He is only acting on the professor's orders. A soldier is not at fault for obeying the orders of his commander."

"That is a lie the commander tells so the soldiers will do his bidding. Tiberius made his choice."

"What would you have him do instead? Die?"

"Yes," she snaps. "Yes, I would have him die. I would have him throw himself on his own sword rather than murder six women for the ambition of one man."

"Tiberius doesn't have a sword," Jacob murmurs.

Khurana spits out a Punjabi curse and strides to the curtained window, turning her back on them.

After a heartbeat's pause, Maia asks in her gentle way, "What would you have us do, Max?"

The demon hitches his arms higher around his waist. His gaze flits over to Jacob, who tries to give him an encouraging smile. "Tiberius will have evidence. We can use it to have the professor arrested."

Silence reigns as the room considers it.

"Pemberton would have to listen if we threatened to include the papers," Jacob says. "If the public knew that a government official was suspected of murder and *The Times* printed the proof, he'd be finished." As would the Agency, but now doesn't seem the time to point this out.

"What makes you think Tiberius would be willing to help us?" asks Khurana, which is better than the flat denial he'd expected.

"I can persuade him." Max drops his arms, stands straighter. "I *will* persuade him."

Khurana looks at the demon for a long, tense moment. "Very well," she says, eventually. "But if he refuses, then he will die."

CHAPTER TWENTY

I wake at a knock on the door, blinking blearily at the window. I'd forgotten to shut the curtains and the view is a blur of white and grey. It's snowing again. Or still. The knock comes a second time, and a woman calls through the door, "Bist du wach, Fräulein?"

Curled into the crook of my arm, the imp makes a sleepy noise. I cover it with a sheet and scramble out of bed. Opening the door a crack, I find the maid who'd dressed me yesterday holding a tray of covered plates.

"Danke schön," I murmur, not having to feign sleepiness. The events of the past few days must have drained me; I haven't slept that deeply in months. "Danke, Fräulein."

"Frau Bluemel," she corrects, giving me the sympathetic look Maia used to give me when I'd stayed up too late poring over old newspapers and had trouble seeing straight the following day.

"Frau Bluemel." I massacre the pronunciation, but she dimples at me for the attempt. I take the tray from her and try to shut the door in her face as politely as possible.

"Ah, Fräulein, dieser Brief ist für dich gekommen." She hands me a folded piece of paper and then curtsies as I say thank you a third time, finally able to retreat.

I place the tray on the desk, lifting the covers to reveal a fried egg served on diced potatoes with onion and, on another, two triangles of toasted bread dusted with sugar. At the scent of food, the imp scuttles out of bed and claws its way down the covers to sit at my feet, pathetic as a puppy. I feed it small pieces of potato as I open the paper. It's not a letter, just a few lines written in a bold hand—Eve's hand. She's used a simple Caesar's code that I crack in a moment.

Our first day in Vienna, we stopped here. You did not like the napkins. B. No S.

Underneath the words, she's drawn three small suns in a vague triangle shape. The sun at its zenith is underlined. Midday, then, at Kaffeehaus Herzog. And the B... She can't mean Bellemeure? Has she found something?

I tap the folded edge of the paper against the table. It wasn't sealed, so Eve either wasn't worried that someone else would understand her code, or under too much of a time pressure to care. Or it was sealed, and someone *un*sealed it.

I reread the instruction. *No S.* No Steel. That makes something in my stomach twist into a complicated knot. Eve wouldn't separate us to take me back to London, she's not that callous. Whatever she's found out must have something to do with Steel's family and she doesn't want him to know.

I suppose it's a good thing that I didn't make that promise. Still, the thought of using a loophole so soon after we'd spoken makes me despise myself a little. Some partner I am.

A tiny flash of pain brings me back to myself. The imp had nipped me. It makes an odd sound, something between a growl and a mewl. I cut off a slice of egg for it.

"If she doesn't want Steel there, she certainly won't want you." But if I leave it here again and some maid stumbles across it… "I'll have to risk her anger," I tell it, with a rueful smile.

My stomach is turning too wildly to eat, so I put the rest on the floor for the imp and dress in a violet taffeta that buttons all the way to my chin. I spill the box of spare cartridges onto the bed and reload my revolver, pushing the imp away when it tries to investigate. My cloak should be big enough to hide both the gun and the imp, if I'm careful. First, I need to fulfil the promise that I did make.

Steel answers my knock with a bleary *Enter*. His room is still dark, the curtains pulled shut. A tray with covered dishes lies untouched on the table. I go to the window and pull back the curtains, casting a ray of grey-toned light over the bed.

A grumbled protest drifts from the sheets. With apparent effort, Steel levers himself onto his elbows, sleep blurring his sharp edges. His hair is mussed, the blankets bunched around his waist. A loose cotton shirt preserves his modesty. "Hazel?" he asks hoarsely, rubbing one eye with the heel of his hand in a way that makes my heart clench sweetly. His other, half-open eye reflects the dim light like a silver mirror. "What—what time is it?"

"Eight in the morning, I think."

"Are you—" He moves to get up, then his hand drops to the blanket and he stops. I carefully do not consider why. "Uh. You don't look hurt. Is there a—a reason why you're in my room?"

"I need to talk to you."

"At eight in the morning?" he mutters, leaning on one hand and taking in my cloak. "Are we going somewhere?"

I lift the note. "Eve sent me a message. She wants to meet me at that coffeehouse we went to a few days ago."

"Why?"

"I think she's found out something about Bellemeure."

He stiffens, grasping the blanket as if he is going to get up, regardless of whatever clothes he's lacking underneath. "What? How?"

"I'm not sure yet, but it might have something to do with those copper class demons she's been talking to. The ones that asked her to look into the experiments." My arm twitches at the memory. The pain of my wound has dulled, but it still aches. "She wants me to go alone."

"No," he says, instantly. "Absolutely not. I'm coming too."

"Bellemeure might not show herself if you're there."

"I don't care. Besides, you promised—"

"I promised I wouldn't do anything without telling you," I reply, hating the way his mouth tightens at the words. "I'm telling you now."

"You think I'm going to let you go anywhere near her alone?"

"*Let* me?"

"You know what I mean. She's dangerous, and she's already tried to kill you once."

"I know the risks."

"Don't be a fool. Tell me honestly; do you think you can stop her in a fight? Do you?" he demands, when I hesitate.

"No, but—"

"Exactly. I'm your partner, remember. We take the same risks."

"Don't throw that in my face."

"They were your words."

I shake my head. Even more than squirrelling out of the half-promise I'd almost made, I hate the way he's right. Belle-meure *is* dangerous, and even with Cassius and Eve, I'm not sure I could do much if she chose to attack.

"I'm not going to keep arguing," Steel says. "I'm coming with you." And he flings back the covers.

I whirl to put my back to him before I can see anything I shouldn't and slap my hand over my eyes. "*Steel*!"

"What?" He sounds grimly amused. "We've been living together for the last three weeks, you'd see something sooner or later."

"I would not! And don't say *living* together, we haven't been *living* together!"

He chuckles. "You're very easy to scandalise."

"I'm not scandalised!" The higher pitch in my voice calls me a liar. A wardrobe door creaks open behind me and clothing rustles. "This is underhanded and conniving," I tell him.

"I must have been spending too much time with Cassius."

My sense of hearing seems to heighten, and I become aware of every sound, even down to our breathing. I find myself swallowing to wet a dry throat, a heaviness in my chest that seems to turn the air to liquid. The imp, with apparently no sense of modesty or decorum, clambers up the inside of my cloak and perches on my shoulder, chirruping impatiently.

"Wait," says Steel. "You weren't going to take me but you were going to take *that*?"

"It might have been in danger if I'd left it here."

"So would I!"

"You're a little better equipped to handle yourself. Besides," I add, "I'm hoping Eve might take it to these revolutionaries. They'll take care of it better than I can."

"Hmph."

The rustling goes on for a moment longer, then silence. Then a hand lands on my shoulder. I startle despite myself.

"No need to jump out of your skin." I lift my hand from my eyes to see an odd grimace on his face, an expression I don't recognise. "I'm hardly that much of a monster, am I?"

"You're not a monster, you're just spoiled," I reply, exasperated, and my tone chases the look from his face.

"Just as well," he says. "You're too used to getting your own way."

"I am not."

"Good. Then you'll let me come with you."

"I—All right!" I fling my hands up. "All right, you've made your point. But if she refuses to meet because of this—"

"Then I'll find her," he says, baring too many teeth as he speaks. "She won't get away from me again."

I peel the imp from my shoulder and tuck it under the cloak, urging it back into the inner pocket. "We'll need to stay away from people. Does the Count have a private coach we can steal?"

"Even if he did, I wouldn't know how to drive it. We'll have to walk, or hire a cab."

"They're not going to be happy about you leaving."

"I don't intend to ask." He grabs my hand and pulls me out of the room.

The maids are up and active, hiding their weariness with professional distance. Steel has chosen a nondescript black suit and a simple greatcoat, with a hat that he pulls low on his brow. We move through the palace as quickly and quietly as possible, avoiding the servants where we can. I keep my cloak tucked around the imp, who shrinks into the curve of my arm, silent. We almost make it out without anyone the wiser.

A Revenant stands guard at the main entrance. I should have known it wouldn't be so easy. He sits in a chair with its back against the wall, as though he's at a gallery guarding the paintings. At our approach, he stands. "Du kannst nicht durchkommen." The words are uttered in flat monotone, his sleepy half-lidded eyes barely twitching. His blond hair is tousled, sticking up at the back where he'd been leaning against the wall.

Although I don't understand the words, his meaning is clear. "We need to pass," I say, indicating the door.

"Du kannst nicht durchkommen," he repeats and raises a hand to stifle a yawn.

I throw a glance at Steel. He considers the Revenant a moment, looking him up and down, and then says, "Move."

That makes the man blink, and his posture straightens. "Du kannst—"

Steel dives forward and slams the man against the door. I jerk, instinctively raising my hand to stop him, then pull back. If our only way out is violence, then we don't have much choice.

"Move," Steel says again, lowly, clenching the lapels of the demon's jacket. The huge black irises of the man's eyes expand even wider. Light glimmers around his hands, and I brace myself for a fight.

"That's enough," Luka calls from behind me.

I pivot, find him striding towards us, shrugging on a dark greatcoat. "Are we prisoners?" I ask, trying to divert his attention.

"He won't move," Steel says, destroying my attempt.

"Perhaps because you have him pressed against the wall." Luka's voice is dry and he stops in the corridor between a painting of an ancient Austrian monarch and one of a lonely stag on a rolling green field. "Release him."

Steel hesitates, not taking his hands or his gaze off the trapped Revenant. The light around the demon thickens into flames.

"Steel," I murmur.

With a muttered curse, he shoves himself backwards, letting go of the demon. Luka says something in German, his voice the snap of an order. The Revenant glances at him, then back at Steel. It takes another, terser command from Luka before the blond man ducks his head and walks away through the corridor.

"What did you say to him?" I ask, when he's out of sight.

"I said that you were carrying out a task for me." A strand of Luka's short black hair slips free and dangles by his ear. He smooths it back with an annoyed twitch. "And that he could leave Steel with me."

"Thank you," Steel says, with a grudging slowness. "We won't be gone for long."

Luka gives him a look. "You aren't going at all. Von Tier won't be happy if I let you wander off alone. She can go."

"I have a name," I reply, at the same time that Steel says, "She's not going alone."

Part of me—and perhaps it's an uncharitable part—wonders if Luka might persuade Steel to stay where I had failed. Before I can determine who to side with, the imp emits a rough, coughing sound.

Luka's gaze narrows in on my coat. "You still have that creature?"

Another croaking sound and concern knocks aside my caution. Luka already knows about the imp, anyway. I flip the edge of my coat over my shoulder as the imp makes another hacking cough. I quickly place it on the ground, where it draws its leathery wings tight against its back and convulses. Vomit stains the carpet with bile and clots of blood.

"What's wrong with it?" Steel asks.

I shake my head, kneeling at its side, putting a reassuring hand on its shivering spine. "I don't know. It seemed fine this morning."

Another convulsion, another splatter of vomit. Its breath comes in heavy strained pants and it lets out a harsh whine. Something whitish and creamy dribbles from its mouth.

"Water," I say, looking up, "it needs water."

Steel hovers, on the verge of dashing away, while Luka seems preoccupied with the loose sleeve of his coat. The sound of the imp's breathing abruptly ceases, and for a moment I think bizarrely that it must have vanished, but when I look down it's still there, lying motionless on the red carpet.

Gently, I turn its pointed head to the side, trying to feel for a pulse. Its thin pink tongue that had lapped up my breakfast so eagerly this morning flops onto the tile, streaked in blood and white phlegm. Its shivering has stopped. Its *everything* has stopped.

"I don't understand." My fingers tremble against its skin. "It was fine. It was fine."

Steel goes to one knee beside me. "The surgery must have affected it internally."

Internal bleeding wouldn't have caused vomiting, not so suddenly, not without any other symptoms. The thought is quiet but swift, cutting through the tightness in my chest like a blade in the dark. Another follows, just as quick and cutting: *poison* would.

I take a deep breath, let it out slowly. Don't look up, don't look beyond the small pathetic body of the imp. "It must have." Even my voice shakes, which is nonsensical. It was only a demon, not a beloved pet. I'd only known it for a day.

"Take it with you," comes Luka's voice. "You can't leave the body here."

"I'm not going to leave the body here." I don't bother to keep the acid from my voice. "I'll bury it."

"Not on the palace grounds. It won't do to have the gardener turn it up while he's planting new rose bushes."

If I had Eve's skill with daggers, I'd throw one at him. He'd surely catch it, but the act alone would give me satisfaction. "If that's all," I say, taking off my cloak to gather up the fragile body, "you can go back to Katharina."

"Not without Steel."

My partner's hand supports my arm, helping me up. "We're leaving," Steel says. "Tell von Tier if you must. I don't care."

Luka purses his lips. "Very well. Then I will come with you."

"No," I object. Bringing Steel along is dangerous enough given Chang Mei's request that I come alone. Turning up with two diamond class demons is going to have her attack us on sight.

On the other hand, with two diamond class demons we might have a chance to stop her.

"Stay, or I come with you," Luka says. "Those are your options."

Steel growls a little. "Stay out of our way, then."

I note that Luka says nothing, but I'm too tired to protest any further, too distracted by the potential threat implied by the imp's death. The sooner we can find and stop Bellemeure, the sooner we'll all be out of danger.

CHAPTER TWENTY-ONE

We bury the imp in a little patch of ground behind the stables. I hesitate to let go of the body at first, wondering if it might revive itself somehow, and in the end Steel has to take it from me and place it in the hole he's dug. I suppose the ghost was right, back in Paris; it's easier to kill demons than they'd have you believe.

Luka keeps watch, or at least he claims to, though he seems to do no more than stand and inspect our work. By the time we've finished digging and warmth from the exertion is running through my muscles, I'm even less inclined to be charitable with him. The memory of the imp's convulsions and what they signify fill me with the urge to flee the palace, flee him and his fellow demons.

It had eaten my breakfast and now it was dead. The logical conclusion glares at me. But the who and the why—those questions still need to be answered, and to have any hope of answering them I'll need to keep the culprit from discovering that I'm on their trail. So I pat snow over the little mound by the stone wall and stay silent.

"Where are we supposed to be meeting this woman?" asks Luka. When we'd told him of our purpose, he'd only raised his eyebrows minutely. Now, he stands in his greatcoat staring in the direction of the road, looking faintly disdainful of the world's existence.

"A coffeehouse in the inner town," Steel replies, tossing aside the shovel he'd nicked from the stable.

"She said come alone," I add, "so make sure you're not seen."

"Why should I hide? You were going to take my brother. One more demon will not make much difference."

If I'm lucky, she might object enough to murder him on sight. It's only with great restraint that I manage to keep from speaking the thought aloud. "Let's go," I say, instead. "It's a long walk if we can't find a cab. Unless you drive a carriage?"

Luka's lips thin and he doesn't answer.

At this early hour, the courtyard is empty. It seems smaller than it had when we came in, the fountains diminished and the trees lonely. The two guards at the gate are too well-trained to gape as we pass, but their eyes slide sideways in their sockets to follow us out.

Snow has polished the roads and even the river moves sluggishly. A lone rider trots by, the clopping of his horse's hooves muffled. We make our way to the more popular streets, where the snow has been trodden into grey slush and I have to slow my pace to stay upright.

Contrary to my expectations, it doesn't take long to find a cab, but the one that approaches is one of the open air carriages that seems designed to ensnare tourists. Its two white horses pick their way carefully through the ice and mud. The driver, swaddled up to his eyes in a huge layered coat and a muffler, calls out to us. Luka answers in German, flicking his fingers at me, and the coachman nods, jerking a thumb behind him.

"He'll take us to St Stephen's," the demon explains. "I assume your coffeehouse is nearby?"

I don't know if it's wariness or obstinacy that makes me dig my boots into the mire, despite the cold biting at my toes. "It's snowing."

"It stopped snowing an hour ago."

Annoyingly, the mat of clouds above us do not seem willing to contradict him.

"It looks warm enough," Steel says, opening the carriage door. The benches are piled high with furs.

"It will be, if we stop standing around." Luka leaps into the carriage and takes a seat, stealing half the furs for himself. "Or would you prefer to be late?"

I refrain from reminding him that we still have a few hours before midday and take Steel's hand to climb inside. Although I'd rather see where I'm going, the idea of sitting so close to Luka makes my hands itch for my hatpin, so I take the seat opposite, my back to the driver. Steel jumps nimbly inside, slamming the door, and portions out the rest of the furs. A crack of the reins and we're moving, the wind whipping through my hair and icing the back of my neck.

I watch the dreary city pass by. The clouds are so thick that everything looks grey and murky, but a few buildings have hung holly boughs from their windows, and a couple of doors already bear wreaths. Christmas is only a few weeks away.

"It wouldn't have survived much longer," Steel says, breaking into my thoughts. I glance at him and he adds, with a significant look at the driver, "The...cat."

He must think my reticence a result of its death. I can't say he's entirely wrong. "Perhaps you're right."

"It's better off dead," Luka interjects. His eyes are narrowed against the breeze and the gleam of gold looks soft enough to pass as pale amber. "They all are."

It wasn't the imp who was supposed to die. Hanna must have discovered that I was investigating her and tried to stop me with one of her plants. Though given the indulgence of her strange surgeries, I can't imagine she'd need to hide the decision to murder me. "Did you learn who was behind the experiments?"

"I did not. Have you?"

Steel opens his mouth and I cut in, "We have not." If Luka is as good as he seems to think he is, he can't have missed what was happening right under his nose. And if he *isn't* as good as he thinks, then I'm not going to reveal our cards just yet. I lean forward, drop my voice so the wind keeps my words from the driver. "Are you certain neither daughter can use magic?"

"Neither can manipulate fire. Products of crossbreeding," he adds, with a disgusted grimace.

"What about other magic? Rituals? Spells?"

His gaze lifts from the street to stare at me, then slide away. "As far as I know, neither have attempted it."

"Katharina seemed intent on getting you to teach her."

"Katharina desires my time. She only chooses magic because she thinks I value it."

"Do you?"

He gives me a thin-lipped smile and the conversation dies.

Steel, who had been watching in silence, says, "We should be focused on Bellemure. She's our true enemy."

"Our first enemy," I correct.

"You have many, do you?"

"About the same number as you, I expect."

"Isn't the coffeehouse up ahead?" Steel asks, with an air of slight desperation.

We've crossed the Ringstrasse and have moved into the inner city, where the tall spires of the cathedral spear into the clouds. Its roof, just glimpsed through the buildings, is ornately patterned with red and blue tiles.

"Stop here," I call to the driver and Luka echoes my request in German. I'm not quite petty enough to glare at him—the words are practically the same in both languages–but I hop out as soon as the carriage halts. "This gentleman will pay you." I gesture at Luka and my tone carries enough of a translation for the driver to turn to the demon expectantly.

Kaffeehaus Herzog is a few streets away, tucked around the corner in another of Vienna's statuesque white buildings. I examine the genteel facade. We're early and there's no sign of Bellemeure, or Chang Mei. In fact, there's no sign of anyone. At a little before midday, peak lunchtime hour, the emptiness seems eerie.

"Both of you should wait here," I say, about to add that it will be safer if Bellemeure doesn't see the two of them until after I've had a chance to speak to her, but Steel flexes his fingers, his talons starkly black, and shakes his head.

Luka has his gaze on the coffeehouse. "We should attack her before she suspects us," he says.

"Absolutely not. My friend is in there."

"We're going in with you. Bellemeure won't be defenceless," says Steel. "Better that you're not, either."

Annoyingly sensible. "Stay back, then," I compromise.

I walk towards the coffeehouse, alert for any sign of danger. The only sound is the high-pitched cry of a baby from the apartments above. When I duck inside, I think that I must have misheard, for although the cafe isn't full, it's populated enough that there should be more noise. Some customers are couples bent over a coffee, and a few others look like workers who've popped in for a quick lunch. A handful of other tables hold young men with caps pulled low over their faces, their boots stained with mud. I take note of their posture quickly, the way their gazes are drawn to the windows, the fact that none have their back to the door. I see Eve and Cassius seated at a table in the back with two empty chairs.

Eve looks up and scowls. "So much for coming alone," she says, when we reach her table.

"I gave it my best shot." We eye Luka with derision. He either doesn't notice or doesn't care.

Steel shifts restlessly, his claws tucked into his palms to hide them, his gaze searching the cafe's other occupants. "No sign of her?"

"Not yet."

"Sit down," Cassius says, caustically. "You're making us even more noticeable than we already are." He uses his boot to push out a chair as he says it, and Steel clutches its back. Its upholstery tears under his talons.

"I'm fine."

I take it instead and Eve says, with a twist of her mouth, "We didn't order enough coffee."

"They can go without."

Luka takes the second empty chair, flicking his coat out as he sits and clicking his fingers with his other hand, summoning a waiter. The man looks as irritated to be summoned as Luka looks to summon him. The demon gives an order without meeting the man's eyes and the waiter disappears, hiding irritation behind tightly pressed lips.

"Coffee?" I ask him.

"I never drink coffee," he replies blandly.

I turn my shoulder to him.

"What happened?" I ask Eve. "How did you find Bellemeure? Why did she suggest—"

Eve holds up her hand. "We ran into Chang at the tavern where we met the others." She cups her own coffee, which is black and appears to have gone at least tepid, if not cold. "We persuaded her to meet. I chose the place."

Leaning my forearms on the table, conscious of the ears attuned to us, I reply, "These others, are they working with her?"

"I'd put money on it."

The waiter returns and deposits a glass of some amber liquor in front of Luka without a word. He then steps around the demon and bends to place a small piece of paper in front of me. He whisks off to serve another table before I can react.

Eve sends me a speaking look. I unfold the paper—it's folded once, across the centre, although the seam isn't straight. Written in a hurry?—and read: *You were asked to come alone.*

"We're being watched."

Cassius tilts his head at the other tables. "Clearly. His nose should have told you that the minute you got here." This is directed at Steel, who lurks behind me. The sound of upholstery ripping makes me glance back at him.

"I didn't notice." It's uttered with stiffness and his gaze doesn't stop roaming the cafe. He's going to be a liability.

The coldness of that thought stops me. He's my partner, and he has more invested in this case than any of us. It's understandable that he'd be overcome.

It won't help the situation, though.

I fold the note again, then twice more to make it small. I suspect that I'm not going to be rid of either Steel or Luka very easily. But nor will Bellemeure make her appearance with them here.

"Well," I say. "We'll just have to wait her out. I'll get us some more coffee." I stand, tapping my fingers on the table as I do. Eve doesn't look pleased, but she dips her chin, which I take for a nod. "See if you can smell her," I add to Steel, in an undertone. He does better with a task. Sure enough, the demon straightens a little, his weight more even, the restlessness disappearing.

I follow the waiter's circular route to the back of the cafe, wait until he's distracted, then slip past him into the kitchen, ignoring the stares of the staff and the surprised "Was machst du hier?" one throws in my direction. I duck around a confused chef, under a collection of pans and out through a door into an alley.

The air bites and I dig my hands deep into my pockets, waiting. It takes a few minutes for a figure to appear at the other end. She wears a maid's simple wool dress, this time, with a bonnet tied tightly over her glossy black hair.

My skin prickles at her approach, my brain clamouring a warning. The last time I'd seen Chang Mei, she'd almost killed Steel. She had killed von Tier. Intelligent, bold and dedicated. The kind of woman who chooses her path and sticks to it, no matter what.

Best to divert her before she can get too far down it. "This is not ideal," I say, in tones quiet enough that the demons will struggle to hear us. "A more open space would have been preferred."

The woman's eyes widen at my audacity. "Would you also have preferred a hot posset and a blanket for your feet?" she says, sneering.

"That would have been appreciated, yes, but that isn't why I'm here. Nor you, I suspect."

The woman blinks, her arms close to her sides, making me wonder if she has blades hidden beneath her skirts. "If you think that I do not have better things to do than serve some arrogant police agent—"

"I do, in fact," I interrupt, before she can build up steam. "And I'm sure your mistress does, too, so let's make this quick. We won't have much time before the others realise I haven't returned."

"The others," says Mei, seizing on that comment, "should not be here. Our message was quite clear."

"I'm sure your mistress can appreciate the difficulties in managing diamond class demons." The second mistress makes an impact; her head goes back a bit, her nostrils flaring. Perhaps I'm overdoing it. "Eve will keep them busy for a while. I suggest you take me to Bellemeure."

Mei's brows go up. They're thicker than they'd been in Paris, one nicked with a tiny white scar I hadn't noticed before. "Do you? Won't your lover have an issue with that?"

I'm not expecting the probe and, though I hide my reaction quickly, I feel my mouth pull into a moue. Hopefully Mei takes it as distaste. "None of them will be particularly happy," I admit, diverting with honesty. "Shall we?" I say, extending my hand to encompass the alley. "I assume you have another route to wherever she is?"

"What makes you think she isn't here?"

"The excessive number of foot soldiers," I reply, "and the fact that we named it as a meeting place. Even a fool would have to suspect a trap."

"And yet, you didn't?"

"She didn't have to use a trap to find us," I say. "She's known where we are for some time." No, she wants something from me, and I intend to find out what. "So," I say, "shall we?"

CHAPTER TWENTY-TWO

Mei turns left, in the opposite direction to the coffeehouse and the cathedral. I brush my hand subtly against the stone wall as we walk. Not that Steel needs a scent trail to find me; our bond throbs at the back of my head. I expect the only reason he hasn't noticed what I'm doing is because all his attention is honed towards finding Bellemeure.

We cut across another street to a smaller cafe. It has a space for chairs outside, although the snow has chased away any patrons who might try to brave the cold. Mei ducks inside without hesitation. I glance once over my shoulder and then follow her.

This cafe is less than half the size of Herzog and it only has one occupant. There's no cigarette in sight, this time, instead Bellemeure has a cup of something fragrant steaming on the table before her. She wears a dark maroon riding dress with a split skirt and laced boots. Although the toes of the latter are painted with slush, the mud hasn't reached more than the heel.

"Good afternoon," I greet her. No waiters here to interrupt us, but no foot soldiers, either.

"Mademoiselle," she replies. I had spoken in French without thinking. She continues in English. "I hope you do not mind my precautions."

"Not at all." I take the chair opposite her. Dirt edges the metal rim of the table and dust lies between the flagstones under it. I cross one leg over the other and rest my hands on my raised knee. "I hope you don't mind if I do not drink." I indicate her cup with a quirk of my eyebrow. It's an odd greenish colour that makes me think of jasmine, although the scent is medicinal.

She smiles a little, appreciating my volley, perhaps. "It would be rather rude of me to drug you after inviting you here, wouldn't it?"

"It would," I answer and her smile grows. Her brown hair is curled in a rounded, full style, an oddly modern look compared to the older style of the dress. The grey shot through it makes it look silver.

"Besides," she says, "even if I did, it would have little effect. I understand that House Asmodeus has developed a cure."

Ah, is that why she wanted me here? I return her look with bland disinterest. "I understand you've developed some new connections. Friends who might be more useful than a drug."

Her lashes sweep down in a slow blink. She has very long lashes, dark and full. Though aged, her features are strong; broad cheekbones, long nose, full lips. The lines and thin skin at the corners of her eyes and mouth seem to add to her beauty, not diminish it. With a start, I realise that her eyes look normal. They hold no unusual colouring, no odd pupils; nothing to identify her as anything but human.

"Friend," she repeats. "An interesting choice of word. Would you consider all your companions to be friends?"

I feel like I'm playing chess against Monaghan, watching him make moves that seem to lead to nothing, knowing that in ten or twenty more he'll have me in checkmate. But this is a game with three players, and the only way to win is to pit my opponents against each other. "Not all of them."

"Nor would I," she replies, without even a twitch of her brow.

"What would you call them?"

"I would call them monsters," she says, in that same conversational tone. "Or have you not yet seen enough of their palace to come to that conclusion?"

The imp's small pathetic body flashes through my mind. I blink quickly, too quickly, but Bellemeure gives nothing away, not even an acknowledgement of my lapse. "I've seen more than I'd ever wish to of that palace," I reply, deciding to lean into the error. "Perhaps I've come to appreciate the feelings of your companion towards the diamond class." I tilt my head to indicate Mei, standing just inside the door, a stalwart guard.

At the corner of my mind, my sense of Steel brightens, as if his awareness has turned to me. I can't suppress a surge of guilt for leaving him behind and it transmits through our bond like a flare. Bellemeure tilts her head, and for a moment I wonder if I made a sound or gave some kind of signal, but no; I'd managed to keep that to myself.

She listens for a moment, silent. Mei hasn't moved and the street is quiet, empty. How good is her hearing?

"Miss Locke," she says and I wish I had a cup so I could take refuge behind it. "As much as I would prefer to remain here, speaking with you, my time is limited. Allow me to make you an offer."

I go alert. "By all means."

"You have been running from the one they call the Ripper."

No amount of preparation could have helped me disguise the jerk of my hands to that word. "What do you mean?" I say, only just keeping my voice from shaking.

"He owns London," she goes on, as if I hadn't spoken, "and it will not be long before his empire expands. He must be dealt with."

I give up on obfuscating the truth, conscious of the growing strength of Steel's presence at the back of my head. "How did you know?"

"We all have ghosts." Her eyes grow distant for a moment. "Some are louder than others." Before I can ask, she says, "I am willing to help you."

"Help me?"

"By removing him, of course." She says it as though he is a stray thread on a new dress, a hangnail grown bothersome.

"And how would you propose doing that?"

"In due course. I have my own task to complete first. A task that will go much faster with your assistance."

"You mean Asmodeus."

She finally takes a sip from the cup, which has stopped steaming. Her lips purse at the taste. "My medicine," she offers, unexpectedly. "I am older than most, you see, and my kind does not age well. It tastes as bad as it smells," she says, "but it is good for me. Some things, however bad they taste in the moment, will be better for you in the end."

I can't tell if the words are supposed to be a threat, or what the threat is if they are. "How do you expect me to help you with this...task?" I ask, cautiously.

"The night of the twelfth is considered to be a time for celebration," says Bellemeure. "It marks the beginning of Yule. It would be beneficial if House Asmodeus remained at the palace on that night. And, perhaps, if their human servants did not."

Goosebumps ripple down my arms. "What are you planning?"

"That will become clear, in time. Now you should leave." She indicates the door with her cup. "The coffeehouse is on fire."

"*What?*"

CHAPTER TWENTY-THREE

From the distance comes a sudden *whoomph*. A surge of shouting follows it and a word I don't need to translate to understand; fire. Steel's presence in my head swells with shock and alarm. I surge to my feet, knocking down my chair, and run to the door.

Mei has already stepped away, a detail my brain notices and discards as not immediately relevant. What is immediately relevant is finding Steel. I burst into the street and race down the alley. The tall buildings obscure any sign of smoke, but I can smell it on the wind. I trace it back to the coffeehouse.

"Steel!" I shout and a ripple of something spreads through me.

"Hazel!"

I round the corner and see the flames, first, making me think of the lodge in the forest. Then Steel is in front of me.

"Are you hurt?" I ask. "Is anyone hurt?"

"Where have you been? Did you find Bellemeure?" He seems to read the answer from my face, or my mind. "How many times," he grits out, "must I ask you not to leave me? Where is she?"

"She'll be gone by now." Mei will spirit her away to wherever they're staying, safe again. Behind Steel, Eve and Cassius are helping a waiter who's bent over, coughing. Luka stands apart, assessing the fire. His head turns in my direction and he starts towards us. "I'll tell you the rest later," I say, under my breath.

"What did she say?" Steel demands and the raised tone makes me flinch. He rocks back on his heels, looking contrite.

"She talked about the cure," I reply. "She's not likely to use the drug again because of it. And she does not like his kind." I flick my gaze in Luka's direction, turning it into a reason for not divulging everything in this moment.

"And you met her alone, because you thought she wouldn't attack you?" The words are quiet but clipped. "You've seen what she and Chang are capable of. It was idiotic to risk yourself by going off alone knowing there was danger. *Again*," he adds, the word bursting out as if he'd meant to keep it back and failed.

"What do you mean, again?" I ask, bewildered.

"The ghost," he says, in biting tones. "Was this another attempt to use yourself as bait and see what happens? You may not value your life that highly, but the rest of us do."

Luka has reached us, and at this he makes a dismissive sound. "Do not count myself among that number."

Steel doesn't seem to hear him. "How many times do I have to ask you not to put yourself in needless danger?"

I can't believe he's starting an argument in the middle of the street, in front of a building that is currently on fire. "Can we please talk about this later?"

"Yes," drawls Cassius, making Steel jerk and whip his head around, "unless you'd like to entertain the firemen and the police, when they arrive?"

Luckily the flames are small, located far enough within the building that it poses no danger to the houses around it. "What happened here?" I ask.

"Some of her rabble set fire to the coffeehouse to distract us," Luka says. "No doubt they thought better of a meeting with me."

Cassius rolls his eyes. "I've grown so used to the Leviathan's company," he mutters, "that I'd forgotten how far up their own backside these demons can travel."

I move to Eve. "Is anyone hurt?"

"Some smoke inhalation, but nothing serious." She thumps the waiter on his back one more time and he waves a hand at her, coughing hoarsely. "Was it worth it?" she asks, with an undercurrent of annoyance.

"She's my case," I remind the woman. Perhaps not my wisest choice of words.

Eve's spine snaps straight. "Oh," she says. "Of course, do not let me get in the way of you and your case. Because I have my own case, as I'm sure you know. Back in London. Where we should be right now."

"I am grateful for your help. But Bellemeure wasn't going to show herself in front of those two."

Eve folds her arms, looking unimpressed.

"She did us a favour," Cassius adds. He frowns at the waiter as the man lets out another hacking cough. "The less Bellemeure knows about us, the less of a target we are."

I eye him. "I'm already a target."

"But we are not," he replies, overly enunciating the words. "And I do not intend for that to change."

Eve doesn't contradict him. I might have offended her more than I thought. "Did one of her workers start the fire?"

"I think so." She lets out a sigh, then, sagging a little. "It came from the kitchen, though, so there's a chance it could have been an accident."

"You think so?"

"I said there was a chance. More likely it was premeditated, designed to give Bellemeure a way out after a set period of time, or under some signal."

From the distance come the bells of an approaching fire engine. Even with the snow, the streets are clear enough that the horses will be here in a matter of minutes. The flames are eating steadily through the furniture inside, but for the moment they seem contained enough to be put out without too much difficulty.

"The police are going to ask questions we can't answer," Eve says. "We should go."

"Back to the palace?" Steel's voice startles me. I hadn't noticed how close he was.

"For you." Eve resettles the coat over her shoulders. "I don't think we'll be welcome there. Unless there's something we should know?"

Bellemeure's proposal teeter at the tip of my tongue. But if I speak here, Luka will know her plan and I won't have the opportunity to take up her offer. If that's something I want.

"She was looking for information about von Tier's antidote. Though I don't think we should let down our guard just yet."

It's honest enough that Eve reads truth in my face and nods. "I'll see Noah," she says. "There's a tavern they use over in the Favoriten district. I'll see if I can find out more."

"Come to the palace later and meet me in the gardens," I suggest. We'll need to consider our plans for the twelfth.

"You're not going to go running after this woman?" asks Luka. "Is that not your job, as an officer?"

"Agent," Eve and I correct, at the same time. "And she's not an agent anymore," adds Eve. She says it without vitriol, a cold hard fact, but it feels like a jab.

"Fascinating," Luka says, with a tone that proclaims it the opposite.

The sirens are getting louder. "I'll see you at dusk," Eve promises. We exchange nods and she and Cassius walk away down the alley. Their figures make for an odd picture, side by side; Cassius' fox-red hair beside Eve's brown curls, his shiny shoes and elegant gait beside her steel-toed worker's boots and broad stride. It will never make sense, seeing them together.

"Another carriage, then?" Luka slides his hands into the pockets of his greatcoat, his slicked back hair dusted with tiny flakes of snow; the clouds have given up their weight.

Steel is brimming with tension and I dread the thought of sitting in a carriage for another hour, a thundercloud on one side and a serpent on the other, ready to strike. "Would you rather walk?" I ask, half-hoping he'll say yes. He gives me a flat stare instead.

We manage to hail a plain hansom cab, or whatever Vienna calls the small for-hire carriages pulled by a single horse. Unoccupied ones are already growing sparse under the falling snow and I expect the weather will only grow worse.

It's a cramped interior, without any furs to keep us warm, and I close the simple wool drape that covers the window. I can feel Steel's impatience beating at my mind. "We didn't speak for long," I say, giving in. "I mentioned the drug, and she said she wasn't sure it would be useful for her anymore."

My partner lets out a growling sound. "Because of the cure Hanna created."

"Yes."

"Then what did she want?"

"To know my loyalty," I reply. "And whether or not I could be bought."

"Can you?" asks Luka in a low voice.

"I owe Steel everything," I counter. "I would never willingly betray him."

The demon regards me. He's very still, and I can't read any emotion from him.

"I think she heard you coming after me," I add, wanting to steer the conversation into an area I can control. "She seemed to be listening to something."

"Impossible," Steel says. "She couldn't have heard me from where you were. Most of the demons in the cafe wouldn't have heard me and I was closer to them."

"Are you sure?"

"He's right." Luka flicks back the window blind. "Even if her hearing had been good, we move more quietly than most demons, and the noise from the kitchen would have masked anything else."

"Then how could she have heard him?" Unless she had sensed our bond, somehow. I drum my fingers on my thigh. "What is she?"

"What attributes did she display?" asks Luka.

I comb through my memories, filing my thoughts together for an answer. "I couldn't determine her age," I begin, and he cuts in impatiently.

"Age is little indication of bloodline. Those of purer lines will live longer, but those years will not show on our bodies until much later."

I take a breath and start again. "Aside from her indiscriminate age, she doesn't seem to move quickly, like Mei, or display any elemental powers. She has an understanding of magic and apparently science, given that her weapon against Leviathan was a drug. She was drinking a medicinal tea, though she didn't explain what it was for." I spread my hands helplessly. "She kept listening to something. I don't know what, if not you."

"A Phantom?" Steel suggests.

"She did it in Paris, too." I think back to the opera house, the way she had tilted her head and looked right at me. "She said her kind is old, older than the diamond class."

Luka murmurs something in another language and it's my turn to raise my brows at him. "A Shade," he says, his gaze going unfocused.

"Is that a demon?"

"They're an old breed," he replies. "A member of what we called the gold caste. They were destroyed when the Houses formed." He says it passively, as if he and his fellow demons weren't the ones who had murdered them.

"What can they do?"

"They talk to shades."

I give him a sceptical look. "You mean they speak to shadows?"

"I mean that they talk to the dead," he replies in the snidest tone I've heard him use. "They are haunted by the souls of those who cannot move on from this world. It drove most of them mad, according to my grandfather."

"Not her," I say, tucking my hands under my arms to fight off the chill that has seeped through me. *We all have ghosts*, she'd said. I didn't realise she'd meant it literally. "Or if it did, she hides it well."

Steel hasn't said a word in the last few moments, and the sense-impression I have of him is muted. His brows are drawn together. "Her people are...dead?" he asks, slowly.

Luka raises one shoulder. "If she survived, others might have, too. Although I expect it's unlikely."

Her quest is revenge against the people who killed her family, just as Steel's is. I glance at him and he looks away, out of the carriage window.

"Surely not all of the Houses took part in that kind of massacre," I say.

"There are always casualties in the seizing of power." Luka leans back in his seat, managing to take up more room than the three of us in one carriage should permit. "It allows those who are more powerful to take up their rightful positions. There are far fewer demons than there are humans, after all. We must be able to protect ourselves."

In that moment I realise that no matter how much time I spend with this man, how earnestly I try to convince him otherwise, he will always believe that he has a right to power, to wealth. In the same way that Monaghan is married to his position as the Head of the Agency, Luka is convinced that he and his family's duty is to rule, like some kind of infernal divine right. He and I will never see eye to eye.

"If she isn't going to use the drug," I say, "then she'll have to come up with another form of attack. We should be on our guard." I can feel Steel's gaze on the side of my face, but he stays quiet, waiting, and the carriage ride continues in silence.

CHAPTER TWENTY-FOUR

When we arrive back at the palace, we find Katharina in the entrance hall. "Where have you been?" she demands, attaching herself to Luka's side. "You said you'd teach me another spell."

Distaste slithers through the demon's expression before he masks it. "Did I?" he says. "I must have forgotten."

Katharina is not as practised at hiding her emotions and her face tightens with annoyance. "Well, you are here now."

"Where's Hanna?" I ask and the woman shrugs.

"Oh, off performing one of her experiments, probably. Who knows? Raziel, won't you join us? I'd love to know what kind of magic House Leviathan practised." The sound of his true name startles me. I haven't heard it since he first revealed it to me.

Steel catches at my elbow. "We need to change clothes," he says, in repressive tones. "Perhaps later."

"Do human agencies not have warlocks, too?" Katharina asks me. "Can you not learn magic?"

"I...do not know." The Agency held no information on how its agents had developed the first ritual. We'd all assumed they'd found a demon who'd created it for them, but however it was performed, the knowledge of its creation was not recorded. Only the need for blood, for sacrifice.

"Well, you could try." It seems to be a ploy to get both demons to stay with her, but it's successful in making them hesitate.

"Another time," I say, though it takes a degree of effort that surprises me. I should have no interest in the paranormal world; everything I need I already own.

Steel starts walking towards our room, exerting light pressure on my elbow to go with him. Katharina starts talking to Luka in rushed German, and I glance over my shoulder to see the man watch us as we leave.

Steel says nothing as we walk and again I get the impression of a storm building. As we reach our rooms, I attempt to head it off. "I didn't want to reveal too much in the carriage," I whisper. "Just in case."

"In case what?" he asks, closing the door behind us. He'd pulled us into his room, the closer one, and its unfamiliarity puts me on edge. "In case you decided to side with her?"

Outside the window, flakes of snow drift from a cloudy sky and melt on the windowpane. I take off my coat, clutch it in front of me. "I'm not siding with anyone."

"I can feel your guilt." He taps the side of his head. "What did she say, to make you doubt me? What kind of sob story did she put together to earn your sympathy?"

"I don't doubt you," I reply. "I'm still on this case."

"Then you should have taken me with you."

"I told you, I can't make promises–"

"That's not enough for me!"

I pause, my stomach tightening. "What do you mean?"

He drags a hand through his hair, letting the long strands fall where they will. "You keep saying we're partners, but you don't *act* like it. You keep me at a distance, don't tell me what you're thinking." He throws up a hand as I make to interrupt. "Even if it is the right decision to go alone," he says, flashing his teeth as though he has to push the words past them, "you can at least talk to me about it first."

"And what if you say no?"

"There'd be a good reason. Your safety, for example," he points out.

"I was fine."

"*This* time. Who knows what could have happened if she'd wanted to hurt you?"

I shake my head. "If we keep disagreeing, we'll get nowhere."

"Then we compromise. That's what a partnership is, isn't it?"

"Isn't that what we're already doing?"

He folds his arms. "Withholding information, deliberately leaving me behind or cutting me out—I wouldn't call that compromise."

It feels as though he's tugging at the last knot that holds me together, and that if it comes unravelled, there will be no walking away from him; I won't survive it.

He sighs and adds softly, wearily, "I can't keep asking you to let me in."

It's the tone that undoes me, and it feels like letting go of something that I'd been holding onto for so long its absence leaves me hollow. I let my arms drop. "She offered me a deal.

She wanted me to make sure Asmodeus was in the palace on the twelfth. For an attack, I assume."

Steel digests this, then asks, "In exchange for what?"

"In exchange for helping me to stop Monaghan. She says he needs to be 'dealt with', although she didn't inform me how she was going to accomplish that."

"We need to tell Luka and the Count." The reply is quick, reflexive.

"What if we didn't?" I ask, so quietly I almost don't hear myself.

He blinks once, twice. "Whether I agree with him or not, Luka is my blood," he replies, hotly. "I'm not going to let her attack him. And if she brings these other demons, we'll need the Count's help to stop her. Are you so willing to let her massacre all these people?"

"*People* is not the word I would use," I reply. "*People* do not experiment on living creatures for some twisted purpose and leave them to die in agony."

"Then they'll face justice," he snaps. "We bring them to justice."

"There's something else." I hesitate, reluctant to bring forward this suspicion given his reaction, but there are no walls left between us to stop me. "I think the imp was poisoned."

"What?"

"It was perfectly fine before it ate breakfast—my breakfast. Frothing at the mouth, vomiting blood, sudden death..." I wave my hand bleakly. "Internal bleeding would have shown symptoms before today. It was poison."

"You think someone here wants to kill you? Why?"

"To get me out of the way, perhaps. To make a move against the Agency. We need to investigate."

"Or it could be Bellemeure," Steel says, "striking at you here so you'll be more likely to help her."

"That's..." A perfectly reasonable suggestion and I should have thought of it earlier. "You might be right."

"This woman had my mother killed," he goes on. "Not to mention the rest of House Leviathan and who knows how many other demons. Why would you even *consider* helping her? It's not as if you'll see Monaghan again."

Silence expands to fill the pause after his words.

"You won't, will you?" he asks, his tone less certain.

"When we're finished here," I say, meaning both Bellemeure and Asmodeus, and whatever comes of Luka. "Khurana and Jacob and the others will need our help. Right now, they're at Monaghan's mercy."

Steel shakes his head. "He's too powerful. He'll kill you as soon as you step foot in England."

"I have to take that risk."

"But..." He looks nonplussed. "But why?"

"What else can I do? I can't run forever."

"You could stay," he says, with an undercurrent to his voice I can't identify. "Or—if Luka..."

"You've found a family," I say, keeping my heart in a grip of iron, holding it together while it cracks. "You shouldn't let that go."

He snorts. "I would not call Luka family. And I don't think he'd be particularly happy to call himself that, either."

That teases a smile from me. "Well, perhaps that will change in time. You might have a chance to be happy. You deserve that."

"So do you," he says, quietly.

I watch the snow fall outside the window, blurring the view of the forest.

"What are you going to do?" Steel asks, eventually. "About Bellemeure?"

"We've made it this far without her help." I look up and find him watching me. "We can manage the rest without her," I say and he smiles at me.

Agent E. Wilson

Eve has Cassius hunt for Bellemeure's trail, but after wandering about for a bit he stops and shrugs at her. The streets are busy enough that it wouldn't be a challenge for Chang and Bellemeure to disappear among the workers, despite the weather.

"You shouldn't have let her go alone," the Phantom demon says, shuffling his greatcoat up to cover his ears. His face is scrunched up in irritation, although this seems so close to his normal expression she's not sure if it's because of Bellemeure or the snow.

"I thought you didn't care if Hazel lived or died?" The crunch of her footsteps is immensely satisfying. She wonders if London will see snow come Christmas. Or the sludge that passes for snow in London.

"That isn't the point. If someone is going to stop Bellemeure and bring her head back to the Professor, it should be us."

"I didn't realise you were a trophy hunter."

"I'm a realist."

"You think we can stop her, just the two of us?"

He gives her a cold look. "I think we would do better than those idiots and your freckled friend."

"Our idiot, perhaps," she admits, "but the other one...I'm not so sure." A son of the First House. That would make him a prince in the demons' insulated society. "What do you know about him?"

"Lucifer's spawn? Only rumours. Humans don't survive an encounter with them and it's rare that us plebeians do." He looks bitter at the idea.

"Not ones to cross, then."

"Not if there's the slimmest chance they might survive your first strike."

Pity. Something about the strange demon makes her want to attempt one. The way he looks at her and Hazel, maybe, as though he'd lifted his boot and found them stuck to it. "You seemed to know a lot more about Steel," she comments.

"News of a House's downfall spreads quickly," he replies. "And it's better for us peasants to steer clear of the noble Houses. You learn how to recognise them."

"What about this cure? Don't you want it?"

"What use would I have for it?" He makes an oblique gesture, taking in the quiet city around them and the gently falling snow. "Bellemeure actually seems to appreciate copper class demons. I doubt I'm at risk from her."

A doubt is not as good as a certainty, but she thinks he's right. Eve does not like the relief she feels at the thought. In most respects, she'd be better off without the man, but he's still a demon and, for now, she needs him.

She stays silent as they approach the tavern. Its windows are shuttered so she can't see its inhabitants. As they grow near, the door swings open and someone leaves, their shoulders hunched against the snow and their cap pulled low. Eve catches the door as it closes and lets Cassius go in first.

"So kind," he mutters as he precedes her.

It's less occupied than last time, although there's a tense air that makes her scan the room twice, noting the position of its customers. Noah sits with a young man—boy, really, with the scruff of a sprouting beard—off to the side and she makes for him.

"You have all of it?" Noah asks. The boy nods and replies in a German thickened by a rural accent so strong she doesn't make out more than an affirmative. Noah's gaze lifts and he sees her. He leans back and dismisses the boy with a nod. The kid ducks away, his heavy factory boots marking his exit.

Eve slides into the empty chair. "We met Bellemeure."

"Yes?" he says, inviting her to explain.

Eve folds her hands on the table. "We'll help her attack Asmodeus." She ignores the sharp sound of Cassius' indrawn breath. "My friend can get people in. Or out, if that's your preference."

Noah is built solidly, a Reaper's frame, and his broad barrel of a chest rises three times before he speaks. "How do we know we can trust you?"

"Look at us." She includes Cassius in her gesture. "If it comes to it, do you really think we'd side with a Count?"

"It *will* come to it," he warns.

The words speak to some bloodthirsty part of her that wants nothing more than to rout the demons from the palace and burn the place down behind her as she goes. "Good," she says, levelly.

"Then be ready by dawn," he replies, shoving off from the table and standing. "Meet us at the palace gates."

Dawn gives them very little time to warn Hazel and persuade her to help. "Wouldn't it be better—"

The door bursts open, banging against the stone wall and tearing off one hinge. Shouts of "Don't move!" and "Stop!" reverberate through the tavern as what seems like a horde of people pours in through the door. The handful of customers in the tavern leap up, hurtling furniture out of their way to escape, or attack.

Cassius hauls her out of the chair and slams her against the wall, bracing his own body over hers. "What in Lucifer's name is that woman doing now?" he spits out. But the strangers wear the blue uniform of the Gendarmerie. It's a raid.

"Noah!" she shouts.

The big Reaper demon is on his feet, talons bared. One of the strangers tackles him to the floor. Eve hesitates. Even if this isn't her agency, she owes it the loyalty of a colleague. She should support them in taking down the insurgents.

But Noah is her ticket to Bellemeure and to ending this case so she can go home. She swears and grabs the nearest weapon; a tin cup discarded on the floor.

It's too late; her hesitation has caused more agents to swarm Noah. She can't see him at all.

"You there!" someone shouts and suddenly the liaison agent appears in front of her, a sword pointed squarely at her throat. He levels her with a cold smile. "Miss Wilson," he says. "What a surprise to see you here."

She lunges at him and Cassius throws an arm across her chest, keeping her pressed to the wall. "Don't be stupid," he hisses.

The demons who attacked Noah have stopped fighting and two of them are standing back up. She can't see the third, or the Reaper. Damn it.

"Agent Gruber," she says, searching for composure. "I've been investigating this group on behalf of the London agency. We believe they're in contact with our rogue demon. Call off your dogs before they make an interrogation impossible."

That cold smile does not fade. "I think not," he says in English, throwing her. Then he digs into his pocket and holds up a slip of paper; a telegram. "No British agents in Vienna," he reads. "Impersonators to be arrested and extradited. London supports lethal force."

A shiver begins somewhere in the soles of her feet and travels slowly up her body, making the whole room feel as though it's caught in an earthquake.

"You and your partner, miss Wilson," the agent says, "are under arrest."

CHAPTER TWENTY-FIVE

I pace between the trees, rubbing my arms to keep warm. My revolver bumps against my thigh as I walk, a comforting burden. Steel had agreed to wait in the palace to keep anyone from following me, but I feel his attention as though he's watching me through a spyglass. It was easy, earlier, vowing to bring Asmodeus to justice. Now that I have to actually do it, I find myself grasping at loose threads, unable to weave them together into a coherent plan.

The Gendarmerie is corrupt, so arresting the demons will do nothing but anger them. That's if we can arrest them; we are altogether outnumbered and overpowered. Our sole hope is to use surprise or trickery. But then what? The only kind of law Asmodeus will obey is the kind enforced by its own hierarchy.

Which means we need Luka. He's the answer my brain keeps coming back to. The Count would have to listen to a representative of House Lucifer, and with Luka's help, we can implement whatever manner of justice their world enforces. If Luka agrees.

Wind gusts a flurry of snow around my ankles, whipping my coat around my legs and sending a blast of cold through me. The sun has almost set and the ground in front of my feet is barely visible; I've been treading a path on muscle memory. Eve should have been here by now.

It's too cold to wait for much longer. I peer through the trees once more and, seeing nothing but snow, turn and make for the palace. Luka's leverage, my brain suggests, is his reputation. It's one of the only things he cares about. That and his bloodline. We can use both.

Something makes me stop. The trees hiss in the wind, a steady *shh-shh* as though they're urging me to stay quiet. Around me the branches make black contours against the white snow and the gloomy shadows beyond. The palace is visible through them, a dim square dotted with the occasional glow from a lit window. There's nothing out here but me.

And yet I can't shake a sudden awareness of my limbs heavy by my sides, or my heartbeat, quickening with every breath. The palace is far enough away that it would take more than five minutes to reach if I sprinted.

From somewhere nearby comes the crack of a gunshot. Steel's attention shifts away from me, his spot in my mind dimming like a lamp sputtering out. Bellemeure's promised attack, come early?

But as I listen with held breath, no more shots come. There's the sound of shouting—a lone voice, a guard—and a high-pitched whinny. Then another, sounds of horses in distress. The stables.

The wind drops and in the moment before it howls I hear a slow, raspy exhale.

My eyes widen, the sensation oddly tangible and distant, as though my mind is cataloguing the sensation. *It was the wind,* says my rational self. *It was the wind in the trees.*

It was not the wind.

I listen intently as my brain scrambles to come up with a plan and fails: the distance to the palace is too far; Steel is distracted by whatever's happening at the stables (*conveniently,* my brain notes); I won't be able to reach my revolver in time.

The wind has picked up again, blowing against the back of my head, sweeping my scent away. I replay the noise in my head, the breath of air, the hoarse growling undertone: it must be ten feet away at least. There's a chance—a slim one—that it might not have noticed me yet. Very, very slowly, I turn my head.

The darkness of the forest masks the gaps between the trees. I can't pick out any movement, not even the shine of eyes in the shadows. There are six cartridges in my revolver, but I need to see the thing to have a chance of shooting it.

I lower into a crouch, card my fingers through the snow. I discard a couple of small twigs, keeping my gaze pinned on the darkness of the forest, before I seize on a fallen pine cone. I clutch it in one hand, my eyes so wide they water. The trees are hissing again, obscuring any sounds that might give me a clue as to what's out there.

Holding my breath, I flick my wrist. The pine cone sails through the trees and lands somewhere in the distance with a soft thud. There's a rustle and a snap of twigs. *Something* leaps through the trees after it. I don't wait to find out what.

I run in the opposite direction, away from the palace, and dig in my pocket for my gun. Six shots and I'll need light to make them count.

The wind in the trees blends with the crunch of my footsteps in the snow. I dodge the largest of the fallen branches, but a smaller one cracks under my heel. My breath catches; I dart left, cling to a broad trunk and freeze.

There's a shuffling sound; something moving through the snow. It pauses, then starts again. This one is slower than the creature we met in the lodge. I should be able to get a better shot.

Where the hell is Eve?

Whatever it is, it's between me and the palace. I take a step back, keeping the tree between me and it. No quick movement follows, just the same scuffling sounds. I keep going, holding my revolver in one hand and steadying it with the other, feeling out each step before I shift my weight. In my mind's eye, I picture the layout of the gardens. If I head north, I should be able to circle around and reach the gravel walk behind the palace; the stable side, where Steel is.

I graze a low-hanging branch and a swathe of snow falls to the ground, making a muffled *thump*. Pivoting, I change tack, walking backwards and getting as far from the tree as possible. The wind is blowing into my ear, now, dampening the sound of its gait. Still keeping my scent away, though, and I make sure to keep it that way as I move.

The lights of the palace have vanished behind the trees. It's impossible to tell how much distance I'm covering in the dark; every minute feels an hour, and my face and fingers are going numb with cold. I won't have to wait for it to kill me; much longer and my hands will be too frozen to shoot properly.

A sense of space opens at my back. I pause, looking over my shoulder. The black silhouettes of trees against the blue-black sky make a rough circle. Squinting, I step into the clearing. The vague skeleton of a building rises against the clouds; wooden posts spearing into nothing, a door frame without a door. The burnt remnants of the lodge.

The fire may not have reached its cellar. I can hide there until the thing passes and make my way back. I duck in through the empty frame, find the stairs—what's left of them—and awkwardly lever myself into the cellar. My boots thud on the hard earth; there's no snow down here, only a dusting of frost from where the cellar door has been burnt away. Someone has moved the bodies, or disposed of them; the tables are all empty. At the other end of the cellar, the door that had been closed before now stands open.

Clutching my gun in a grip that makes my palm ache, I move to the side of the door and peer through it. A small oil lantern on the floor sheds enough light to illuminate an inexpertly carved tunnel braced with wooden beams. I pick up the lantern; the wick is freshly trimmed, the oil plentiful.

A noise comes from above me. Holding my breath, I lean back on my heels, peer up towards the dark square where the trap door used to be. Slow, crunching footsteps, the sounds too close together to be bipedal. Whatever it is, it's heading my way.

I make the decision in an instant and duck into the tunnel. The roof is uneven and the walls marked with indentations. I trail my hand against one to keep my balance.

The second time in a month that I've ended up in a tunnel. At least this time I don't have a ghost and an aristocrat to watch out for.

Ahead, the shaft splits. I pause at the junction, listening for any sound of pursuit. Nothing yet. Both branches look the same, and further down one I see another split. It reminds me of a story Jacob read to me years ago, about a labyrinth and a hero. Hadn't there been a monster in that one, too?

The wind is a distant murmur and my sense of Steel is faint. Dying down here would be a fantastically stupid idea.

I make my own mark on the wall, a straight line crossed twice—once feels like it's tempting fate—and start down the left hand path. If the tunnels are headed towards the palace, this route should take me in that direction. If.

The wooden beams that hold up the ceiling are little more than logs. Someone didn't care to make this place attractive, or long-lasting. I can't help but think cage, which makes sweat break out on the back of my neck.

Shadows ahead swallow the light. I lift the lantern higher, then realise I've hit a dead end. No, not quite—a door blocks my path. I press my hand against it, note the heaviness of the wood. A small section is cut out at my eye level. It's barred, too much like a cell door to be a coincidence. Peering through, holding up the lantern, I glimpse a long table and a collection of what looks like glass objects. What I wouldn't give for supernatural strength right now.

From somewhere behind me comes a scraping noise.

There's no handle on this side of the door, no padlock or bolts, either. My brain throws out a wild suggestion to dig around it, which might be amusing if there wasn't something stalking me. I put my shoulder to the door and shove, clenching my jaw when it only shifts. I'm not strong enough to kick it down and the bars are too narrow to reach through. It would take a demon to break it.

Which gives my brain an even more ridiculous idea, and I swear under my breath. But with a locked door in front and a who-knows-what behind, I'm low on options.

I tuck myself against the wall where the hinges are. Judging by the padlocks and the bolts on the door that had led me into the tunnel, this one probably has the same kind of reinforcements. But almost no one looks at the hinges.

The scraping noise gets closer. Footsteps, but now the sound is louder and I can hear one step dragging, as though the thing's injured. I put my hand over the lantern, blocking most of the light and directing the rest to stream over the floor. It'll see me as soon as it turns into this part of the tunnel, but that's what I'm counting on.

More slow footsteps, and with my other hand I grip my revolver, take aim at the curved wall at the far end of the tunnel. I count my breaths to keep them steady.

Then something slides into view, a leg—no, a paw—then a shoulder, furred, and a torso, part fur and part skin. It lumbers around the corner, dragging a hind leg that looks almost completely human. Its head swings to look down the corridor at me and my heart jumps. It has a wolf's head.

It's also steaming. Curls of heated air waft from its humanoid parts, just visible in the light, and evaporate before they reach the ceiling. Revenant body parts stitched to a wolf. A new breed of demon.

CHAPTER TWENTY-SIX

"**W**hat do you think?"

I start so hard that I bang my spine against the door. Down the tunnel, the wolf-creature's muzzle wrinkles and it emits a low snarl. I turn my head, trying to keep one eye on the demon. A shadowy figure stands behind the barred window.

"Hanna." I drop my hand so the lantern reveals her. Though they're not Revenant black, her eyes seem to swallow its light. "What the hell is going on? What are you doing here?"

She clicks her tongue thoughtfully. "I thought you might have found this place sooner, but, ah well. I suppose I should be impressed that you are still alive."

"This is your doing." I gesture to the creature, whose gaze seems to be fixed on the barred window, on Hanna. "And the others, too."

"Who else would it be? But you knew that already—I noticed you poking about in my rooms. Find anything interesting?" Her voice is calm, as if we're speaking of a new novel over tea and cake.

"I should have confronted you then." If I had, if I'd done *something*, I might have been able to put a stop to this.

Her lips stretch but don't quite form a smile. "Then you would have died sooner and I would not have been able to complete this experiment."

"This is an experiment?" In the corner of my eye, I see the wolf-creature take a slow step forward. I can't tell if Hanna notices. I can't tell if she would care even if she did; her expression is flat, empty.

"It steams, you see, but it does not light. It has not faced anyone with a revolver, though," she muses. "Perhaps I should have shot it."

The fragmented pieces come together to form a picture that I'd glimpsed but hadn't seen in its entirety. "You're trying to create magic."

"That is not inaccurate," she allows. "Although I would perhaps use the word—what is it in English—transfer?"

Another slow step. It will be a gamble; the thing could well be coming after me, but the way its eyes are white at the edges and so unerringly fixed on the window... I tighten my clammy grip on the revolver. "And you thought the best way to give yourself Revenant abilities was like this? Stitching body parts together to see what lives?"

"Natürlich," she says. "Science is already beginning to outstrip what we can do with magic. If we cannot keep pace with you humans, you will eradicate us."

"Perhaps that's for the best. Perhaps you'd deserve it."

A look of condescension. "I am sure I would think the same, were I in your position."

My stomach is tight and sick at the thought of what other experiments she might have done, the others she must have planned. There's nothing else she can say that I want to hear.

In a quick movement, I leap to the other side of the tunnel, and yank my revolver up to aim at the topmost hinge. In the small space, the shot makes the world go strangely, throbbingly silent even as I feel the vibration of a growl rip through the cavity of my chest. The hinge fractures, coming loose. I throw myself to the ground, still clutching the lantern, trying to aim my revolver in case I'm wrong and this is how I die.

But the wolf-thing jumps over me in a flicker of shadow. Sound returns with the crash of the door bursting open under its weight. Hanna yells something, but the words are swallowed by the sound of snarling and shattering glass.

I toss the lantern over the battered door now half embedded into the tunnel wall. The creature pins Hanna to the floor, snapping and growling. Steam pours off it in waves, and a faint flicker licks over its skin. Hanna struggles, shouts, and it sinks its teeth into her throat, cutting off her cry in a gurgle. Shaking, I check my revolver and click back the safety. The creature ignores me, savaging at the Revenant with teeth and claws. The woman rakes at the wolf's body, her own blunted talons leaving ragged tears in its skin. But even though it yelps, it doesn't let go.

I stand behind the wolf, aim my revolver so one shot will go straight through its skull. Then I hesitate. The woman's motions grow fainter. Without a Revenant's special brand of magic, she's weak. I lift my aim, just a little, and pull the trigger.

The bullet leaves a hole in her forehead above her left eye. Her arms fall limp, though the monster tearing at her throat does not seem to notice. I click back the safety a second time—four bullets left—and take a second shot.

This one goes through the base of its skull and out the other side, tearing open a bloody wound and rupturing Hanna's face a second time. The monster shudders, once, and the fledgling flames on its body wink out. It slumps, dying with its teeth still inside her.

I shoot a third time, just in case. The wolf's body jerks at the impact. Hanna's eyes are wide open, the colour brown and human despite all her plotting.

Putting my revolver back into my pocket—my hands should be shaking, but somehow they're steady—I take a look around. Glass beakers lie shattered on the floor and a nearby table holds the remains of some kind of chemical station, all tubes and wires. The walls are better supported in here and another closed door leads out of the space, this one unbarred. I push it open and close it behind me, blocking the view of the bodies. The corpses that I'd put there.

Quickly I cut off that thought. Now is not the time.

There's a little stairwell that leads into a storeroom filled with barrels; an old wine cellar. Slipping the gun into my coat pocket, I move through the silent casks and emerge into a white and gold corridor, back in the palace. It takes me a moment to get my bearings; I'm not far from Hanna's rooms. It would only have taken her a couple of moments to walk from her bedroom to this...laboratory.

I'll have to tell Steel. The question of what to do about the monsters has been resolved with Hanna's death and if—when—the rest of Asmodeus finds her body, there won't be any hiding the bullet holes.

My fingers pluck aimlessly at my skirts. I realise I haven't moved, have been staring blindly at the carved gilt frame of some oil painting. It is another long moment before I recognise the sound of approaching footsteps. I turn my head, watch a tall, dark-haired figure round the corner. Not Steel, I tell myself, though I rock forward on instinct. Luka.

The demon walks towards me in his neat, precise stride. His eyes flicker to the door behind me, to my hands. "You look as though you need a drink," he says, curtly. "Did something happen?"

"I..." Words don't come. My brain seems strangely blank and stupid.

Luka's hand grips my shoulder. "You need wine. Or whatever it is they drink in your country." He steers me in front of him and keeps walking, herding me through the corridor until we reach a dainty parlour. "Sit," he orders, pushing me into a chair, then goes rummaging in a cabinet. "I am sure Hannah will not mind if I raid her supplies," he mutters and I startle, look around with more awareness.

The bookcases are filled with crates and vials, and the cabinet Luka is rifling through sits next to a bar topped with bottles of various spirits. Dust collects in the corners and a spider has made an elaborate home under the drapes by a window.

"Here." A small tulip shaped glass appears in front of me, filled with an amber-coloured liquid. I glance up, find a similar glass in Luka's hand. He drinks it in one mouthful, meeting my gaze, and I take the one he offers me.

It has too much burn to taste anything and I cough into my fist. Warmth seeps through my chest, easing a chill that I had long ago stopped noticing. "Kind of you," I say, when I can clear my throat.

"Do not fear, I do not make kindness a habit." He takes the glass from me and puts it on a round table by my chair. The table is set for afternoon tea, one plate filled with the scraps of bread and butter, a second empty, the cutlery beside it untouched. "Something happened," he says, standing by the second chair. He's as still and as beautiful as a sculpture.

"Where's Steel?"

"The stables. There was an attack."

"Bellemeure?"

"If so, she was unsuccessful. They only slaughtered a few of the horses."

The word *only* snags at me. I look away, my gaze falling on the table. The knife's handle is engraved with a dainty leaf pattern.

"I think," says Luka, "that we should discuss what Steel is going to do next, after Bellemeure."

"You shouldn't be having that discussion with me," I reply. "Have it with Steel."

"He is confused. You have confused him."

The parlour is uncomfortably warm. I shrug out of my coat, drop it over the arm of the chair. "You've not shown much interest in what he does or why he does it," I say. "Why is this suddenly so important?"

"It was important the moment I realised Lyr had a son. He was not supposed to—" Luka stops.

I ponder the pause, swallowing. The drink has left a bitter aftertaste on my tongue. "Supposed to happen?" I guess. "What, you assumed he would live an empty life?"

"I assumed he would know better than to threaten the authority of the First House."

"You said yourself he has no claim on the throne, or whatever it is your House uses."

"We do not permit mistakes."

"What does that mean?" My heartbeat picks up, registering a threat in the cool way Luka looks at me. "Steel is not a mistake."

"If I let him leave, he will be."

"He doesn't want anything to do with House Lucifer."

"But he has a brother, now. Family."

"Why does it matter?" The room blurs, as though the walls are coated in a fine layer of steam. Luka isn't a Revenant, though.

"We have not become the First House by allowing cast off scions to reach their full strength."

"Lyr was strong." Something flashes through his expression, something that makes my body go tense for new reasons, though it's gone in less than a moment. "Until he was killed," I say, slowly, "by Revenants."

"A pity."

"Did you know?"

Luka watches me, stroking the thin stem of his glass.

"If you want me to persuade him to stay with you, you're wasting your time," I say and stand. The world tilts sideways. Gasping, I clutch at the chair to remain standing.

"How disappointing," Luka says, as if from a great distance. "I thought you would be smarter than to accept a drink from a demon."

CHAPTER TWENTY-SEVEN

The door, Steel—

I sway forward, reaching, but my fingers meet cloth. Luka's there, stopping me. "Now, now," he murmurs, his voice arctic, "we have not finished our discussion."

He pushes on my shoulders. I fold back into the chair, grabbing at the table for balance. My head aches, heavy and full. "Drugged," I breathe. I'm a fool, I'm an *idiot*.

"What did you do to Hanna?"

The question swims through my mind as I stare at the leaf-patterned cutlery on the table. "What?"

"She and her little pets should have taken care of you by now," he continues, dropping to one knee in front of me. "What did you do?"

Taken care of... The guilt that I'd been carefully not looking at burns away in anger. "I stopped her."

"You?" His laugh is scornful. "What could you possibly do to one of us?"

"Go into the tunnels and find out."

The amusement in his face seeps away, leaving a wintry expression that makes his familiar visage look suddenly alien.

"Was it you who poisoned me?" I ask.

"If not for that imp," he says, "we would be half way to my House by now, this petty nonsense with Bellemeure behind us. If she even truly exists."

I ignore the way the edges of my vision have gone dim and say slowly, steadily, "You're a monster."

"Perhaps." His hand touches my knee and I jerk in shock. "It would have been easier, if you had died by another's blade—cleaner. He'll know if I do it. But if I cannot kill you, then I will ruin you for him."

His meaning takes my lethargic brain a moment to understand and when I do I flinch from him, lean heavily on the table. "You don't want me."

"Of course not," he admits easily. "I have no interest in you whatsoever. But when Steel learns that you threw yourself at his own brother... Well, there will be nothing left for him here."

"He won't—" Slowly, deep breaths, keep my pulse steady. "He won't believe you."

"I am his family. What are you to him?"

"I..." I don't have a weapon. I need a weapon. *My kingdom for a sword*, my addled mind sings.

Luka's hand bunches my skirt, his fingers brushing bare skin. His other hand slips to my back. "You may not be a beauty," he murmurs, "but you'll be sweet for me, won't you?"

His touch is soft, but sure. He hasn't even bothered to restrain me or hold me down. He's left himself vulnerable because he doesn't think I can do anything about it. The same way

Bellemeure thought me so insignificant that she handed me off to her men to dispose of. The same way Rayne hadn't imagined I could fight back. I was nothing to them.

My fingers curl and the handle of the knife bites into my palm. I'm tired of being nothing.

When the blade touches his neck, he freezes. "Now," I whisper, wrapping my other hand around his cravat, making him look at me, "let's finish our discussion."

"A kitchen knife?" Luka mocks. "What do you think you can do with that? It is not even Blessed."

In answer, I press harder, forcing his chin up. "Quiet," I tell him. "Did you know about Lyr?" My voice is low and hoarse, though the words come without exertion, without thought. My control is in tatters.

"I did not give the order."

"That isn't what I asked."

He looks down at me through his thick lashes. "Why take this from him so soon after he has found it?"

"You are not his family," I say. "You are nothing to him."

"Are you willing to put that to the test?"

The door opens. Steel. *Steel.* "Hazel?" His footsteps pause and then; "What the fuck are you doing? *Get your hands off her!*"

Luka wrenches his hands from me and holds them up, visible. "I am not the one holding a knife," he protests.

"Do not." Now my hands are shaking. "Do not address him." Blood trickles down his neck, beading on his collar. I'm not close enough to the carotid artery to do any permanent damage. I shift the knife to a better position.

"Hazel? Are you all right?"

I ignore Steel. "Tell him the truth."

Luka's mouth twists.

"Tell him what happened to Lyr." In the blurry corner of my vision, Steel pauses.

Luka grinds his teeth, his jaw flexing, then says, "I did not know until after it was done."

"What?"

"I swear it," Luka continues. His throat bobs, and a fresh bead of blood seeps down his neck. "The decision was made without me. They could not take the risk that Lyr would return to challenge them. They...made sure he would not."

The silence in the room is as heavy as freshly fallen snow. After a long moment I turn my head slightly—the room tilts again—to see Steel staring at Luka as though the demon had stabbed him in the chest. Well. That's not so inadequate a comparison, I suppose.

Then in a blur of movement, Steel takes Luka by the scruff of his jacket and rips him from my hands so quickly I lurch forward. The demon goes sprawling on the floor, coughing and clutching his throat.

"Get out," Steel demands, his voice thrumming. I sense his magic in the air like the scent of rain before a storm.

Luka picks himself up. "It would be safer to be brothers than enemies," he warns.

"Get *out*!"

The door bangs against the wall as he leaves. Steel grabs it and flings it shut, then stands facing it, his head bowed, his shoulders heaving.

My vision ripples and I grunt, shake my head. A moment later Steel is kneeling in front of me, reaching for the knife. He has to pry my fingers away one by one before he can put it back on the table. His expression, when he looks at me, is shattered. With a suppressed sound, I reach for him.

His face twists and he takes my hands. "What happened?" he asks, his voice a rasp.

I droop forward, resting my head on his shoulder and trying desperately to soak up his strength. After a moment, I feel his arms come around me. My heart is melting. *I* am melting.

"You are not yourself."

This strikes me as hilarious. Who else would I be? Who else *could* I be, if I wanted? The world lurches as Steel lifts me into his arms. I forget how strong he is.

"I am a demon, you recall. I'm quite strong."

Yes, that is handy. He is quite useful, all around. I tell him so.

"Glad to be of assistance," he replies, dryly.

Dry as parchment. Dry as bleached bone.

"Do you know you're saying all this aloud?"

My head rolls back, and the ceiling moves. Wooden engravings, some strange fat fish. Dorado, perhaps. Or salmon.

"Why are you naming fish?"

Silly. If I were naming a fish, I'd name it Fred.

"Who is—You know what, never mind. I'm taking you to bed."

Thank goodness for the drug. If I was sober, I'd be blushing.

The ceiling passes in a blur, music coming from far away. It seems only a moment later that Steel's laying me down on soft bedding. My hair has come loose and it tickles my neck.

The surface dips as Steel sits beside me. He touches my face just under my eye with his thumb. "Your pupils are dilated," he says, quietly. His own are thin, serpentine.

Darkness clouds the edges of my vision, but I can still see Steel. Steel is the only thing I see. I reach up unsteadily and put my index finger to the deep line carved between his brows. He blinks, his dark lashes masking his eyes. My hand trails over the line of his eyebrow, smoothing the tiny creases as I go, then down the curve of his face to the sharpness of his cheekbone. It doesn't actually cut me, though for a second I think it might.

Steel catches my hand before I reach the corner of his lips, grips it with his own. His throat bobs. "You're drugged," he says, hoarsely, as if he's reminding himself as well as me. "You are—you are not yourself."

Words trip out over my tongue with no barrier to stop them. "You're very beautiful," I say, solemnly, though I don't just see beauty, anymore. I see the faint line at the side of his mouth where his smirk lives, I see the sparkle in his eyes when he laughs at me, I see the wrinkle in his nose that only appears when he doesn't want to do something, and the shift in his jaw when he decides to do it anyway.

My chest can't possibly be strong enough to contain this feeling.

His mouth tightens and he looks away. "That's the Leviathan blood," he mutters, bitterness crushing the words even as they leave his mouth. "It's always the face they like best."

"I don't like your face."

He snorts and says, dry again, "Well, that's a relief."

"It's true," I protest. It seems important that he knows this. "I like—I like—"

At my hesitation, his gaze flicks back to me and there's pain in it.

"I like that you make me laugh." Stupidly honest, *dangerously* honest, but I would do stupid dangerous things to take that look away. "I like that you never let me hide. I like that you always have my back. Even when you shouldn't." My voice is barely a whisper, like my mind is still trying to hold back the words but my heart—my heart that I'd never known, never cared to listen to before Steel—won't let them go unspoken. He curves over me as I speak, his breath fanning my fingers, my hand that he still holds. "I like that you care, though you pretend you don't. I like that you can take the silence away when I'm drowning in it. I love your smiles, even when they hurt. I love the way a room brightens when you're in it." I stop, finally out of words.

Silence falls between us, then he says, very, very softly, "Love?"

My hand twitches in his. Mute, I gaze up at him. My brain is silent, for once, its defences gone.

"Do you mean it?" he whispers and for some reason that stings.

"I mean everything I say," I retort and his breath huffs out in the shadow of a laugh.

"Why don't you—Why didn't you—?" I don't know what he means to say and he gives up part way through, presses my fingers to his lips instead, sending a tremor through me. I wait, exhaling carefully, and he pulls away, leaving my hand cold.

Then he lets out a strained breath and drops his head to my shoulder. "You're drugged," he says again, and I wonder if my confession damaged something in his memory.

Then my own memory wakes. I try to bolt upright and am stopped by Steel's weight against me. "I killed her."

He lifts his head a little at the words. "What? You killed who?"

"Hanna. She's in the tunnels with the wolf. I killed them both."

"The wolf…? All right, all right, we'll deal with it in the morning. You need rest."

"Luka," I whisper. "He—Your father—"

His hand tightens around my own momentarily, then he lets go, letting his hand fall to the bed alongside me, his thumb brushing my arm. His head goes back to resting on my shoulder, on the dip of my collarbone. "I don't want to talk about that," he replies, his voice tight.

"I should have killed him."

Steel's shoulders tremble and a muffled snicker escapes him. "I appreciate the thought."

He stays like that and though his voice is steady I can feel an ache, a distant pain that isn't my own. Seeking to comfort him, I rest my abandoned hand lightly on the nape of his neck. His hair is shorter here, soft as silk under my fingers. Only his forehead touches my shoulder, the rest of his body held above me, a distance between our bodies. Still, it feels like a weight on my chest, making me fight for every breath. My fingers twitch out of my control, stroking the delicate strands of hair within their reach.

"Hazel," he whispers, his voice thick, and abruptly I'm aware of the length of his body as it curls over me, the broad strength in his shoulders, the heat of his torso so close to mine. Warmth unfurls at the pit of my stomach. He pulls away and looks down at me, his eyes soft, his mouth tender. An expression that will haunt my dreams. "You need to sleep." He goes to leave and without thinking I clutch at his shirt. He's dressed for a party; impeccable black jacket, white shirt, silk cravat. I hadn't noticed.

"Stay?" I whisper, beseeching. The shadows are long and dark, and I can't see what might be in them. "Please?"

He hesitates a moment, something both painful and furious flashing through his face, then says, "Of course. Of course I will." He touches my hand, waits until I let go of him. "I'll sleep on the floor."

He always does that. "No, no, I will." I roll over to do so and nearly pitch over the edge of the bed. Steel catches me and gently hauls me back.

"No, you stay here."

"You always sleep on the floor, or the chair, or the—" I struggle to remember where else we've slept.

He doesn't seem to understand the importance of the situation; his mouth is curled up at one corner and his gaze is warm. "Yes."

"*I* will sleep on the floor," I say, doing my best to enunciate in case he didn't hear me. I try to fight him, but that amounts only to a vague waving of my hands. Still, the fact that I'm trying at all makes him let out an exasperated sigh.

"If I sleep up here, will you stop?"

"Yes." Besides, I don't have the energy to do much more than fall off the edge of the bed.

He clambers fully onto the mattress beside me, awkward in a way I've not seen him before, and then lies on his back, clasping his hands on his stomach, staring at the ceiling. He says nothing, his legs very straight. I turn on my side, curling inward, and reach out to touch his arm.

He twitches at that, turns his head to look at me. "What is it?"

"Just..." I tuck my hand against him so my knuckles rest against his arm. "I want to know you're there."

He pauses, then he turns fully on his side and clasps my querying hand with his own, holds it between us. "Better?" he asks, his eyes gleaming in the dark.

"Yes," I whisper in reply. "Thank you." With the reassurance of his hand and the rhythm of his breathing, I let my eyes fall closed and drift into sleep.

AGENT E. WILSON

"You're making a mistake," Eve calls. "We're British agents, you can't keep us here. Are you even listening to me?"

"Don't waste your time," drawls Cassius. "They're not going to keep us here; the telegram said extradite. They're going to send us back."

She throws him a glare. Sitting on the lone bench in their cell, he lifts his eyebrows and flicks his fingers at the brick walls. In the bowels of the Gendarmerie there are no windows. The cell is too small to be designed for anything other than transient criminals arrested before processing. The reinforced bars and the two armed guards standing at the door suggest this isn't the first time they've arrested a demon. Outside, Gruber bounces his ring of keys on one finger, expression triumphant.

"Let us speak to whoever's in charge," she says. "We're not impostors. Look—" She digs out her warrant card and presses it against the bars. "See?"

"Your agency disagrees," he replies.

"That telegram was false. It could have been sent by anyone."

"Then you can discuss it with them when you return to England. You should be grateful that my agents did not shoot you on sight."

She glares at him through the bars. "You've been looking for an opportunity to arrest us ever since we told you we were investigating Asmodeus."

"Count von Tier and his family are advisers to the Emperor." The agent hands the keys to one of the guards and straightens his jacket. "They have nothing to do with this."

"How long have they been lining your pockets? Does the rest of the agency know how partial you are to bribes?" The guards at the door don't blink, so either they already know or they don't care.

"You will be sent home on tomorrow's train," Gruber continues, ignoring her. "Members of your agency will meet you in London."

"Where's Noah? What did you do with him?"

"The insurgents have been dealt with."

"Meaning?"

"Dead," murmurs Cassius.

The agent glances at him, frowning. "You will not move from that bench, Phantom."

"That may become rather messy. Not to mention fragrant."

"Agencies only use lethal force if absolutely necessary," Eve says, drawing the other man's attention back to her. "Those demons should have been arrested and tried in a court of law."

"Agencies exist outside the law. Surely as an agent you would know that?"

"Not like this," she grits out.

"I do not have time to debate our working practices. You two," he says to the guards. "Watch them. If they try anything, shoot them." He marches out of the jail, slamming the door shut behind him.

Eve pushes herself off the bars and paces across the stone floor. The cell is ten feet by eight, and she covers the distance in seconds.

"Well?" Cassius tilts his head against the wall and watches her. "Do you have any other brilliant ideas?"

"You're the demon," she replies, gesturing at the bars. "You're the one who's supposed to get me out of situations like this."

"Phantom," he reminds her. "If you wanted brute strength, you should have bound a Reaper."

"None of this is what I wanted." She stops pacing and stares at the bare brick wall, keeping her back to Cassius and the guards so they can't see how hard she bites her lip. Three weeks of work and she's behind bars, waiting to be extracted.

Monaghan knows that she turned against him. God knows what he's going to do to the others. What he's already doing to them. It was a stupid idea, following Steel and his bloody family drama.

"Wilson." She's so deep in her thoughts she doesn't register the word as her name at first. Then Cassius says, "Eve," in a low, urgent voice, and she turns.

The demon jerks his head at the closed door. She frowns at him, causing him to roll his eyes and tap one of his ears. Tilting her head, she tries to hear whatever he's picked up. Nothing at first, just the murmur of people talking and moving that the door can't quite muffle. Then the sound of splintering wood cuts through the faint noise and the room outside erupts with shouts. Gunshots sound in the distance.

The guards twitch, turning instinctively towards the door, but their feet stay fused to the ground. Eve seizes her opportunity.

"The agency's under attack," she says, striding forward to grip the bars with both hands. "It could be demons." More crashing noises come from the other room; furniture being hurled into a wall.

"Your agency is understaffed," Cassius adds. "I doubt it'll survive a full frontal assault."

The guards look at each other, doubt making their faces slack and stupid.

"If they kill us in here because you idiots were too slow to stop them…" She trails off, but it's enough.

"Don't move," one commands, as they flank the door.

"Where are we supposed to go?" mutters Cassius.

The way they brace themselves and clutch the hilts of their sabres makes Eve think they might actually succeed. Then they fling the door open and run straight into Chang.

She makes quick work of them, so quick Eve doesn't catch more than a spray of blood and a scream of agony. When it's over, she kicks the crumpled bodies aside and takes a step into the jail. Her outfit is a nondescript set of worker's overalls, her hair a long tail.

Eve greets her with a scowl. "Come to free us?"

"Free you?" she repeats. "How do you think they found us? Or do you think they just stumbled in while they were on patrol?"

"What do you mean?"

"I mean you were *followed*." Dirt smudges her cheek and her eyes are forbidding, black and bottomless in the dim light. "House Asmodeus were tailing you and you led them straight them to us."

"That's not possible. I would have realised, or Cassius would have smelled them." She looks at him to confirm it.

For once, he doesn't try to hide behind sarcasm or wit. "I would have," he says, simply. "My nose is not the best but it's good enough to scent Revenants."

"See? There's no way they could have followed us."

Chang just looks at her.

"The only people who knew where we were going were Hazel and the others. She would never have given us up and Steel—Steel wanted Bellemeure more than any of us." She glances at Cassius who protests, "Why would I arrange to have *myself* arrested?"

Which only leaves... "Luka," she breathes.

"Careless," says Chang, turning away. "I expected more."

"Wait! You can't leave us here."

"Why not?" The demon looks over her shoulder, one hand on the doorjamb. "Why should I care about you and your pet?"

"Because we're the same, you and me." The words are dredged from somewhere Eve doesn't want to think about too closely. "We want to protect our family."

The woman scoffs. "You're so desperate to be one of them that you've fastened the collar around your own neck. We are not the same."

"What would you have done? Starve to death because you're too proud to take what you're given? I'm not ashamed of wanting to make something of myself."

"Perhaps you should be."

"And become a murderer, like you?" Eve shoots back. "Those men were human. But it doesn't look like you give a damn from where I'm standing."

Chang pivots to face her. "Behind bars? Because that's where your so-called morals have led you."

"Not through her own fault," Cassius interjects. "The London agency put us here because they don't want us helping. *Anyone*, not just humans. That's all she's been trying to do since she got here—help. Much to my irritation," he adds, under his breath.

Eve wraps her hands tighter around the bars, feeling the rough iron imprint her palms. "That's all I want," she says, quietly. "To help my friends. My family."

The other woman examines her in silence for a long moment while Eve tries not to hold her breath. Chang glances away, scowls, then looks back. "I wasn't given orders to kill you," she says begrudgingly, as though she's still angry over the fact. "And if I left you here, you'd just starve to death." She kicks over one of the guards and tears a set of keys from his belt, then tosses it at Eve. It clangs against one of the bars and lands at her feet.

Eve scoops it up before the demon can change her mind. "Thank you."

"I wouldn't," she replies, as Eve flicks through the keys. "Not if your goal is to save your friend."

She stops, looking up. "You mean Hazel?"

Chang hesitates, then says, "If you make it to the palace by dawn, you might still save her." And with a flick of her dark hair, she's gone.

AGENT J. HORNER

Jacob checks his pocket watch for the hundredth time. Ten minutes past three. A little over fifty minutes before Khurana considers him a lost cause. He tucks the watch into his breast pocket with trembling fingers. Max is watching him warily.

"I am *fine*," he says, stressing the last word. "There is nothing to fear."

"I could do this alone, if you prefer," Max offers. Khurana had taken them through the ritual amendment last night and it was still new and odd, being able to go so far from each other. Jacob had to fight back an instinctual surge of anxiety every time Max stepped over that invisible twenty foot mark. He almost missed the pain.

"I'm not going to leave you." Not unless Max asks, which he hasn't done yet.

Hooves clatter on the cobblestones behind him as a cab passes. The agency's black double doors have been recently painted and a new gold plaque on the wall beside them reads *Her Majesty's Private Investigation Agency: Professor John Monaghan.*

Inside, the Agency is quiet. His boot heels click on the stone as he passes the kitchen. Where Maia would be bustling around the fire, the new French chef is snoozing in a chair beside it, his apron ties drooping. There's no one else around. Though the place smells of lemon and fresh paint, it feels hollow.

"The professor will be in his study," whispers Max.

Jacob nods, takes the stairs without looking into the dark empty dining room. He doesn't have time to linger.

The first floor seems deserted; even the desk where Miller normally sits is empty. Drawing in a deep breath, Jacob starts down the passage. A short, sharp sound emerges from one of the parlours as he passes its open door. He takes another two steps before recognising it as a cry of pain.

Stopping, he turns, peering through the gap the door leaves. Blythe's Reaper demon sits in an armchair, his talons clawing through the fabric. Thick ropes keep him tied to it, motionless, and blood runs in rivulets down his bared chest. Clara's Hound faces him, holding a dagger.

Horror fuses him to the floor. He can't help but watch as the demon adjusts a knife in her hand and makes a cut—another cut—in the Reaper's skin. Jacob recognises the blade; it's one of the blessed weapons they keep locked up in the trophy room.

"What happened to the others?" comes Clara's voice. "Where is Khurana?"

The Reaper demon lets out a grunt but doesn't answer. Valerian. His name is Valerian. Jacob finds enough control to move slightly, to shift his view so he can see the young woman standing by the window, her back turned to the sun.

Something tugs at his sleeve. He forces himself to look away, to meet Max's gaze. "We must go," the demon murmurs. He looks sick, like all the life has drained from him. "We must see the professor."

Jacob wobbles. He has fifty minutes before Khurana considers him dead—closer to forty five, now. He cannot waste a moment.

And yet. He looks again at Max's drawn face and cannot turn away.

The door swings open and comes to a stop before it cracks into the wall. He pauses in the doorway, a mouse facing down two feuding alley cats. Clara stares at him. She wears her pretty teal ribbons again, though a few locks of hair have comes loose from her bun.

"Horner," she says. "You came back."

Jacob's brain works feverishly. She'd been asking where they were, what happened to Khurana, so the Reaper has told her nothing. "What are you doing?" he asks, gambling for more time. "Why is this demon injured?" He catches Clara rolling her eyes and flushes. "Do you have permission for this?" he adds, gesturing to the ropes, the blood, avoiding the dark eyes of the Hound.

Clara folds her arms. "Just because you're a Reaper agent doesn't mean you outrank me."

He seizes on this avenue. "That is exactly what it means. Max." He flicks his fingers towards the bound demon, hoping Max can read his intention. "This demon's agent is dead. He needs to be assessed for redistribution." Max, passing him, flinches and Jacob stumbles over his words. "I'll—I will speak to the professor about where he can do the most good."

"It isn't human," Clara says, with a surprised kind of smile. "You don't have to call it 'he'."

Oh, this is much worse than he thought. "We are not in the habit of partnering with monsters," he replies, stiffly.

Max growls at the Hound demon, who backs away. Her expression is thoughtful and she watches as the Reaper demon is freed.

"You said his agent was dead." Clara moves to the door, her gait casual, her position anything but. "How did you survive?"

"I had Max," he replies, pivoting to keep an eye on her. Out of the two of them, he isn't sure which is more dangerous. "But Khurana did not."

"Ah. That's a pity."

"How can you do this?" he bursts out. "How can you think of them as inhuman?" Her smile falters. Only for a moment, but he pounces on it. "You don't, do you? Think of them that way. This is just for Monaghan."

"You've seen what demons can do to a person," says Clara, throwing him. "You've seen how easily they can peel off our skin and rip out our organs. And that isn't taking into account what they can do with magic. They could *rule us* without doing more than clenching their fist. If you can't see that," she goes on, "then you're a fool."

"This is not a line I am willing to cross," he says, gritting his teeth. Max has freed the other demon and stands with their arm slung around his shoulders. "And this isn't you. He ordered you to do this, didn't he? What does he expect to gain?"

"Am I to assume that you mean me?" The professor stands in the doorway. Tiberius is with him, and as the man steps inside the demon slinks around him, advancing on Max. Max, who is burdened with the other Reaper's slack form and cannot raise his hands to defend himself.

Jacob's hand flies to his dagger, but then a knife presses against his throat, cold and startling. "A-ah," breathes the Hound demon in his ear. "No moving."

Shit, he thinks. "Yes," he answers the man, because there's no point lying any more. "What is all this for? What do you want?"

"In the summer, I sent you to eradicate those Blood Drinker demons. You saw what they did. Can you truly not understand why I would make this choice?"

He thinks of the nest they'd found on that case, the gruesome pile of limbs, and twitches from the memory. "You can't kill all of them."

"No," he says, unexpectedly. "But once we alter the summoning ritual, we will be able to subdue the rest."

Alter the ritual—he's trying to use magic?

"Tiberius," Max whispers, with such pain it makes him ache. "Help us. Please. Don't listen to him."

The scruffy demon looks at his partner. His amber eyes are the eyes of a tiger sizing up its next meal. "I would rather be at the head of what remains," Tiberius says in his gravelly voice, "than crushed under the heel of progress."

"This isn't *progress*," Jacob cries out, "this is *murder*!"

"You will be gratified to know that you will not die," Monaghan says, ignoring him. "I may need you to bridle the

Leviathan. Agent Ward, take him downstairs. You will obey, demon, if you care for his life," he adds, to Max.

"Don't—" he protests, but the knife at his throat cuts and a warm trail tells him it's drawn blood.

Max wilts. "I will obey," he whispers.

"Good. Ward."

Clara nods and Jacob is pushed out of the room, the threat of the knife never leaving his neck. His last sight before the door closes is of Max watching him leave, the professor behind him, expressionless.

CHAPTER TWENTY-EIGHT

Awareness comes back in fragments: soft cotton under my cheek; my stays pinching my waist; the sound of breathing not my own. Slowly, cautiously, I open my eyes.

Steel lies sleeping, his face half smothered in the pillow and his mouth open. He still holds my hand, his fingers laced through my own. The night before comes back to me in a sudden rush. I'd said—I'd told him—

I hold myself very still, desperate not to wake him until I've parcelled my feelings together. I was honest—too honest—about how I felt. He hadn't said the same. But he'd stayed. I watch his eyes shift beneath their lids. He'd stayed with me.

Dawn light filters through the window, glinting off a layer of dust coating the wardrobe. My room, though getting here is something of a blur. I remember Steel carrying me, and before that the parlour where Luka...

I pause, waiting for rage or shame to well up at the thought of the demon, but instead I'm just cold. My fingers twitch, and, beside me, Steel stirs. His eyes flutter open, bleary and glazed. They focus on me and his expression tightens, his hand gripping mine, then abruptly he softens. I can almost see the memories trickle through his mind.

"Good morning," he says, in a voice still rough with sleep.

"Good morning," I whisper.

"Are you all right?" He lifts onto his elbow, frowning at me. "Any lasting effects?"

I sit up hesitantly, waiting for the room to tilt, but the world stays where it should be. "I don't think so."

"Do you—" He pauses and lets go of my hand. I hold my breath. He says, "Last night you said you killed someone."

Oh. Shame finds me then, and dread, and by the flicker of his expression he senses it. "There was another demon in the woods."

"What?" His gaze sweeps over my body, searching for injuries. "You're not hurt?"

"No. I heard it while I was waiting for Eve and hid in that laboratory we found." I rub both hands over my face in an effort to avoid his gaze while I piece the rest of the night together. "There are tunnels under the garden connecting it to the palace."

"So it *is* Asmodeus."

"It was Hanna. She was trying to replicate their fire magic. The demon...attacked her." He waits, and I drop my hands to meet his gaze. "I shot them both."

"Ah," he says and we sit in silence for a moment.

"They'll find her body," I add. "If they haven't already. Luka knows."

At the demon's name, Steel's fingers gouge furrows in the sheets. "I'll deal with him," he promises.

I give it another moment. He says nothing, focused on smoothing over the rents he's made in the cotton, not looking at me. "Steel. What I said last night..."

His gaze snaps to mine. "Yes?"

"I—"

Footsteps pound down the corridor outside and someone shouts, "Im Wald! Sie sind im Wald!"

Steel gets up and pulls the door open. Someone in servant's whites dashes past. "What's going on?" Steel calls after them, but he gets no answer.

I slide off the bed, the remnants of the drug making my skin feel hot, my muscles sluggish to respond. "Im Wald?" I murmur, wishing I spoke German.

Glass shatters and Steel ducks. Something hits the wall in the corridor and rolls jerkily across the floor; a rock. From outside comes more shouting. I yank on my coat. "It sounds like it's coming from the gardens."

He looks over his shoulder at me. "Bellemeure."

"She said she wouldn't be here until the twelfth."

"Then she changed her mind. Or she lied," he replies, grimly. "Come on."

He leads the way into the corridor, moving cautiously but quickly, staying away from the windows. As we ease down the stairs to the ground floor the sound of yelling grows louder, along with an odd roaring noise that takes me a moment to place; fire. The Revenants are fighting.

"We need to get out of here," I tell Steel, snatching a breath as we pause to peer around a corner.

"We need to find Bellemeure." He presses himself to the wall by a window, peels back a drape to see outside. I can't see much in the dim grey fog, but he exhales heavily. "They're fighting in the woods. She must be with them."

"Along with an army of demons," I remind him.

"Go to the stables," he orders, letting the curtain fall. "It's on the other side of the palace, they're not fighting there. I'll meet you once I've found Bellemeure."

"I can't just leave you."

"What can you do against them?" he asks, with an edge of ruthlessness that reminds me of his brother. "You're human."

"What if it's a trap?"

"I'll be fine. You need to be safe."

"But—"

"Trust me. I can do this." He lopes down the corridor and disappears.

The clatter of bullets ricochets off the stone walls. They brought guns. I curse, then turn and run in the direction of the stables. Fire flashes through a window as I dash past. I reach the lobby, find the butler and one of the valets cowering behind the huge Christmas tree.

"They're outside the south wall," I instruct. "Go back to the northern exit, head for the city." As it is now, the attack can still be passed off as a rebellion. Bellemeure's men won't venture into the city centre, won't risk being seen by humans.

The humans stare at me, and I haul one up by the sleeve of his shirt. "I said, go." It takes me forcibly pushing him into a run for him to stumble away, and the second follows. How many other servants are still here?

"Fuck," I mutter, and change direction, run towards the kitchens.

The corridors are quiet and I bang open each door, in case others are hiding behind them. I don't find anyone until I reach the kitchen. There, the cooks and most of the maids are huddled underneath the table. "Get out of the building," I bark at them. "Get to the city."

More empty stares. For God's sake.

"Get *out*!" I yank one from under the table, but my shout spurs the others; they claw their way to the door and spill into the corridor. I follow them towards the stables. As we pass a turning into the west wing, a sharp cry catches my attention. I swing into the corridor, find the maid who'd dressed me stumbling out of the library. She looks shaken and soot streaks her cheek.

"Are you all right?" I grip her shoulders. "Are you alone?"

She shakes her head, gestures back at the library, sputtering something I don't understand.

I push her in the direction I'd come from. "That way, back to the city. You'll be safe there."

A sound behind me makes me turn. Luka stands in the doorway to the library. Smoke wreathes the ceiling behind him, obscuring the murals.

I don't have enough time to do more than open my mouth before he grabs the lapel of my coat and hauls me into the room with him. I stumble backwards against a shelf and a handful of books tumble out, hitting my shoulders with sharp corners. Long hands wrap around my throat. I scrabble at his arms, but they're as immovable as iron rods, his hands so tight on my throat I can't draw breath to scream. His eyes are narrowed to thin slivers, his face a mask of concentration.

Grabbing his arms for leverage, I kick him. Once. Twice. My heavy practical boot lands on his thigh. He gives a startled hiss and releases me, stepping out of range. I clutch at my throat, slumped against the shelves, sipping at the tiny shreds of air that are all I can draw in.

I have to get away. I have to get out.

Luka plucks me up with one hand and crushes my oesophagus with the other. From far away comes Steel's voice, calling my name. My mind is so foggy I can't sense him.

Luka releases me. The cool rush of air is heaven, but there's so little of it I have to fight to keep breathing. He slams my wrist against the floor and holds it there. My hand explodes with pain. I jerk it away from him, cradle it to my chest, and he tugs my other wrist. I open my mouth to scream but all that escapes is a strained breath.

He has a book in his other hand. The spine is thick and heavy and he smashes it against my spread fingers. The crack of bones breaking is swallowed by a whoosh of fire. When he releases me, I hunch to the floor, curled over the throbbing agony of my hands.

"Hazel?"

Fire licks at a bookshelf nearby, crackling the pages. Luka's boots take a step back, away from me, then another, then the door is closing, leaving me alone.

"You." Steel's voice, so close. "What are you doing here?"

"The palace is on fire," Luka returns crisply. "We need to get out."

"Hazel—I thought I felt—"

"That woman was chasing the servants out. Help me bar this door, we need to keep the fire from spreading. Those idiot Revenants—" He cuts off and there's a thud, the doors shuddering.

"But I have to—"

"Are you going to stand here like a fool and die? I'm getting out of here before the whole damn place caves in."

"I need to find Hazel. I can't feel her."

"Their magic is swamping your senses. You need to get clear of the building. Watch out."

"What—" Steel's voice cuts off with a hard thud and a wrenched cry. Then there's silence.

Gasping, I push myself onto my elbows, crawl towards the door. My hands throb in agony every time they graze the marble.

"Idiot," mutters Luka, on the other side. There's a shred of a gap between the two doors and through it I see Steel, crumpled on the floor. Luka picks him up with a grunt and throws him over his shoulder. With one last glance at the doors, he strides away and they vanish from my sight.

CHAPTER TWENTY-NINE

S moke coats the air, clogging my lungs. Part of my mind has walled itself off from the pain and is still, somehow, turning over. Luka has Steel. He barred the doors so I can't leave, broke my fingers so I can't get out. Choked me so I can't scream.

Think, Hazel. *Think*.

The fire eats up one wall, crisping the books in its path. Any longer and it will cover the exit completely. If I'm going to try for the door, I'll need to do it now.

I get one knee under me, push myself to my feet using my forearms. Even that movement sends jolts of pain through my hands. Smoke sears my throat and I press my mouth to my sleeve, huddle in on myself to stay as low as possible. I skirt the fire, feeling the press of heat on my face. So many books, all devoured by these demons and their war.

I stumble towards the door, slam up against it. Flames lick at the threshold, beautiful in their menace. I reach instinctively for the handle and the burn almost puts me on my knees. Choking on the smoke, I use my clothed elbow instead, pressing against the door with my whole body.

It doesn't move. Acrid fear bubbles up my throat. I swallow to keep it down and the muscles in my neck throb. With a crackle, the fire leaps up another shelf. The only way out is a window.

I half stumble and half crawl away from the door. The library is vast, large enough that it'll take time for the flames to reach its other end, so I make for the furthest window. It's just about wide enough for me to crawl through. I loop my arm around the back of the nearest chair and drag it under the window.

It could be worse, my brain tells me. He could have shattered my ankles.

Squinting through the smoke, I examine the window. A golden latch at its centre keeps the twin panes shut and there's a key protruding from a lock beneath it. All I have to do is turn the key and open the latch.

I take a breath, wincing at the pain, and clamber onto the chair. The low roar of the fire creeps closer. I reach for the key, another foot over my head. My fingers are swollen and jut in strange directions, the skin purple with bruises. Another breath. I grip the key between the meat of my thumb and forefinger, grit my teeth, and twist. The key is old and clearly hasn't been turned in months. It resists my effort, and my hand slips, smearing blood on the pane where my skin has split. I let out a weak, pained noise.

This should be simple. I should be able to do this. Smoke stings my lungs and I pause to cough, straining my throat. I *can* do this.

I try again, pressing my weight against the key, holding my breath against the throb of my broken fingers. It shudders and then clicks into place so suddenly I lose my grip. Hurriedly I reach for the latch, smothering my mouth in my elbow, breathing as shallowly as possible. It takes a few tries to grasp, too dainty for my swollen fingers. I hook it finally and a cry escapes me, half pain, half relief. I give the window a shove with my shoulder. It swings open, letting in a gasp of icy air.

I throw both arms over the sill. It comes up to my chest, even standing on the chair. Thank God I'm tall. Leaning over as far as I can, dragging in breath after breath of crisp cold air, I put one foot to the wall and haul myself up. My hands scream as I press them into the stone for leverage. I lever my chest over the windowsill, then my hips, then gravity takes me the rest of the way and I fall hard onto the gravel that surrounds the house.

Small stones bite into my face. I roll onto my knees, then my feet, then stagger away from the building. Further down, one of the windows bursts in a shatter of glass. There's a roar of flames and a sound like a crack of thunder. Everything blurs.

Cold stings my hands and my cheek and I realise I'm looking at the world sideways from the snow, huge clouds of smoke billowing across my vision. My ears ring and wet warmth seeps down my cheek. Gasping, I push on my hands to rise and pain spikes through my whole body. My vision goes black.

⁓ ℓℓℓ ⁓

I wake to a splitting headache. The pain streaks through my skull and down my neck with every beat of my heart. Slowly I open my eyes. I'm in a pallet bed, sheets tucked up to my chin, something cool and wet around my throat, something heavy on my hands. There's a faint light coming through the window; afternoon, judging by its golden tone. Two chairs sit against the wall and Eve's in one of them.

"Eve," I say. Mean to say—what comes out is a wheeze. She looks up and shock ripples through me at the sight of her hollowed cheeks, the dark smears under her eyes.

"Don't speak yet," she says, standing, grabbing a glass of water from a table near my head. "Drink some of this." She helps tilt my head up enough to reach the glass and I take a few cautious sips. A bead of water escapes the corner of my mouth. Eve wipes it away with her sleeve. She's avoiding my eyes.

I dig my elbow into the bed and push myself backwards, prop my shoulders against the wall and look down. Each of my fingers is splintered and strapped to its neighbour. Bandages leave a triangle of bare skin at the back of my wrist. I use the gap to feel my throat, encounter damp cloth.

"Don't touch that." She pulls my arm away, gently puts it back on the sheet.

She drags the chair a little closer and sits back down as I take in the room again. Small, with log walls and a wooden ceiling. The window looks out on a dense forest of trees I don't recognise. The acrid scent of antiseptic stains the air. I glance at Eve again, note that the second chair is empty.

At my look she gestures to the door. "Cassius is outside. I can ask him to come in if you like."

I shrug one shoulder, then think better of it and nod. He'll probably be listening at the door anyway.

He enters at her call, looking just as worn as Eve, his red hair matted, his clothes torn and burnt. He seems mostly uninjured, so whatever he fought only gave him temporary wounds.

I inhale carefully, ignore the pain, and say, "What...happened?" My voice is a rasp, barely audible even to myself.

"You really shouldn't be speaking," Eve protests, her hands fluttering up in uncharacteristic nervousness, as if she intends to smother my mouth to make sure of it.

"She's hardly going to sit there in silence, is she?" Cassius drawls and then, to my surprise, he adds, "You were thrown from the building—it took us ages to find you."

Eve reads the questions in my face. "Some chemicals caught fire and exploded. You were so close to the building you were thrown clear, but the impact gave you that head wound." She seems to calm as she says it, the wounds becoming a list of simple facts. "Your fingers are broken, as well as a couple of bones in your hands. Your neck—" Here she pauses. "There are bruises on your neck and the tendons were damaged. Your voice should return if you rest it."

I glance at my hands and back.

"We... We're not sure how much utility you'll have," Eve says, hesitantly. "With some exercise, you might be able to hold a pen."

I wince at the word *might*. Fine. It's something to deal with later. I search the room again. Wherever we are, it's almost silent save for birds calling to each other outside. "Where...?"

They exchange a look and Cassius makes a *go on* gesture, his mouth slanting. "You might as well tell her," he says. "She's not going to like it, either way."

"Like...what?" Where the hell are we?

"We came late to the party," Eve begins. "The Gendarmerie raided the tavern and arrested us. They'd telegrammed London, and Monaghan apparently wasn't interested in protecting us. Chang broke us out." Eve waves her hand as I give her an astounded look. "Not for any altruistic purposes. There's a cost." That sounds cryptic and worrying, but she goes on before I can interrupt. "When we got to the palace, we saw the battle. The Revenants weren't discerning about who they attacked. Obviously we had to defend ourselves." She sounds defensive. I try to signal with my expression that I understand. "They took that to mean we were on her side, Bellemeure's. And Bellemeure's lot thought the same. Just as well," she adds. "We couldn't have fought them all.

"Von Tier fled," she goes on. "I don't know where his daughters got to. The other Revenants were killed, I think. It was hard to see what happened, in the smoke, and we were trying to find you."

I wait, tamping down the urge to interrupt, to ask the question that pulls desperately at my heart.

Cassius grimaces. "By that point, all I could smell was fire and blood."

I'm not sure what he means until Eve adds, "They helped us find you, in the snow. Brought us here and tended to your wounds. We couldn't have done it without them."

"Them," I repeat, in my hoarse whisper.

"Bellemeure's people. The demons and—and Chang. This is their place."

"Is Bellemeure...?"

"She's here." Eve looks at me with a tense expression. "She'll see you, when you're well enough."

I shut my eyes, blocking out Eve's face, Cassius's presence. All this time and effort to stop her and now we're in her power. In her *debt*, with the amount she's done to mend my injuries. And even if the Count and Katharina are still alive, House Asmodeus has fallen. Exactly as she wanted.

"Where... Where is Steel?" I ask, opening my eyes. Just in time to see Eve twitch and look away. Dread seeps through me. "Where is he?" My throat twinges in response to my raised voice.

"We don't know," she answers, sorrow in her face. "He and Luka vanished during the fight. No one knows what happened to them, if they were caught in the blast or..." She trails off.

No. No, he's not dead. I'd know if he were dead. I reach into myself, search for the glimmer of awareness that will tell me where he is.

But there's nothing. That tiny flutter at the back of my mind—it's gone. Steel is gone.

EPILOGUE

He wakes slowly, feathering up from the darkness. Ice tingles at his temple and the tips of his fingers. He blinks, waits for the world to swim into vision. The ground is snow and scattered leaves, smeared with streaks and curls of blood. He's drawn patches of water to him in his sleep, and they've frozen solid under his face and hands. Trees wave above, dancing over a star-lit sky.

No wounds, he recognises. He's healed, although a faint throbbing at the back of his head tells him *something* hit him.

He'd been looking for her, for that flicker of feeling in the corner of his mind. He'd found Luka instead, Luka and the fire. Then pain, then nothing.

Hazel, he thinks, with an ache like a knife.

Growling, he pushes himself to one knee, listening for the sound of an attack. Footprints around him have turned up the snow, scattering the blood.

A scent makes him turn; petrichor and burnished metal—Luka—and the crisp smell of burnt sugar—Katharina. He tenses, clenching his fists. His brother—*not his brother, not in any way that matters*—steps out from the trees, dragging Katharina beside him.

She struggles weakly in his grip, her face dripping with blood, her teeth bared. A thin red line like a second smile splits her neck. "Let go of me," she hisses. "Traitor, fiend—" She lapses into German.

Luka does not blink. "You're awake," he says, addressing Steel.

"Where are we?" he demands. "Where's—" He bites off her name. This demon knows too well what she means to him, he doesn't intend to give the man any more rope to hang him with.

"North of Vienna," Luka answers. "I carried you far enough that Bellemeure's people won't find us."

The old rage surges through him. "*Let* them find us."

A tired look. "The two of us, against her army? Be realistic, brother."

"Don't call me that."

"It is the truth, whether you like it or not."

Steel runs his hands through his hair. Fuck this. "How do I get back?"

Luka regards him for a long moment, ignoring Katharina as she scrabbles at his arm. "She's not there," he says, abruptly.

"What?"

"Your human. She was in the palace when Hanna's chemicals exploded."

Something inside him turns icy. "You're lying."

"Can you feel her?" Luka asks, his face expressionless.

He searches, clenching his fists so tight that his talons tear into his palms. He can't. He can't feel her. "That doesn't mean—" He shakes his head over and over. "That doesn't mean—"

"She was trying to get the humans out, to save them." Luka shakes the woman. "You were at the doors, weren't you? The servants. Was the woman with them?"

Steel forces himself to look at her, not wanting to hear, desperate to know.

"No," Katharina mutters. "The servants were the last to come out before the palace went up. No one else."

It punches a wounded noise from him. He doesn't believe it. He can't believe it.

Of course she'd try to save them, another part of him thinks. *Why couldn't she have run?*

Hazel, he thinks again, hunting for that trace of cool composure tethered to his mind. He finds nothing. *He finds nothing.*

"Let me go," Katharina cries. "You have what you want—"

Luka grabs the woman's head and shoves her to the ground. He slams his boot down on her neck, again and again, until the snow is crimson and the muscle fibres of her neck rip, flopping like worms. Steel can't summon the energy to turn away, can't even retch. He's hollowed out, nothing left inside him to be horrified.

When the body is motionless, Luka wipes his boot in the snow. "The Revenants only set the fire," he says, impassive. "It was Bellemeure who arranged the attack. Her people caused the explosion." He waits, as if Steel might reply, then when he doesn't, continues, "She's the one who deserves to face justice. Let me help you deliver it."

Justice. Some shred of dampened anger stirs. Hazel wasn't supposed to get caught up in this war. He was the one who'd brought her to it, who'd asked for her help. She was the one who'd paid for it. Because of Bellemeure.

He meets Luka's golden eyes. "How?" he rasps.

"Come with me to my House," the demon says, his voice cold, as cold as Steel feels. "Help me get the power to face her."

"Lucifer's House."

"The ones who had your father killed." Luka tilts his head. "Justice," he says, again. "For your father. For your mother. For Hazel."

Steel stares at the blood marring the snow. His hands twitch, empty. He wishes he knew what to do. Hazel would know what to do.

On a crushing, smothering wave, the thought comes; *Hazel is gone.*

And then slowly, among the cresting despair; *I'll kill them all. I'll drown them in their own blood.*

"Show me," he says and his brother smiles.

Also By

Thank you for reading *The Palace of Shadows*. If you enjoyed it, I'd be incredibly grateful if you could leave a short review or rating. Your feedback will help other readers to decide whether to read the book, too.

To read the short story prequel, *House of the Serpent*, and get notifications of new releases, join my email list by visiting my website, www.lemedlock.com.

House of the Serpent

A once great house, fallen. A perilous quest for revenge.

Follow this vengeful journey of a demon as he seeks justice for his slain family.

A companion short story to the Locke & Steel series.

ACKNOWLEDGEMENTS

A huge thank you to Damonza for an absolutely stunning cover. It's so pretty and the colours work together so well, I genuinely gasped aloud when I first saw it! Thank you to Tessy for your feedback and suggestions on the early version of this novel, I hope the adjustments I made earn your favour.

Thank you to Becky and Liam for traipsing around Schönbrunn Palace with me in the cold. Not to mention visiting the catacombs under St Stephen's, queuing for Lindt chocolates and laughing as I almost brained myself on the gold Mozart in Café Frauenhuber.

And thanks go to Mum, Kevin and Dad for all of your support, and to all my family for nudging me to keep writing. This book wouldn't exist without you all.

ABOUT THE AUTHOR

L. E. Medlock has been writing stories since her first school writing assignment, and reading books long before that. She initially decided it wouldn't make a great career choice and went to University to study Egyptology and Classical Civilisation, but the writing never stopped. At the end of her master's degree, she decided to try and turn professional. Some fourteen years and six novels later, she published her debut, The Agent's Demon (the "light-hearted" one). She enjoys stories about flawed gods and monsters who look like us. She's much too addicted to video games and dreams of one day being a cat owner.